MW00942608

Copyright © 2019 by Ivan Kilgore.
All Rights Reserved.
Published in the United States by UBF Productions, an imprint of the United Black Family Scholarship Foundation. https://www.ubfsf.org

Library of Congress Cataloging-in-Publication Data is available upon request.

ISBN: 9781074457839

Printed in the United States of America.

Cover design by Illustration Paragon
https://www.deviantart.com/lmahlati

Editor: Kathi Gardner

Interior book cover design by Ivan Kilgore and Quaitie Siverly.

UBF PRODUCTIONS PRESENTS:

KING

The Early Years

by ivan kilgore

Dedicated to my loving mother Reiletta "Sticky" Kilgore.

Rest in peace Mama. Forever in my heart and thoughts.

Chapter 1

The Amos Temple Methodist Church sat atop the hill, a lone structure. In the distance, its red brick walls stood in contrast to the streaked billowy white clouds looming in its backdrop. The air smelled of rain, and despite the fact it was some two miles from Pecan Street, the church's spire stood as a celestial monument over the humble township of Boley, Oklahoma.

Founded in 1903, Boley was home to a proud African American community, considered by many, to be the embryo of the infamous Black Wall Street. At its height, it rivaled neighboring white communities with the nation's first black college, chartered banks, agricultural industry, and many other black-owned businesses. Booker T. Washington once said of it that it was "the most enterprising, and in many ways the most interesting Negro town in the United States. All this, of course, had been reduced to a ghost town in the years since 1903. Economic woes coupled with racism had caused all but four hundred of Boley's former 4000 residents to abandon it, reducing this once thriving community to a post office, funeral parlor, general store, and prison—the John Lilley Correctional Center.

Of the many red brick buildings that lined Pecan Street, most had been boarded up and tagged with graffiti of the sort. Some were in need of demolishing. Others, including the Prince Hall Masonic Lodge, which had been built in 1912, had been reduced to ash. A skeleton of a new lodge stood in its initial stage of construction at the end of the street. It was one of several historical development projects intended to preserve Boley's rich history.

Pecan Street itself was a patchwork, tattered with potholes, threadbare as a worn-out pair of favorite jeans. The sidewalks were simple dirt pathways overgrown with Johnson grass and other weeds. The maze of dirt roads connected to it, which led to the church, seldom was graded.

Outside the church stood a long line of mourners listening to the PA system as it broadcasted Bishop VC Little's eulogy of the revered life of Daddy Redd. Inside, it was just as packed. People stood from wall to wall in the back of the building and along the aisles, anticipating the final viewing of the man who'd attempted to spark the torch of Boley's history.

"We are gathered here today," the Bishop's voice trailed off before continuing, "to celebrate the life of a man who loved his community like he loved his family." His voice was calm as he stood atop the pulpit with an empty gaze that told nothing of the fire he was about to unleash as his lips parted again. In sermon like fashion, his voice boomed, "No man should have died in the manner he did... shot and left to die—"

A hysterical cry suddenly broke his momentum, mid-sentence, and others joined in, filling the pews with wails of sorrow.

Startled, King jumped to his feet and went to his father's side. "Daddy, get up!" he cried as he stood on his toes attempting to shake his father to consciousness. "Daddy get up, get up!" he again plead but with more eagerness and dissatisfaction as his little hand braced a handle of the casket, while the other reached into it to find the cold feel of his father's corpse.

"Sticky, get that child!" Betty-Jean cried out loud in the midst of the commotion.

The panic in her voice caused King to jump to attention before seeking refuge behind the casket as a pallbearer sought to grab him.

"No! Leave him be... He don't understand," Sticky uttered between tears of pain. "Redd... his daddy... is gone."

"No he's not! He's right there! See? See?" King pointed defiantly, peeping from around the side of the casket. The awkwardness of the moment hardly went unnoticed. A crowd of mourners sat with their mouths agape, others joined in the hysterical cries filling the church.

"Mama, is Daddy playing dead?" King asked, a puzzled look on his face. "Daddy get up! Let's ride Big Red."

Instantly, Sticky's hands swept up to her face to catch the tears. Her son's words shot through her soul—Daddy Redd was *gone forever*.

Four years earlier.

"Man, if it wasn't for this rodeo, black folk wouldn't know we existed. I mean… Look around. There's nothing here but abandoned homes, dope and gangs," Pumpsie reasoned, twitching from an obvious addiction.

"Well, you sure don't mind considering every dime I pay you to clean them stables goes to the dope man!" Redd said, reflecting on the fact that Pumpsie was a pitiful sight compared to his former self.

"You ain't right for that Redd. How is you going to judge me? Hell, you've done a line or two yourself. And you still backing them crap tables and bootleggers," Pumpsie shot back.

Redd smiled, knowing Pumpsie had a point. His remarks were simply his way of antagonizing Pumpsie with hopes of steering him back on the right path. He couldn't stand seeing his big brother strung out. He tried to help, but Pumpsie's addiction had gotten the best of him. His days of slammin' Cadillac doors and rocking $1,500 alligator boots were over.

To make matters worse, Pumpsie was stealing from him. They both knew it. Nonetheless, Redd turned a blind eye to it and often would intentionally leave something of value laying around to pacify him. In Redd's eyes, whatever his brother stole would never compare to the sacrifices Pumpsie made over the years to assure he had the best of everything growing up. Then too, his brother had taught him all he knew about hustling.

"Man, I just want to see you back on your game. That's all. It just don't seem right me out here having things and you—"

"You what!" Pumpsie interrupted. "Shoveling shit? Digging up people's yards for wild onions to stay high?"

"Come on bruh, I ain't mean it like that."

"Fuck you mean then, nigga?"

"I jus—"

"I just what? We both know if I hadn't knocked that straw from your nose, your ass be digging up onions too." Pumpsie said. It was his defense to guilt-trip Redd every time he tapped a vein.

Again, Pumpsie had a point. He had been Redd's sobriety in his younger years, keeping the gorilla off his back by checking him for blowing his nose. "This shit ain't for you baby boy. Leave it be." Redd recalled. It would only take Pumpsie having to put a foot in his ass before he finally got the point.

Undeniably, Pumpsie had shown Redd all the things not to do by his example. In many ways they were alike. But Redd obviously benefited from his brother's mistakes. For that he would forever be in his debt, yet Pumpsie was not the driving force behind his success.

"Who knows," Redd responded half spirited as he looked across the rodeo arena with dreamy eyes. "To be honest, if it wasn't for shorty right there," he pointed in Sticky's direction, then continued, "I'd be up shit creek, if not dead or in the penitentiary."

Down in the rodeo pit, Sticky could be heard at work directing several workers who were hanging up Budweiser and other sponsorship signs.

Redd's words were salt to Pumpsie's wounds. "Fuck you mean, nigga!?!" he exploded, making no attempt to conceal his envy for his brother's fortune.

Redd inherited the world the day he planted his seed in her. He knew Pumpsie despised their relationship, not to mention the good fortune Sticky had brought him. With her father's blessings, Redd was given the opportunity to back and promote the black rodeo circuit. Overnight, he went from home-distilled spirits on the small scale and inferior stuff not even suitable for cleaning the toilet, to a respectable businessman.

The rodeo circuit had expanded his side hustle beyond the Tri-County—Okfuskee, Seminole and Potawatomi—area to include the Okmulgee, Rogers, Creek, and Oklahoma County. Because liquor was only legal for purchase up until a respectable hour of the day, come Sundays and after five o' clock, Monday through Saturday, Redd got every spent quarter a wino could muster. Even during business hours, his liquor operation was doing so well that local liquor chains registered a ten percent drop in sales in the region where he was distributing his bottles.

Vendor rights included, Redd was now hosting seven rodeo events each summer, which catered to a million rodeo goers, including radio and TV circuits that competed for broadcasting rights, and paid advertisements for the *Cowboys of Color* event in OKC.

Certainly, he had come a long ways since the days Pumpsie and he hustled crap tables for small change. His operation had money pouring in hand over fist.

"Now we know Redd was no saint. Like any man, he had his vices," the Bishop stated matter-of-factly. *Young pussy being one of them,* he thought to himself as he looked in Sticky's direction. "Some may want to judge him for his womanizing and questionable business dealings. But this ain't for man to decide…"

Sticky's eyes shot up to the pulpit like infrared beams trained on a tight target. The expression on her face read: *I know this nigga didn't. Much money Redd put up in this raggedy-ass church.*

Betty-Jean gently placed a hand on Sticky's forearm. "Baby…" she said in a soft voice before continuing, "Baby, Redd was a good man. But—"

"Mama, don't go there," Sticky shot back, thinking of when she first let Redd know of her intentions. Several of her girlfriends and she had been out celebrating their high school graduation and had been trying to get into Pooches Gentlemen's Club for over an hour. It was a hole in the wall strip club Redd co-owned with a silent partner over in Wewoka.

Wewoka, another black settlement located just south of Boley, in Seminole County, was founded in 1886 by the Black Seminole Indians. Unlike Boley, however, oil was discovered in 1923, causing a large influx of white settlers to descend upon the settlement.

Cultural clashes rapidly sprung up amongst the Natives and settlers, leading to several fatal encounters which resulted in the Natives being forced onto a reservation located just beyond the city limits.

Legend had it that after having been forced onto the reservation, a Native Shaman had cursed Wewoka with a powerful dark magic that took effect when one drank the town well water. It was said to have driven the settlers mad.

Over the years, what few blacks remained in Wewoka seemed to be affected by the curse. The black business district on Cedar Street stayed busy with criminal activity of the sort. Pooches was one of several business establishments located there that was a magnet for dope dealers and women desperate to *eat*. It stayed packed with pimps, tricks and players, except on Thursday nights when male strippers were brought in.

Outside, Daddy Redd pulled up in a candy apple red, 1957 C4 Cameo truck. Six, 15-inch Rockford Fosgate woofers sat in the bed of the truck, gasping for air as the base from MBJ's song "My Life" sent reverberations throughout the crowd. It was Thursday.

"Girrrrrl… Is that Redd?" one of Sticky's girlfriends asked.

"That nigga stay in something wet," another observed.

And know how to make his presence known, Sticky thought to herself.

He was stunting' southern-style in a classic he had found in a field and restored himself. It was a chariot, sitting on 22-inch, hundred spoke Daytons, with low profile Vogue tires. A chrome blower peeped from under the hood, concealing a ZL1 427 CI Stingray Corvette engine he had salvaged and rebuilt with a Pro Racer Kit. It was by far the cleanest and fastest ride on the block.

It wasn't the first time Sticky had noticed him. She often heard her father speaking of their business relationship. Several times he had visited the ranch to purchase cattle and other livestock.

Redd was a handsome man. His reddish brown complexion told of his biracial background which sprang from a joining of African and Native lineage. He stood 5'10" with a bedroom body build, and curly tapered afro, which was usually kept tucked under his cowboy hat.

Seeing him mounted atop his prized possession, Big Red, was breathtaking. He commanded the stunning roan like a professional. At any given rodeo event, Daddy Redd led 50 or better members of the *Cowboys of Color Rodeo Club* in parade procession atop elegantly draped and trained thoroughbreds, all of which trotted in unison. The riders, Daddy Redd included, were dressed to the nine in festival-like cowboy fashion.

Redd, in particular, sported a pair of custom-made gator skin Tony Lama boots, which bore the revered Masonic insignia of the Creek Freedmen—a Red Tail Hawk, its wings spread eagle with a rattlesnake wrapped around its left talon and a broken shackle and ball and chain on the other. The backdrop consisted of the traditional compass and square, which formed a six-point star customary to the Freemason tradition.

History had it that Boley was settled by the Creek Freedmen, whose ancestors had been held as slaves of the Creek at the time of Indian Removal during the 1830s. After the Civil War, the federal government forced new treaties on the tribes that allied with the Confederacy. It required of them to emancipate their slaves and give them membership in the tribe. The former slaves became known as the Creek Freedmen, who after being allotted 160 acres under the Dawes Commission organized the township under the self-governing principles of the Freemasons.

Over the years Sticky had developed a childhood crush on Redd, which eventually grew into something more by the time she was 18.

Seeing him the prior week at the Wewoka Rodeo Parade, she realized she had to make her move or forever remain just another girl in the crowd screaming his name.

Now it was time.

As Redd parked, he hit a switch and the hydraulic system gently lowered the truck on all fours. He sat there for a minute as the music came to an end. By then, Lenny, Redd's chief of security, along with several bouncers had made their way over to escort him through the crowd.

Lenny was a longtime friend of the family. Both Redd and Pumpsie had known him since the sandbox. He was

Redd's right-hand man and someone he had grown to count on over the years.

"That muthafucka clean!" someone in the crowd observed of the truck.

"Say fam, help me with these," Redd motioned to the bouncers, then pointed to the rear of the truck. He then hit another switch to open the canopy covering the bed of the truck, as he jumped out with a black money bag under his arm.

As soon as the canopy popped open and slowly lifted, a professional speaker arrangement and four humongous Rockford Fosgate amps, along with several cases of liquor were exposed.

Sticky joined in with the spectators after seeing Lenny part the crowd. "I see you…" she flirted as Redd walked by.

He grinned with confidence hearing a familiar voice as he turned to see Old Man Blue's daughter. He and Blue were gambling buddies who occasionally worked together during the rodeo season. Blue was the founder and chairman of the Board of Commissioners for the Historical Black Rodeo Commission, which oversaw the licensing rights to host rodeo events statewide.

Over the years, Redd watched as Sticky had grown into one of the baddest redbones in the Tri-County area. Both Betty-Jean and Blue were Black Seminoles, and Sticky had inherited all the stunning characteristics of the Native and African mix; high cheekbone structure, long silky hair, and a frame built like a Clydesdale. The Roper jeans she stood in seemed to be painted on her country thick, hourglass figure. The scenery was just too much to take.

"You know it's my graduation?" she smiled. Her eyes did a once-over, then stopped on Redd's bulging manhood.

True to the cowboy he was, he was wearing a tight pair of boot cut Wrangler jeans that betrayed his clam appearance.

"Oh, so you grown now?" he teased as a sly grin spread across his face, admiring her assets.

Sticky bit her bottom lip, then pouted, "So where's my present?" Her seductive eyes left no doubt as to what she wanted.

"Girl, look at that ho. Over there throwin' VIP pussy at Redd," one of Sticky's girlfriends snickered.

"I hope her ass get us up in this bitch with some VIP action," another said.

"See... Now you need to cut that shit out for you get both of us in trouble," Redd said before turning back toward the club and saying, "And you ain't gettin' in!"

"Stop playing Redd," Sticky shot back. "We've been waiting over an hour to 'Make It Rain'."

"You mean make it dribble," he laughed.

"Aggghhhh! You got jokes. Oh, Oh, okay, okay!"

Redd then looked over and saw several of her girlfriends standing at the door observing the exchange.

"Come on y'all can roll with me," he waved and extended his elbow.

Sticky eagerly grabbed his arm and strutted past her girlfriends like a queen, "You bitches coming?" she snapped her head at them, thrusting her nose in the air.

The girls looked at each other as if to say, *no doubt,* and then fell in behind them.

Once inside, they quickly made their way through the crowd. The club was packed with mostly older middle-aged white women who were throwing money at a male stripper performing on a stage. There was a small group of men, including Sticky's older brother, Dekoven, enjoying the show. The DJ was playing the Ying Yang Twins song "Wait 'til you see my…." The crowd screamed with pleasure as the dancer was now twirling his anatomy like a cheerleader twirling a baton.

"Chiiiild," Dekoven gasped with incitement, his head making circle motions in sync with the dancer's anatomy.

"Unh, unnnh," a woman standing next to him retorted as he threw several singles at the dancer.

Redd shook his head as if to say, *that's a damn shame*, and moved along in the direction of his office with Lenny and the bouncers in tow.

"Thanks fellas," he said as they finished stacking the cases of liquor in a corner and turned to leave.

"Anything else bro?" Lenny asked.

"Nawl! Just see to it I'm not disturbed."

"No prob."

After they had left, Redd immediately walked over to the door and locked it. He then slid a heavy metal barricade into place, locking the door, adding reinforcement.

The stakes high when you in the game stacking chips. He'd been forced to tighten up on security after a failed robbery attempt.

Within minutes of getting situated, a slight tap came at the door. He had just cracked the safe. At first, he paid no attention to it, mistaking it for a loose window pane rattling from the club's sound system. There it was again, yet with rhythm. "Tap, tap… Tap dad da tap…."

Who the fuck this? He knew it couldn't have been one of his bouncers. When he said he did not want to be disturbed, they knew not to bother him unless they wanted to be unemployed.

He hastily placed the money bag in the safe and locked it before grabbing his .45 Llama. With the hammer locked and loaded, he swiftly moved across the floor to the window and peeked through the blinds. "Peeeewww," he sighed in relief. *Now how the fuck did she get past security* He shook his head in disbelief, opening the door, Llama in hand.

Seeing Redd standing at the door with a gun only made Sticky's pussy wetter. He was a real gangsta, and not one of those busters that ran around Wewoka throwing up gang signs. Several times they had tried him, only to get body bagged.

"What your ass want!" he spat, knowing damn well why she was standing there. In the backdrop, the DJ's song selection, Guy's "I want to get with you," could be heard as it inconsequently coincided with her response.

Sticky boldly walked into the office, ass swinging hard like a pendulum, and threw her panties in his face.

He was immediately caught off guard. Redd, no doubt, was used to women pushing up on him. But Sticky took the cake with this one. At that very moment he felt like Teddy Pendergrass in a ladies' only concert.

She wasted no time. After she threw the panties, Sticky took him by the belt and unzipped his Wranglers. His dick popped out at her like a jack-in-the-box, surprising them both.

Wasn't but a half an hour ago I was sightseeing, now she gagging on my dick!

The many tongues of love now tickled his Johnson as Sticky's moist, full lips consumed the girth of his manhood. He was too much. With each dive she took, she gagged, she choked, and almost spit up, but she was determined. She licked and sucked like a newborn calf on a wet tit.

With both hands firmly planted on his shaft, her mouth slid over, up and down on his manhood like a porn star. Several times she backed off, only to spit on him for lubrication, while her hands eagerly stroked his loins as she sucked harder and more enthusiastically.

She was intentionally violent and had complete control.

Beads of sweat rapidly formed on his forehead. "God damn!" he cried between clenched teeth. She was a beast. An explosion was building as his helmet grew sensitive to her touch, and he began trembling as his toes balled up in his boots.

Sticky could feel "Big Redd" literally swell in her mouth. With a swift movement, she pulled back as cum shot in her face. Quickly, she consumed him again as if to preserve every drop of his precious seed. Her mouth grew full. She swallowed.

Caught up in the moment, Redd hadn't noticed she got up just as fast as she got down, and wiped her face clean with the panties. He was ready and primed for round two, three....

When he opened his eyes, he was surprised to see her walking towards the door. Before he could fix his mouth to say anything, she turned, threw the soiled panties at his feet and said, "Next time you want to play… Remember those," she pointed to the panties, then turned back to the door and walked out.

"Look bitch! Tell that nigga Redd we got his punk ass brother. If he ain't at the drop spot with $200k in an hour, we sending this muthafucka home in pieces! 'Click!'" The voice on the other end of the phone abruptly ended.

Sticky had been doing the books at the office early that morning when the phone ring. Over the years, Redd and she had become somewhat of an item. At first, she was patient with him, never one to fret over his exploits with other women. But things changed shortly after she let her interest in him be known. Eventually the sexual escapades led to her pregnancy, and they now had a three-year-old son, Javon Michael Reed, Jr., who Redd had affectionately nicknamed, "King Cowboy.

"That boy got more fire in him than a cock with metal spurs," he often boasted.

It was obvious from King's first steps that he was going to be one hell of a cowboy. He was a spitting image of his father. However, he had the added effect of being born slightly bow-legged, which added to his swagger. He often posed with his little chest poking out and his fists clenched like dynamite ready to explode.

"Sticky, you and that boy are the joy of my life," she recalled Redd saying as he got down on one knee. *It wasn't but a week ago*, she glanced at the five carat diamond engagement ring on her hand as tears and anxiety built in her eyes. King was all a proud father could have ever wanted. They spent every hour of the day together. On this particular day, when the ransom demand was made, they just so happened to be out fishing at Edward's Lake.

Sticky dropped the phone a nervous wreck. She sat there for a moment, speechless. She had feared something like this would eventually happen. Time and time again, Redd had to bail Pumpsie out of debt with the neighborhood dope dealers.

It's only a matter of time, Redd, before somebody snatch his ass up, she thought of the many times she had warned him.

Inside, she wished she'd never answered the phone. Better he die anyway. Pumpsie was a liability that Redd didn't quite know how to deal with. No matter what it was, he was always saving his ass. She knew he would give his last, if not his life, for Pumpsie's safe return. *Now everything we've built is at stake behind this pitiful nigga.*

Realizing she had no choice, Sticky jumped in her car and sped out to the lake.

Chapter 2

"**N**ow Pumpsie, that boy you shot done identified you. We know you killed your brother," agent Jeff Sisco of the Oklahoma Bureau of Investigation stated matter-of-factly, as he searched Pumpsie's eyes for a clue.

Pumpsie sat with a stern face, cuffed to a table in a small interrogation room. He had been charged with attempted murder on Jay-5 and Redd's murder.

"Boy, you best give us something or your ass up shit Creek!" Sisco slammed his fist onto the table, thinking Pumpsie was sure to break.

Pumpsie, unaffected by the agent's display of anger, took a long pull on a Newport. It was the first time in years he'd gone without a fix in days. "I ain't got shit for you," he finally said coldly, blowing a cloud of smoke in Sisco's face.

"Well, we'll see how long you hold up once that gorilla get to pounding on your back," the agent quipped, using one hand to wave the smoke from his face, while the other violently jerked Pumpsie's arm to expose the needle tracks. "I see you've graduated from sipping syrup to slamming smack. We're done in here. Take him back to the cell."

Kicking wasn't Pumpsie's biggest problem. He'd been down that road before. Redd's murder somehow got pinned on him and Jay-5 had lived. And by the looks of it, he'd turned State. Pumpsie couldn't believe none of it. *Redd's dead and that bitch nigga Jay-5 must have nine lives or something. I hit that fat fuck seven times, plus domed him.*

Sticky couldn't believe her ears, *Redd is Dead!* She had pleaded with him to let Lenny or one of the other bouncers make the drop. But he was adamant.

"Look I got this," he assured her after stuffing the money bag.

"Redd please, please! I got a bad feeling. It ain't good. Please, just… jus—"

"Just what? Let them kill Pumpsie?" he snapped, having read her thoughts.

"No! I'm not… I'm not saying—"

"Fuck you saying then?"

"I just, I just think you shouldn't make the drop," she uttered, wishing she had the courage to speak her mind. "Think about it. Redd if this was about the money, why they demanding that you make the drop?"

She had a point. He knew this was personal.

"Just get King and go to your daddy's. I'll be back in an hour," he promised before kissing her on the forehead and disappearing out the door.

P umpsie slept for what seemed like an eternity. His body was exhausted and in agony. He'd been booked into the Seminole County Jail on a no bail bond and was to be arraigned the following morning.

After a week of the shits and vomiting, he was seriously considering the agents offer. He was jonez'n bad for a taste.

"Hey anybody got any candy or fruit?" he shouted down the tier to the other inmates, gripping his stomach in pain. He desperately needed to get some sugar into his system. It was the next best thing to methadone to knock the edge off his withdrawal symptoms.

R edd shifted into sixth gear as his '96 *SS* Impala sped down Highway 9 towards the drop off location.
"How did these niggas get my number?" he wondered out loud. *I don't get it. They only asked for $200k. I got millions. It just don't add up. Lightweights trying to chip at my stack.* He laughed and shook his head, determined to see otherwise.

After some negotiation, he'd convinced the kidnappers to hold off on the drop until nightfall. He needed the evening's veil to provide cover if his plan was to work.

He finally pulled off the highway onto the dirt road leading to Noble Town Elementary. A quarter mile had passed as he ghosted downhill with the engine and lights off. He left the hum of the highway for the crunch of the dirt road, creeping into the school parking lot.

The school was seven miles northeast of Wewoka and had been closed since the late 1980s. Occasionally, the old gym was used for summer league basketball tournaments. It was a familiar place to the kidnappers.

Redd parked and got out of the car and did a quick recon of the area. There was barely enough light left in the day to make out the details of several small buildings scattered about the campus, along with the main administrative building and gym, which were a short distance away from where he was standing.

The campus grounds were overgrown with weeds. And from the looks of it, there hadn't been much, if any, traffic on the road leading to the school. But none of that concerned him at the time. He waited patiently for a sign. Then it came.

"Coo coo coo," Lenny sounded off with a distinctive sound.

Redd gave a slight grin, feeling reassured that they were in position.

Lenny and three other snipers lay about the compound, armed with .308 Remington sniper rifles, equipped with night scopes.

Sticky had been so shook up about the whole situation, Redd could not risk explaining to her he had them in position the moment he renegotiated the drop-off location. They knew the grounds well, because they had attended the school as children.

Within half an hour of arriving, he could see in the distance the headlights of two vehicles slowly approaching the school. Eventually, they came to a stop within a few yards of where he stood.

The driver of the first car hit his high beams, intentionally blinding Redd, who was now attempting to shield the light with his forearm in an effort to make out the occupants of the vehicle. At his back rested the cold steel of the Llama. He clutched his fists, ready for action. *As soon as Pumpsie is in the clear, we blazing these muthafuckas!*

"Glad to see you. I'm sure Pumpsie is too!" the driver said to Redd as he opened the car door and stepped out before continuing, "Now drop that hammer and kick it over, so we can get down to business."

Redd was in the blind. He couldn't make out their descriptions, or figure out how many men had gotten out of the vehicle. By the sound of it, he knew there were several of them scurrying about. One of which he assumed was his brother, because somebody was frantically mumbling as if gagged.

Lenny and the shooters had their sights trained on the men, but feared shooting, not knowing which one was Pumpsie. "Redd, we have a problem!" he held his hand up to his ear piece and whispered.

Redd slowly removed his pistol and set it on the ground before kicking it over as instructed.

"Search him," the driver instructed as he bent over slowly and picked up the Llama. Another masked man quickly stepped forward and pat-searched Redd.

"He's clean!"

"Where's Pumpsie?" Redd asked.

"Relax! Now here's what we're going to do. I figure you probably have a few shooters out there in the bushes somewhere. So how about you telling your boys to join us," the driver said.

Redd stood his ground firmly. "Just me and these boys here," he pointed to the money bag.

"Humph" the driver responded and laughed. "Okay. How about we take our business into the gym. Wouldn't want anybody taking a crack shot once we make the exchange. You three come with me," he pointed at two masked men and a hostage.

Lennie was within earshot of the conversation and patiently awaited the opportunity to make his move.

The driver hit the lights on the car, and for the first time, Redd was able to assess the situation. There were eight men standing in front of him with tear gas masks concealing their faces. Two of them were bound by duct tape with their hands tied behind their back.

Which one is Pumpsie? Redd questioned himself. The other obviously was a decoy, which had kept his shooters from letting loose. *Shit!* At that moment Redd realized he had underestimated the kidnappers.

"Look Mr. Jackson, the deck is stacked against you on this. Weaver's testimony could very well result in your conviction at trial. If you don't cooperate, you're looking at a possible life sentence if we take this to the box," Pumpsie's public defender advised, hoping to soften him up and make his job a little easier.

"Fuck that! You must take me for a goddamn fool? The DA's witness is a fucking murder suspect!" Pumpsie growled. Having kicked, Pumpsie had come to his senses and was no longer under the influence of the gorilla.

"I'm aware of the credibility issues, Mr. Jackson. But, forgive me for saying the obvious. If you didn't kill your brother, and I believe the D.A. knows this as well, then he figures you'd be more than willing to cooperate, considering it is your brother's murderer he is trying to build a case against." The public defender paused for a moment before realizing there was no give with Pumpsie, then continued, "I uh… I believe that given the credibility issue, I can probably get the D.A. to consider a 20-year deal if you're going to insist on not cooperating."

Pumpsie noted his lawyer's changing tune. Yet he was distracted with his thoughts, which were reeling from what had just occurred at the preliminary hearing. *Bitch nigga all in court testifying, claiming a gangsta. No doubt, we got some unfinished business!*

"Pop... Pop...." The sound of multiple gunshots rang loud, just as Redd and the kidnappers were within feet of the gym door. Lenny had opted to open fire, fearing the kidnappers would kill Redd once they were inside.

Suddenly all hell broke loose. The head of the kidnapper standing next to Redd, exploded from the impact of a high-velocity slug. Brain matter and skull fragments splattered across Redd's face. More gunshots rang out, killing the men standing next to the second car, sending the hostage they held to the ground.

Within a split second of hearing the first shot, Redd sprang into action, lunging at the driver, sending them both crashing through the glass door of the gym. The driver was out cold. Redd quickly recovered but was barely back on his feet and spinning around, when he saw the second kidnapper standing in the doorway, leveling a sawed-off shotgun at his chest.

"Boom!" The flame of the shotgun spit fire, sending Redd flying backwards. He hit the floor, sliding on his back and clutching at his chest as the heat from double-ought buck burned through his bulletproof vest.

"Ahhhhhh!" he clinched his teeth in pain, quickly removing the vest and getting to his feet. He then staggered across the floor to Pumpsie and cut loose his hands.

"Watch out!" Pumpsie screamed, tearing duct tape from his mouth and diving for the Llama, which sat on the floor a few feet from him.

Redd spun, only to be caught in a volley of bullets that tore at his already blistered skin and shredded his insides. Death's shadow quickly swept across his face as the light behind his eyes went out. Pumpsie was too late. The Llama barked seven times, cutting the driver down. As soon as he fell, Pumpsie was towering over him, arm extended, with the Llama trained on his temple. "Please.... Please, please!" he pleaded. "You, you can take my—" were his final words before the Llama barked for the last time.

"We found Weaver's body riddled with bullets and barely alive at the crime scene. GSR confirmed he fired a weapon. Problem is, without Pumpsie's testimony, we can't pin Redd's murder on him," U.S. Attorney Jim Olsen reasoned, citing the nature of the case to Agent Sisco.

Olsen was new blood in the Eastern Division of the U.S. Attorney's Office. He had come from a long line of prominent prosecutors who had successful careers in politics, and was eager to cut his teeth and make a name for himself. Unfortunately, Redd's death had cut short an eighteen month investigation Olsen and a multi-agency taskforce had been building to indict him on tax evasion and illegal manufacturing of a controlled substance—alcohol.

Typically, it wasn't the sort of case the U.S. Attorney Office concerned itself with. In fact, there hadn't been such a case since Prohibition was lifted. But then, Redd's operation wasn't your typical backyard hobby. Records generated during the investigation indicated it was pulling in anywhere from seven to ten million dollars a year, tax-free, which was a substantial amount of money that Uncle Sam couldn't afford to overlook.

"Now that Redd is dead, what's our next move?" Olsen wondered out loud determined to see the investigation through.

"Well, GSR evidence showed Weaver was bound after firing a weapon, which supports his testimony that Pumpsie tied him up after shooting him," Sisco replied, certain of his assessment.

"Not necessarily! Weaver's testimony won't hold up in court. And there was neither money nor Pumpsie at the crime scene. Thus, there's no evidence to corroborate his testimony."

Agent Sisco couldn't believe his ears. Multiple murders, extortion and kidnapping, none of it made sense. To top it off, everything rested on the testimony of a witness who was not cooperating for the very reason he was possibly the mastermind behind the whole plot.

"This is bullshit! I'm going to break that fucking bastard if it's the last fucking thing I do," he vowed in frustration.

"We will, but let's not write off the last eighteen months. If we can't get Redd, his assets are the next best thing," Olson said.

Chapter 3

An EKG monitored Jay-5's heart rate as his life hung by a thread. Several times he had coded, having to be resuscitated by doctors and nurses who scampered about to perform CPR and jolt his body with the shock of a defibrillator. An IV pumped fluids into his bullet-riddled body as he lay in the ICU. Blood-stained bandages covered his chest, neck and head. A potentially fatal bullet had entered his temple at a downward angle, severing the optic nerve in the left eye and shattering his lower right jaw.

"He will live," Sonya thought out loud as she sat at his side cupping his hand in hers. It would be months before he recovered, the doctor had said.

"He will be slightly disfigured with a charismatic scar that will run the full side of his jaw, which has a metal plate and pins holding it together. He's blind in the left eye. But he's lucky….he will live."

"Ja'Monte," Sonya cried softly, whispering Jay-5's government name. "Why do you do this to yourself? To us? To your daughter? What do I say to her?" Defeat consumed her as she stared at him intently, hoping he would wake from the coma to answer.

For years, Sonya James had asked herself these very questions over and over again. Jay-5 as well. And each time he would answer the same, "You know what you signed up for!" She was paying the price for a thug's love. Yet she wanted to tax him so badly for all the pain he had caused her from jump.

It wasn't the first time his life hung in peril. Jay-5 had been in and out of trouble his entire life. Ironically, it was because of his troublesome nature that the two had become acquainted.

"Ja'Monte, I don't get you! I mean, you know these guards playing you like a pawn, right?" Sonya asked. Sitting before her, bruised eye and bloody nose, the seventeen-year-old tough had pounced two opponents in a gladiator-style fight set up by the prison guards. It wasn't the first, nor the last time he would be sent to her office.

"Maybe I just needed a reason to see you," he smirked with a devilish grin.

"See, there you go with that foolishness," she smiled and gave a slight giggle.

The two had been flirting with each other, back and forth, and making small talk for months now.

Barely out of college, Sonya was a bit too approachable as a youth counselor at the California Youth Authority. She had yet to learn where to draw the line and objectify the wards. Time and time again, she attempted to remind herself Ja'Monte was a minor, an inmate, and a convicted criminal who had attempted to kill his own father. Still, the more she became familiar with him and his story, the more he grew on her. Even more, he was an extremely violent ward with a fierce reputation for being quick with his hands which excited her. He was a savage: an autonomous creature of the wild she had become infatuated with and determined to tame.

"All you had to do was request an appointment," she continued, flattered by his advance. "You sure you don't want to get that checked out?"

Jay-5 tilted his head back and pinched his nose with two fingers in an attempt to stop the bleeding. He squirmed about with obvious discomfort as the AC blew cold against his paper-thin state issue, which provided little insulation against the cold steel bench he sat on.

"Nah, I'm good. But I sure could use some of that shit you sitting on!" he shot back with a wry smile and wink, licking blood from his lips and glancing down at her phat thighs.

Sonya was undeniably thick, standing at 5'4" and 130 pounds with curves like a *Sub-Zero Phat Puffs* magazine cover model. Her coffee and cream complexion complemented her African and Cambodian features, a broad nose that spread across a perfect smile and studious lips. Her hair cropped in a bob, was gelled to a curl. Her eyes, a hazel brown, betrayed her thoughts.

Seeing Ja'Monte lick his lips electrified her inner thighs. She jumped from her seat in an attempt to shake it off, trying to put in perspective the fact that he was an inmate, a minor. But he had swag, and carried himself with an air of confidence that piqued her attention and caused her to look beyond his hard looks.

Simply put, Jay-5 was an ugly motherfucker who had been beat with an ugly stick at birth. He was a real life version of a Planet of the Apes makeup job, gorilla chest and all. His hands were unusually huge, like sledgehammers, and calloused from years of punching on the bag without gloves. Nevertheless, what he lacked in the looks department, he made up for with his confidence and intellect. He was uncharacteristically shrewd for a boy of his age. A leader; word was he and his crew reigned over the prison yard.

Right away, Sonya's thoughts filled with rank fantasies of him playing Three-Card Monte with his tongue in her mouth, pussy, and asshole. She was a freak like that and wanted that thug love. The thought of him inside her drove her to do the unthinkable. She took a deep breath, walked over to the office door and locked it.

Ja'Monte's head dropped to find her lifting a knee to rest a three-inch Jimmy Choo heel on the bench beside him. Despite her modest income and profession, she was a fashion statement. A short form-fitting Dolce & Gabbana dress hugged her curves and climbed her thighs to expose a pair of lace red Victoria Secret panties. His gaze quickly shot to her fresh pedicure before slowly making its way up to a fresh manicure resting impatiently on a knee.

He quickly picked up on the invite.

Before Sonya could realize what she had committed herself to, Jay-5's hand was up between her thighs sliding her panties to the side to slip a finger, then two into her tight, wet pussy. She tilted her head back and closed her eyes before letting out a soft moan as she began to gyrate her hips, making slow, circular motions on his hand.

Within seconds, his fingers were drenched in nectar. He pulled away from her, smelled them, and then begin to suck on them. *Sweet!* He was as curious as any teenage boy. What did it smell like, taste like, feel like.

She giggled.

"What's funny?" he frowned, somewhat embarrassed. She was his first.

"You like how I taste?" she asked and looked on him approvingly.

Before he could respond, she took him by the back of the neck and gently pulled his face into her crotch.

Jay didn't hesitate. Like a starved pup, he began licking at her inner thighs as though he was lapping at a warm bowl of milk. His inexperience was ever the more obvious.

Frustrated, she stepped back and, in one motion, swiftly pulled her panties off.

"Now that's what I'm talkin' about!" Jay-5 said, jumping to his feet in excitement.

She then leaned in and pushed the panties into his pocket. His dick was rock hard, and by the feel of it, huge. She grabbed it firmly and led with it to her desk.

"Now, let me show you how I like it," she murmured seductively, leaning back across the desk to pull a knee into her chest, providing a full view of her juice box.

The glamorous presentation between her thighs immediately caught his attention as she set up on an elbow, licked two fingers and begin pressing her 'love' button. Her pussy glistened like the flesh of a fresh picked peach; ripe, soft, clean-shaven, with an abundant clitoris nesting between a pair of full lips.

Jay-5 quickly took a knee and began a trail of passionate kisses up her thigh.

"Here," she instructed as she guided his lips to her luscious clit. "Here, suck here. Suck it like you sucked your fingers, but harder!" She then pressed his face into her pussy.

He did as instructed, sucking and pulling gently at first. Within seconds he had picked up the pace and inserted two fingers into her velvet folds, then her tight asshole, double-dipping, back and forth, rhythmically.

"That's it! Harder, Faster!" she panted between short breaths and bit her bottom lip in an effort to resist the urge to scream. Her body grew tense as she tightened her grip around his head. "That's it! Oh shit. That's it!" she cried. Her body trembled uncontrollably. Her pussy throbbed. Suddenly, she went limp and gave a long sigh, what had been building in her loins released.

Before Sonya could gather her senses, Jay-5 was up and standing over her, anxious as a kid in a candy store.

"My turn!" he said.

She opened her eyes and gasped.

He stood within an inch of her mouth with his dick in his hand. It was short, but four fucking fingers thick at its midpoint and torpedo shaped. Before she could object, he shoved it into her mouth, immediately causing her to gag and choke. He then began to thrust hard and roll his hips as his dick slid in-and-out of her mouth, stretching her jaws like a blowfish.

The sight of her head hanging off the edge of the desk, chin up, consuming his girth, was hypnotizing.

"Y-y-y-yeah! Suck that dick, bitch!" he rocked hard and rocked fast as her lips made slurping sounds and saliva flung from his balls, smacking her square in the forehead with each thrust.

He was swelling by the second.

Her mouth stretched more and more.

"S-s-s-suck that dick!" he stuttered, barely able to contain himself as his voice grew sharper and cum exploded into her warm jaws and began running down the side of her face into her hair.

Sonya gulped several times before sitting up to lick her lips and grab a Jolly Rancher from the candy jar that sat on her desk.

"You like how I taste?" Jay-5 smirked.

"Kiki ha-ha," she faked a laugh and looked at the clock, then said, "That's what the candy is for... To give you flavor. Now come on. We only have about 5 or 10 minutes before the guards return." She then motioned for him to step behind her—doggy style—as she bent over to expose her yam.

He swiftly slid up on her and firmly gripped her phat ass with both hands as his thumbs begin probing her poop chute like a gamepad.

She grabbed his dick and began pressing it up against her clit until it grew hard. "Shove it in me!" she ordered.

Without hesitating, he drove into her with full force, thrusting with all his might, and stretching her walls. Sonya gasped.

"Be easy now—damn!"

"You the one said shove it in."

"Yeah, but Goddamn! It's the size of a fucking eggplant!"

A sadistic grin swept across his face. He enjoyed the fact that he was causing her pain. A wild ecstasy began to stir within his scrotum as he intensely watched his dick slide in and out of her tight, wet pussy, which wrapped around him like a glove.

"Oh shit! That feels so good! Just take it easy, young dick!"

"I got your young dick!" He began pumping harder and faster, and in a frantic, pounding motion.

"Y-y-yes!" she screamed, unconcerned with her surroundings and whether they would be heard outside the office door. "I'm coming!" she cried out loud for the world to hear.

Jay had also built to a peak.

Her knees buckled, giving out from underneath her as she literally cried, "I'm coming! Oh shit! I'm fucking coming!"

Without indication, he froze and with a final thrust exploded in her hot, wet pussy.

Sonya couldn't help but laugh at herself as she sat at his bedside recalling that first sexual encounter. She had fully succumbed to the thrill of it, the danger of being in his presence.

Certainly, Jay-5 was an exciting person to be around. Since meeting him, there was no questioning the fact that her boring middle-class lifestyle had been filled with one harrowing adventure after another.

Suddenly, without warning, his EKG flat lined and caused her to snap out of her thoughts. As his body began to twitch, her thoughts shifted gears to panic mode, fearing the worst.

"Don't you die on me, muthafucka!" she cursed as the nurses rushed into the room.

Little did she realize he heard her every word, had heard them when the lights went out as he slipped in-and-out of consciousness, constantly living the memory of Pumpsie towering over him, gun extended, the flash and burn of steel pressed against his temple.

"Please, please, please Pumpsie! You can take my...."
Jay-5 pleaded for his life. Suddenly, he was reliving his childhood. He was 13 years old and his father was striking him with a closed fist.

"You ain't shit! Ain't ever gon' be shit! Little muthafucka," his father yelled as his fist smashed into Jay's face, sending blood spraying from his nose. The putrid smell of alcohol radiated from his father's breath as he continued to beat him to a bloody pulp.

"Bang! Bang! Bang! Click! Click! Click!" Jay-5 was reliving the moment he emptied a .38 cal. into his father's back. Gunpowder burned in his nostrils and flashes of light erupted from the gun's muzzle.

Miraculously his father survived. However, a hollow point bullet cut through his spine, paralyzing him from the neck down.

"Mama, he'll never hit you again!" Another scene burst into his memory. He was speaking into a phone. His mother sat on the other side of a Plexiglas window crying. It all seemed so real.

Suddenly, he was filled with rage.

His mother was torn between her love for her husband of 28 years and her son's fury to see him dead. The irony was more than surreal. Her son had been convicted of attempted murder for shooting her husband and sentenced to a juvenile correctional facility until he was 18 years old. As complicated as it was, she somehow managed to support them both, often visiting him in lockup and providing convalescence for her quadriplegic husband

Jay-5 was simply dumbfounded. He refused to even try and understand why she continued to love an abusive man.

"He's dead to me!"

"Son, Jesus—"

"Click!" The phone slammed hard into the receiver. He long since resolved to never adopt her religious views. He might as well have been an Atheist because in his eyes her blind faith was the cause of years on end of suffering abuse at the hands of a man he vowed to kill.

Darkness suddenly turned to light as Sonya appeared in his world to test his belief that angels did not exist. She was polished, educated with a Baldwin Hills upbringing, a square from West LA. He was rough around the edges with an upbringing in one of East Oakland's toughest neighborhoods, an ESO thug. She was benevolent and optimistic. He was nothing more than an opportunist. The two would have made for an ideal couple if not for the circumstances to which they met. Still, fate had it in the cards that they would become an item.

Several months on the job, Sonya and a newly-hired counselor were walking through the facility when a disturbance broke out in the gym. They quickly responded and were the first to arrive at the scene where they found two wards fighting. A small crowd of boys anxiously looked on as the taller of the two fighting threw a punch and connected with the other's midriff.

"That's all you got?" Jay-5 needled the boy.

The boy threw another punch.

"Hey! You boys knock it off. Now!" the counselor shouted.

The boys ignored him.

"What's up nigga?! I know you got more in you than that!" Jay-5 needled the boy some more after side-stepping a wild haymaker. He was intentionally trying to throw him off his game, figuring if he got inside the boy's head and got him mad enough, he'd get wild and he could nail him.

The opening came.

He hit the boy with a quick right to the jaw, a left hook to the stomach and another right to the solar plexus, bending the kid over at the waist as he gasped for air, having had the wind knocked out of him.

Sonya was both shocked and impressed. It was all over as quickly as it started. The guards rushed in just as the kid hit the floor, face first.

An hour later, Jay-5 was sitting in Sonya's office sharing his aspirations of becoming a professional fighter.

"You seen my hands. They worth millions!" he boasted, making a quick display of his speed. "I study all the greats. Jack Johnson to Mayweather. I get in the head like Ali. I hit hard like Tyson. And I light hem up like Sugar Ray Leonard."

"Okay Apollo Creed," she teased.

They both laughed.

It wouldn't be long after that Jay-5 had her breaking laws and packing her pussy with balloons of heroin and smuggling cell phones into the prison. By the time he paroled she was pregnant.

Out the gate he wasn't ready to play daddy or settle down. Sonya did not expect him to. However, she could only hope someday that would change. That day had yet to come, and it had been almost five years since they met.

It all flashed before him. He had hit the bricks revenue retrieving. Within months of his release, Sonya's uncle had plugged him with a direct line to the poppy fields in Southeast Asia—Heroin No. 4. It was a wrap after that. He went hard organizing his clique of goons. From City to city, they took the show on the road: Seattle, Phoenix, Dallas.... They became a *BMF Rise & Fall* story.

Then the feds kicked in the door!

Kingpin Runs Drug Ring from Cambodia to Los Angeles.... read the headline on the front page of the *Los Angeles Times Newspaper*. The article went on to read:

Kim Chan, 69, was arrested Thursday morning at one of his toy factories located in the Warehouse District in downtown Los Angeles, California. Chan, a native of Phnom Penh, Cambodia, migrated to the US during the early 1980s and quickly established himself in the Los Angeles drug trade. According to authorities, he had been deported several times after suffering convictions on minor drug charges, assault, and illegal residence.

In addition, authorities report that the Chan Syndicate had been under surveillance for over a decade with numerous arrests leading up the chain.

"We finally got our man," said U.S. Attorney Kenneth Kingsbury.

The arrest involved multi-agency operations composed of a number of government organizations ranging from the Department of Homeland Security to local authorities. "It was the first of its kind," Kingsbury further commented at a press release. "We were able to derail a major pipeline pumping tons of heroin into our nation's streets."

Of those arrested, notably are Los Angeles County Superior Court Judge Dale Drozd, 56, recently retired L.A. Chief of Police Antonio Hernandez, 56, and Oakland city councilman Jerry Brown, all of whom have been indicted on corruption charges for allegedly accepting bribes to thwart criminal investigations and convictions involving the Syndicate. A total of 542 arrests were made statewide with another 120 by Cambodian and Hong Kong officials.

In an innovative approach to trafficking, the Chan Syndicate operated what authorities dubbed "Operation Toy Factory." The heroin was reportedly processed at several toy factories in Hong Kong after chemical agents were added to the opiate base to form a plastic like property. It was then used as a substitute to make children's toys, which were then shipped to various ports around the world....

Jay-5's thoughts skipped from one memory to another.

"Mr. Weaver, could you please point to the leader of the Chan Syndicate?" the prosecuting attorney asked as he stood poised before the jury.

Jay-5's hand slowly lifted to extend a finger to point at Sonya's uncle who sat with a team of lawyers at the defense table.

"The man who you testified supplied you multiple kilograms of heroin, is that the man you just identified?"

"Yes!"

The choice between the witness or defendant came easy for Jay-5. He thought about Sonya's uncle rotting in the pen with little, if any feeling. It was every man for his self. *Get down first*! A life sentence in prison wasn't in the cards for him.

In exchange for his testimony, he would avoid a prison sentence altogether. However, death threats would eventually force Sonya and him into a federal witness protection program. She was easily persuaded to go along after agents informed her that her uncle had ordered a hit on her and her daughter for bringing Ja'Monte into the fold. After months of being moved from one state to another, they were eventually relocated to a suburb on the Northside of Tulsa, Oklahoma.

The channel changed.

Suddenly, Pumpsie appeared out of the blue. He was scratching, jonez'n and jiving and acting like a flea-ridden junkie performing tricks for a treat.

"I'm in the medicine cabinet looking for that codeine/goddamn stomach got me feeling like a fiend/I need some lean/Visine/Bay Hitta/Jay-5 the chip Getta..." Pumpsie rapped and danced about, imitating a minstrel, hoping he would be blessed with a balloon.

Within months of being relocated, Jay-5 was back up to his old tricks. A hole in the wall strip club had brought him to Wewoka as a potential investment. The vibe was good. Wewoka was just like Oakland, a Chocolate City, but smaller. He quickly set up shop and soon realized the competition was fierce.

Twice his flunkies washed up at the local lake after he sent them after a cowboy. The cowboy was a formidable challenge. Still, he had a weak link. Pumpsie was that link and Jay-5's meal ticket.

It all flashed before him. Every tragedy, every pain, every bad decision he had made or experienced before waking up from the coma a month after Pumpsie had shot him in the head.

"Thank you Mr. Weaver… You may step down from the bench," Olson said.

Jay-5 stood from his seat and stepped off the witness stand. He sat there for more than three hours recalling it all, and occasionally glancing over at Pumpsie with a look of contempt on his face that told of betrayal.

Chapter 4

"It just isn't fair," Sticky cried, tears building in her eyes. "Mama... Why? Why, he do this to us? And that snake bastard!" Her demeanor suddenly went from sad and filled with pain to mad and furious in an instant of rage thinking of Pumpsie.

Sticky had just left the courthouse, confused and outraged. Olson had informed her and the family of Pumpsie's refusal to cooperate early on. Still, she couldn't quite understand how it was he'd wind up with a murder charge and attempt, and Jay-5 all of a sudden was the victim. And if that wasn't enough, Lenny was being all tight-lipped about what happened at the gym.

"He got himself killed behind that snake bastard! I tried... I tried to warn him," she cried before jumping to her feet and pacing the kitchen floor.

"Baby..." Betty-Jean said, "you have to stay focused and be strong. Strong for King. Strong for this family and yourself." She then took her daughter by the shoulders and looked her squarely in the eyes before continuing, "Now get yourself together child!"

Sticky was a nervous wreck. It had been several months since Redd had been laid to rest. Stress and depression had wilted her once voluptuous figure to a stem.

"I'm…, I'm trying." Sticky said, sighing. Her entire world had been turned upside down. Still, her mother was right. She couldn't continue to allow King to see her in such a state. She had to be strong for them both so as not to allow Redd's death to discourage them in life. This was especially for Jr. It was in that moment she realized how short life was and just how short their time together had been.

"That boy hasn't had his father but three years," she trembled at the thought of her words.

"I know baby… I know," Betty-Jean replied. "But, you best believe Redd blessed that child with his spirit. Look at him," she reached over and pulled back the kitchen window curtain and pointed to the yard.

Outside, King danced around the yard on a stick horse, throwing a hand into the air and yelling, "ya ya," mimicking a bronc rider. He was playing his favorite rodeo game, pretending he was his father competing in a Bronco busting contest.

Sticky looked out the window and smiled.

"He seems so unaffected." She fought back tears, brushing them away with the back of her hand.

Blue sat on the porch sipping a cold beer. As he looked out across the cornfield, he couldn't help but shake his head. Redd had worked hard to bring them to harvest. Golden-blonde corn silk sprouted from ripe ears of corn as far as the eye could see. The stills waited. After everything that had happened, it was a bittersweet moment.

Over the years, Blue had watched as Redd amassed some 1000 acres of fertile land. He'd worked with him to cultivate the soil. He remembered selling him his first calf. Now, several hundred cattle could be seen grazing in the distant hillside. Behind them, the sun set in a fusion of a blue, white and orange haze. A classic style red barn with white trim sat three football fields from the house and was enclosed in a wrought-iron barnyard fence. Big Red, along with several mares, rested around the enclosure. Chickens scratched about the yard aimlessly.

Suddenly, his moment was interrupted by a low growl.

King had since discarded the stick-horse and found a more suitable challenge to ride—Flight Risk, Redd's Great Dane.

True to his name, no cage or chain could hold him. Each time he broke free his long legs would stretch the length of a field as if a greyhound.

"Grrrrrrr!" the dog growled, exposing its teeth. It was more irritated than threatened by King jumping on its back. It snarled again and snapped at the boy.

Blue quickly got to his feet and peered around the side of the house, fearing the worst. Thinking Flight Risk was onto a snake or something potentially dangerous, what he saw initially caused great distress, then sudden laughter.

King snapped back! Biting down hard on the dog's back before taking a firm grip on its ears to steady himself.

Flight Risk yelped and shot to his feet in an instant, twisting and turning and biting at the boy's boots, which were heeling into the dog's ribs like razor-sharp spurs.

"I got him Papa… I got him!" King shouted as he and the dog struggled and he tossed a hand in the air as Flight Risk danced across the yard in a fiery speed and determination before slamming on the brakes to a dead halt.

King went flying through the air, looking like the Caped Crusader. He hit the ground hard, knocking the wind out of his lungs, with dust flying up around him.

Old Man Blue was in stitches, tears spurted from the corners of his eyes. All the commotion sent Betty-Jean and Sticky running to the porch just in time to see the dog and King striking across the yard.

"See? I told you. He's Redd all over again," Betty-Jean laughed as she wedged an elbow into Sticky's side.

"I don't know if that's a blessing or a curse," Sticky replied, crying tears of joy. Seeing her son get to his feet and dust himself off without so much as a whimper, encouraged her.

In fact she would need it. For there was a storm brewing, and she would soon find herself engaged in a battle of another sort.

"Ja'Monte, this is too much. Things have gotten way out of hand and we seriously need to relocate," Sonya begged in fear. The media was having a frenzy with the story. *Seven bodies found murdered, brother held over after preliminary hearing...* read the headline of the *Seminole Producer, Daily Oklahoman* and *Tulsa World* newspapers. Next to the Oklahoma City bombing, it was one of the most gruesome mass casualty incidents in the state's history. One by one, media outlets across the nation were picking it up, and this terrified Sonya, who feared their identities, or worse, their location would be compromised and their whereabouts revealed to her uncle.

"Look bitch! I done told you... I ain't running no more! Fuck your uncle!" Jay-5 growled, then spat, "I got these country niggaz foaming at the mouth ready to tear up some shit first sign of trouble."

Defeated, Sonya sat there trembling, tears staining her face. By now she realized it was a pointless argument to continue. She knew the real and finally saw through all the talk. It was just that—talk! The man who had swept her off her feet with his thug appeal, had proved pussy when the feds came knocking and the bullets started flying.

She couldn't continue to deny it any longer. The nigga she had given her heart to, who put a baby in her, had no sense of loyalty. Her love for him had blinded her to this very fact. He was a grimy ass street nigga who, along with his team, lived by the rule *Get-Down-First*, the new fake nigga-real-shit where the rules about snitching no longer applied and bitch niggas slammed hammers and claimed goon. This, without question, made Jay-5 the most treacherous type of street nigga there was. He was dangerous. Not because of any propensity to murder, but because niggas fucking with him caught life sentences and died because he didn't know how to keep his mouth shut.

And to think... He got the nerve to call me a bitch! Sonya bit her tongue and wished to herself things had turned out differently. Time and again, she'd thought of the what-ifs. What if he didn't turn state on her uncle? What if, like her uncle, he received a life sentence in federal prison? It definitely would have been better than constantly having to look over their shoulders, she reasoned. After three years in witness protection she knew deep down in her heart she would have played her role like a boss bitch, knocking down penitentiary doors and keeping his lawyers paid, his locker full of zoom zooms and wham whams, a cell phone, and holiday and weekend visits just to keep the bond strong between their daughter and him. Hell she might have even caught religion and stayed prayed up.

Yet that wasn't the reality. Jay-5 had made a deal with the devil and the snitch jacket he now wore was not bulletproof, despite the feds protection. Sonya now realized this more than ever. It was only a matter of time before her uncle's goons caught up with them and carved happy faces into their throats.

Redd's body hadn't been cold in the ground a good six months before there was a loud bang at the door of the ranch house. Outside, the alphabet boys sped up the driveway in a fleet of Ford Ranger XLT modified trucks, black with black glass before coming to a screeching halt in the driveway. Droves of federal agents jumped out of the vehicles and fanned out around the house, weapons drawn, waiting to move in.

"Bam... Bam... Bam... Police!"

Sticky grabbed her house coat thinking to herself, *what the hell is all this about?*

"Bamm... bamm... bamm... police!" a husky voice again announced.

"Hold up! Hold up! I'm coming, damn!"

As soon as she extended her hand for the door knob, there was a sudden explosion that sent the door flying off its hinges and crashing into her. She was immediately knocked backwards and stumbled halfway across the floor before falling to the ground.

"FREEEEZE! Don't move!" another officer yelled as a team of federal agents stormed through the doorway and spread out through the house.

"Clear!" another shouted as they began to secure each room.

"What the fuck—" Sticky looked up into a barrel of a MP5 submachine gun within inches of her face.

"Stay put!" another interrupted.

Her eyes quickly shifted about the room as the agents begin ransacking the house, tossing everything that wasn't nailed down. She attempted to keep track of their activity. It was hopeless. They all wore ski-masks and were dressed in black Nomex SWAT gear and body armor with ATF, FBI, IRS, or DEA stenciled across their backs. A sea of black soon enveloped the house as some 300 agents, from multiple agencies, descended on the ranch.

Sticky sat in total silence, recalling to herself what Redd had instructed her to do in the event she found herself in a jam with the police. "Don't talk! Ask for a lawyer... Don't say a fucking thing or answer even the slightest question under any circumstances without a lawyer!" His words sounded off in her head as if he was standing over her shouting them in her ear.

Before she realized it, she drifted off into a daze. Redd had handled the police with such authority when they raided the club. He somehow always found a way to use their own tactics against them. It was in that moment that she found her footing and snapped out of it. She grew enraged as a familiar face appeared in the doorway.

Agent Sisco stepped into the house accompanied with a plain-clothed officer and made a beeline for her. "Ms. Williams, I would say good morning, but it seems a bit out of place at the moment," he stated matter-of-factly before handing her a copy of the search warrant and continuing, "This is Officer James McKinley of the IRS. I believe he has some papers and questions he'd like to ask of you."

"IRS!" Sticky snapped with surprise before saying, "I'd like to call my lawyer first!" Frustrated with the entire charade, the surprise on her face quickly vanished.

"Ms. Williams, my apologies for the inconvenience. Unfortunately, these things are never quite pleasant," McKinley stated as he reached inside his vest and removed an envelope to hand her.

"What's this?!"

"It's a notification. The IRS has placed a freeze on the late Mr. Redd's assets pending the outcome of federal court proceedings."

"A freeze! For what?"

"Back taxes!" Sisco interjected.

Sticky stood speechless for a moment to allow his words to sink in. She was frozen, stunned, finally bringing herself to tear open and scan the letter.

"$2.5 million!" she gasped as she zeroed in on the amount owed. "You're fucking kidding me right?" It was a rhetorical question. As much as she wanted to discount what was happening, Sticky knew Redd wasn't on the square when it came to his taxes. The bulk of his money was made illegally. Blue had repeatedly warned him about how he *washed* it, cleaned it up. The only real surprise about it all was they had waited until he was dead to charge him.

The letter went on to give a detailed account of Redd's finances. There were a number of banking accounts and other investment accounts that were now frozen. It also included a lien on the ranch, his livestock, car collection, club, rodeo properties and rights, and a long list of commercial and residential properties.

"You mean to tell me that all this..." she paused and looked over at the upholstery that had been torn from the couch cushions and other items scattered about the house. After gathering her senses, she continued, "I can't believe this shit! All this to serve a fucking letter?!"

"I'm afraid so," Sisco said.

Sticky shook her head in frustration. On paper Redd wasn't worth but half of what he owed. However, the good thing about it was, the money and other financial accounts the IRS had frozen was front money. In order to maintain the appearance that his businesses were legit, the accounts had been set up and funded with the proceeds he made from the rodeo events and other business ventures. The bulk of his money, the illegal money, had been squirreled away in an old bank vault he'd salvaged from a construction job and reset in the foundation of the new lodge. This, she knew, was the reason the agents had stormed the house and other properties. The Lodge, fortunately, had been listed in a fictitious business name and was not amongst the list of properties registered with the County Clerk's Office.

"Ms. Williams… We have a few questions we'd like to ask if—" Agent McKinley said.

"Are you arresting me?" Sticky asked cutting him off mid-sentence, knowing he wanted to question her as to Redd's finances.

"—No! But, but we—"

Sticky quickly took control of the conversation, which was a tactic Redd had taught her to employ when confronted by the police. "Well then, I guess you need to speak with my attorney. I'll gladly retrieve his phone number. Any questions you have, he will answer on my behalf for the late Mr. Reed and I," she stated matter-of-factly, then turned to retrieve the number from Redd's office.

"Now... Now, Ms. Williams. This thing is about to get a whole lot uglier if you don't cooperate," Agent Sisco said, following her into the office.

"It doesn't have to be like this," McKinley said soothingly, placing a hand on her shoulder and continuing, "I know all of this has been somewhat overwhelming, having recently laid Mr. Reed to rest."

"Look!" Sticky said, shrugging her shoulder in disgust to remove his hand. "This good cop, bad cop shit ain't working with me. Now! If we done here, I kindly ask you leave. I have your notice and my attorney will be in touch. And by the way… He will be sending a bill for the damage and cleaning cost."

"Okay… alrighty then! Have it your way. Don't say I didn't try to warn you," Sisco threatened as McKinley and he turned to exit the house. "Wrap it up boys!!!"

"We tossed the whole fucking place! Every building… Every property, everything! Didn't find a goddamn thing," Sisco cursed, slamming his fist into the steering wheel of his cruiser. Both Jay-5 and he had met discreetly out on Old Bowlegs Road west of Wewoka.

"Look, I know that's where he stashed his loot," Jay-5 responded. "Had to be…" he whispered under his breath. For months, his crew and he had scouted Redd's ranch with plans to rob him. When that went bust, and he found himself at the center of a murder investigation, he decided to turn the tables to his favor and manipulate the D.A.'s office to agree to a ten percent reward for information leading to Redd's nest egg.

"Well… I know your ass best come up with something or else!"

"Or else what?" Jay-5 shot back unaffected by the threat.

"Or else your ass is going to be stewing in the cell next to Pumpsie's! There's a lot of people pissed with you right now. And the way they see it, there is plenty of room where they're sending Pumpsie for you too," Sisco threatened.

"Yeah well… Fuck they feelings. I don't give a flying fuck about who's pissed. Let's not forget who needs who! I'm the muthafucka that got you the records you needed to bring those tax charges in the first fucking place. I'm the one who made the charge against Pumpsie stick! And if you or any of those pink muthafuckas in the D.A.'s office don't want to see me recanting my testimony, then y'all best get some act right!"

"Relax Weaver," Sisco countered.

"Relax? Relax my ass! Try tellin' that shit to my fuckin' wife. How about you keeping my fucking name and face out of the goddamn newspapers. How the fuck I'm supposed to relax with that shit out there like that?"

"I know... I know. Trust me. We're working on it!" Sisco replied.

"Well, you need to work on it a little harder. My old lady is freaking the fuck out and is worried that Pumpsie's, I mean Redd's, people might come at me," Jay-5 lied. It wasn't either Pumpsie or Redd's people that worried him. He knew Sonya had spoke the real about her uncle's goons possibly catching wind of the press coverage of the story and didn't want to blow their cover.

"We're on it," Sisco repeated, clueless as to Jay-5's motives. "Now, about Redd's records. Just how was it you were able to get your hands on them?"

Jay-5 paused. He had to be careful not to incriminate himself. "Let's just say, I have my connections," It was a dead issue.

"Well! I guess that's that!" Sisco said, indicating their meeting was over. He knew Jay-5 was a manipulative son of a bitch. He had seen his kind a thousand times and chewed on them like bubblegum for information. Once they ran out of flavor, he spit them out to the wolves they had caged. *Dumb nigger... He don't realize who's working for who or that he's working against himself with this trying to be slick shit.*

Sisco started the car and slowly pulled off after Jay-5 opened the door and got out. His focus was on nailing Pumpsie. And if that meant he had to play a sucker and use Jay-5 like he was using the D.A.'s office to get what he wanted, then he would chew on him until he ran out of flavor.

"Ms. Williams, let me explain the nature of the proceedings. It's a very complicated matter. The indictment is for tax evasion. Something to the tune of two or three million dollars. It alleges the money to which the taxes are due were generated from Mr. Reed's entertainment company, the rodeo events, and other business dealings. Now, we both know Redd used these enterprises to launder the proceeds he made from his illegal gambling and liquor operations. The government knows this as well. And to put it nicely, they aim to strip you and your son of any claim to any of his assets and financial investments—" Sticky's attorney attempted to explain.

"The hell they will!" she interrupted.

"—please allow me to finish."

Sticky reluctantly bit her tongue knowing the worst had yet to come.

"Now...," the lawyer continued, "in light of Mr. Reed's recent demise, the government's case has suffered tremendously. My contacts inside the U.S. Attorney's Office tell me that their inability to indict him on the liquor and gambling charges took the wind out of their sails. A conviction on charges like that would have resulted in the seizure of all his assets—"

"Hold up! I'm confused here. They did seize his assets," Sticky said with a puzzled look on her face.

"No! They put a lien on them. Big difference! Seizure typically results in forfeiture upon a conviction. A lien only seeks payment on taxes owed. It is then removed and you remain in possession of the assets after the debt is settled. And the former is the result of a criminal matter. The latter, a civil. Usually, there's a notice of tax delinquency prior to imposing a lien and a court hearing is held on a Chapter 6 liquidation proceeding. In this case, however, the government aims to gain leverage over Pumpsie in hopes he breaks by threatening to take everything his brother and you established."

"The hell they will!" she again protested. "I'll burn this shit to the ground before they take it. Redd spent too many years getting it the hard way for his son to have to start over. Plus, my daddy put him in the game in a real way—legitimately! These muthafuckas."

"While I can appreciate your frustration, Ms. Williams, I must be frank with you. I'm aware of your father's involvement with Redd's business affairs. But we both know he wasn't on the square. And I can almost assure you the government is watching your every move in hopes that you will lead them to his nest egg. That said, I advise you to consider filing for bankruptcy on behalf of his estate. However, there's a problem."

Sticky looked on and said, "What?"

"Your relationship with Redd. It may not be recognized by law."

"What do you mean 'not recognized by law'?"

"You and Redd were not married! That puts his brother in charge of his estate. At best I can argue Oklahoma's common-law statute if you decide to go forward with my advice to file bankruptcy. However this may prove difficult given the fact that the two of you never established anything on paper—"

"What do you mean, we didn't establish anything on paper?" Sticky interrupted with dismay written across her face.

"Like a joint bank account or utility bill. That would prove y'all shared equal responsibility in the household and businesses as man and wife or partners."

"Boy ain't this about a bitch!" Sticky looked to the ceiling shaking her head and, praying for an angel to end her nightmare, asked, "So what other options do I have?"

"Well, you could pay the taxes or roll the dice with hopes that the judge doesn't enforce the lien. If he does, you stand to lose everything. In the meantime, I can file for an order granting you a temporary fiduciary roll in the continued day-to-day operations of Redd's businesses."

Sticky couldn't believe her ears. It was too much to process in such a short time. So much was happening. So much had happened. There had been no time to grieve. Redd's liquor business and the club kept her busy day and night, not to mention the upcoming rodeo events would greatly overwhelm her time wise. And now, she had this matter to deal with.

After close to four years of being patient, managing his business affairs, a son, and engagement—Redd was dead and everything her and her father had done to assist him to rise to the top was up for grabs.

Chapter 5

Pumpsie sat up on his bunk looking at an old photo of Redd, Dirty Dick Kemp, and himself. Five years had passed since he lost his brother and he wound up taking a 15-year deal for the attempt on Jay-5. Prison was nothing new to Pumpsie. Because of the high-profile nature of his case, he had landed at the Oklahoma State Penitentiary, OSP, or "Big Mac" as it was known, a maximum security prison located in McAlester, some 45 minutes southwest of Wewoka. Needless to say, the day he arrived, both his enemies and comrades were waiting at the gates.

"Look P, we got it good here, man!" Brother Yusuf said.

"Yeah," Pumpsie responded as he walked out of R&R with his property and prison garb.

"Yeah, we got some people with bars and stripes who pull strings for us. Pretty much whatever we need. You remember Lil John don't you?"

Pumpsie paused for a moment to reflect, "You talking about Ms. Burnet's son Lil' John?"

"Yeah. He's a lieutenant here. Been working in the system for ten years. We have a few other folks from the town that work here as well."

"Yeah!" Pumpsie said with surprise. "Like who?"

"For one, you're ole buddy Smitty—"

"Shitty Smitty?"

"Yeah!"

"Get the fuck out of here."

"No shit man!"

"Man, last time I saw him we were getting high!"

"Well, he done cleaned up and got him a job as a correctional officer."

"Man, you shittin' me right? Shitty Smitty? Fuck no! I'll believe it when I see it."

"Well, see for yourself," Yusuf pointed to the security booth just as they walked out of R&R and headed for the housing unit.

Pumpsie looked up and without giving any indication that he knew Officer Smith, gave a nod acknowledging his old friend. Smith returned the nod with a grin.

"Okay, so let me get settled in and I'll get the details on everything after chow," Pumpsie said, turning in the direction of his housing unit.

"Hold up, hold up man!" Yusuf said as he reached into the small of his back and pulled out a steel rod wrapped in black electrical tape. "You're gonna need this."

Pumpsie quickly concealed the weapon stock and said, "Thanks. I take it things get a little off the chain around here from time to time?"

"Well, you know what they say? It's better to be caught with than without!"

"Already!"

"Seriously, we already got some shit to deal with. There's some talk that the boy you domed done put some money on your head. Ain't no telling which one of these fools is going to try and collect."

A week later, Pumpsie was coming out of the prison laundry after exchanging some clothes when two heavily built black inmates suddenly appeared out of nowhere and shoved him into a blind spot.

Pumpsie quickly sprang into action, breaking free of a full-Nelson hold one of the assailants had attempted to place him in. As soon as he did, a six-inch shank thrust past his shoulder into the chest of the assailant behind him. The assailant's hands shot up to his chest clutching at the wound as he fell to a knee and toppled over dead.

Caught off guard, the other assailant was taken by Pumpsie's firm grip on his forearm and served a stiff knee to the elbow, causing him to drop the knife he held. In the same motion, Pumpsie pulled back and quickly retrieved an ice pick he'd concealed in his armpit before shoving it through the remaining assailant's throat.

Blood sprayed everywhere. He had struck an artery. It would only take a few minutes before the man bled out and lay dead at Pumpsie's feet. He frantically looked around to see if any security cameras or witnesses had observed the struggle. He was in the clear. Leaving both men for dead and no witnesses, he hurried back to his housing unit to shred his bloody clothing and flush it down the toilet. Just as he did, the institution alarm sounded off and the prison was immediately placed on lockdown.

Three days later, after things had settled down, he rested on his bunk, stone-faced, flipping through old pictures, almost certain he was in the clear. It was then, while looking at the picture of himself and his brother and Dirty Dick, that he began contemplating why life had dealt them such a misfortunate hand.

King was now in grade school and essentially living with his grandparents and younger cousin, who everyone affectionately called Slim due to his lanky frame and unusual height for a boy of his age. His mother, Regina, was Old Man Blue's daughter from a previous relationship. At age 14, she had found herself in Oakland, California, a teenage runaway.

Three years later, she was pregnant with Slim and forced to step back from the streets that fed her as a renegade prostitute, but not for long. She soon found herself managing a group of *talented* runaways who had their beak wet with everything from pussy to plastic. Their schemes made life good for a change. Despite the money pouring in, things became more and more hectic by the day. The streets of Oakland were cold and no place to raise a child. Forced to reckon with this fact, the decision was made to send her son to live with her father.

There, on Old Man Blue and Betty-Jean's ranch, King and Slim would flourish. For them, it was a 200-acre playground of open fields, hills and forests. There were ponds filled with big mouth bass, which were surrounded by blackberry bramble and plum and mulberry trees. The boys ran about the ranch freely without curfew or worry. They built makeshift camps in the woods which glowed with bonfires and served as mock military stations for their imaginary wars.

Naturally, they came to learn a great deal about how to live off the land. Blue taught them everything about hunting, fishing, and growing just about any fruit or vegetable that would germinate in the soil, even the marijuana seeds King and Slim would occasionally swipe from the ashtrays at Pooches.

Hunting, in particular, was one of the boys' favorite pastimes. It was a ritual rite of passage. One morning, while out hunting, King came across a patch of creeper and bramble alongside the trail leading into the woods. Suddenly, Flight Risk froze in his tracks and began growling. He stood poised. The hair on his back bristled along his spine and his nose pointed, making him resemble a bird dog.

"What is it boy?" King asked in a barely audible voice as he looked to Flight Risk for some indication of what had disturbed him. Flight Risk remained rigid, pointing.

"What is it?" King asked again as his eyes searched the woods. Finally, they rested on a brush patch some 40 yards in front of where Flight Risk and he stood. There in the distance, he could see a set of deer antlers protruding from the bush. An eight-point buck stood partially camouflaged staring at them, frozen like a statue.

"I see it now boy!" King said excitedly, as he zeroed in on the animal with the sight of the rifle. He quickly discarded the notion that it was illegal to hunt large game with a small caliber rifle. A .22 caliber bullet would likely injure the animal and leave it to flee and bleed out if not die of lead poisoning.

Suddenly, several shots rang out. The first round struck the animal in its rear quarter, shattering the bone in his hind leg. The second struck high behind the front leg, piercing a lung. Surprisingly, the third missed its mark and grazed the deer's skull, causing it to struggle violently in death.

Flight Risk quickly sprang into action after the first shot was fired. For all his size and agility, he effortlessly dashed pass the trees and closed the distance between the fleeing animal and himself. The crimson taste of blood would soon fill his mouth as he ferociously latched upon the deer's hindquarter and shredded its hide.

King resembled a native warrior charging the frontline; sprinting the distance to arrive at a dogfight. Flight Risk growled fiercely as he sank his teeth into the animal's flesh again and again. Several desperate murmurs escaped the deer's throat as it desperately jerked to free itself.

Suddenly, both animals cannonballed unto the ground and rolled about in a cloud of chaos. Despite its wounds, instinct and fear now provided the deer the advantage in the struggle as it gouged at the dog with its antlers.

The possibility of shooting Flight Risk made King think twice before taking a close-range shot. As the struggle grew more and more intense, he realized he had to do something quick or his dog would be fatally injured.

It was in that moment he made a split-second decision and launched upon the deer, taking it by the antlers with one hand, while the other swiftly removed the Bowie knife from the sheath tied to his thigh. Without hesitating, he repeatedly stabbed the animal until they both lay covered in blood and it was dead.

Part of the boys' weekly ritual involved attending the Masonic meetings held at the Lodge. Within weeks of the IRS storming the ranch, Sticky's attorney was able to obtain an order from the court allowing her to maintain temporary control over Redd's businesses. Thereafter, construction on the J.M. Reed Masonic Temple had been completed within a year.

It stood a celestial monument to Redd's efforts to restore the crown city to its rightful place as the mecca of black progress. In fact, it was part of a business strategy

Sticky and her attorney set in motion to improve on Redd's business model, and raise money to pay the back taxes.

Minus a few minor changes to the floor plan, the Reed Temple's architectural design borrowed from the original blueprint of the 1912 Lodge. This bestowed upon it the historical air of an ancient palace supported by Corinthian columns right out of the Old South. An ash-gray marble façade offset the red brick exterior of the building, which consisted of three floors. Each floor had a separate entry with the revered Masonic insignia of the Creek Freedmen engraved above the doorway.

The first floor consisted of a restaurant franchise Redd had incorporated prior to his death. Ms. Johnnie Mae's BBQ was a favorite of his as a child. During the 1970s throughout the 1980s, Ms. Johnnie Mae, the sole proprietor of a hole in the wall BBQ joint over in Wewoka, became legendary for her amazing beef brisket and pork butt. Hundred-mile "barbecue-runs" to Wewoka were a regular occurrence during those years.

Even more, Mae's Barbecue was the meeting place for many high-ranking local and state officials whose sons, in time, grew to become public officials themselves and longtime friends of Redd's. Many, in due time, would join him in secret meetings and would eventually become honorary members of the Masonic chapter.

Pumpsie sat staring at the pictures, recalling how it all started. It was there, at Ms. Johnnie Mae's, that he had been introduced to the *game* at the tender age of nine. Redd and he often visited Lenny over in New Edition, a shanty town of run-down homes on the outskirts of Wewoka. The boys often took to Ms. Mae's to buy ten cent boxes of Mr. Lemon Heads, Boston Baked Beans, and other cheap candies she kept in a display case behind the counter.

One morning they stumbled into the restaurant and found the counter abandoned as Ms. Mae was preoccupied in the back office.

"Man what are you doing?!" Lenny looked on with disapproval as Redd stepped behind the counter and reached into the cabinet.

"What it look like!" He quickly filled his pockets.

Lenny's eyes quickly swelled to the size of a cue ball. He blinked twice and panicked as a strong hand caught Redd by the collar and violently jerked him off his feet.

Candy boxes suddenly flew everywhere.

"What the hell!" Dirty Dick barked. "I know you ain't up in here stealing? Muthafucka!" He continued to shake the boy senseless until his pockets were empty.

Dirty Dick, also known as Louis Kemp, was a middle-age player who sold companionship and spirits for a living. Often, he would visit Ms. Mae for a taste of that *sweet,* and a plate of ribs, free of charge.

Figuring he would give the boy a good scare, Dick reached into his pocket and pulled out his knife. The blade suddenly appeared, glistening, sharp, and threatening.

Fearing the worst, Pumpsie sprang into action, taking Dick's massive forearm under the weight of his body.

"Nigga! Let him go!" he cried, struggling to knock the knife from Dick's hand as they wrestled about the restaurant shattering glass and busting up tables.

All the commotion eventually caught the attention of Ms. Mae, who came running from the back office in a frenzy, half-dressed, pulling her clothes on.

"Now what the hell is going on in here!" she demanded, appalled by what she saw.

By the time she reached the dining room, all three boys were engaged in a struggle to free the knife from Dick's hand. The dining room floor looked as if a tornado had hit it. Tables and chairs lay shattered to pieces. Her custom-made display cases were shattered beyond repair. Candy and other items she sold looked like they had been intentionally thrown about the floor.

"Goddamn it! Knock that shit off! Knock it off!" she screamed at the top of her lungs, eventually putting an end to the chaos with a bucket of cold ice water.

Exhausted, wet and shivering, the boys and Dick sat on the floor gasping to catch their breath as they looked at one another.

"Now look what you've done got us into," Lenny cried.

Redd ignored the comment, staring uneasily at the front door of the restaurant.

"Well? Don't just sit there! Somebody needs to explain why my place is busted up," she again demanded.

Dick quickly spoke up. "I caught them three stealing," he responded, still somewhat winded from the struggle. "And when I—"

"A thief ain't shit!" Ms. Johnnie Mae spat before he could continue. She stood impatiently, arms folded, tapping her foot in obvious frustration. The look on her face told of utter disappointment.

"Now what do you have to say for yourselves?" she finally said, staring intently at the boys. "Just trifling… Trifling ass niggas! That goes for you too Louis!"

Utter silence fell on the room.

"Done destroyed my establishment for a box of goddamn candy. I'm of the mind to call the police!"

The thought of going to jail had never crossed Redd's mind. He grew even more uneasy as fear consumed him.

"Now ain't no need in doing all that," Dick interjected. "Besides ain't nothing here that can't be fixed. And if these three can put up like they just did, then I imagine somebody need to take them up under their wing and show them a thing or two before they wind up in the penitentiary or worse," he said, reaching for a dish towel to dry his face.

"Oh hell no!" Ms. Mae frowned. As the words parted her lips, she realized what he was up to. "Hmmmmp!" she said, briefly paused to reflect, and then said, "Okay! I'm going to go with this… but first—"

As if on cue, the boys let out a loud sigh of relief, as though someone had opened a valve on an old tire and all the tension in the room was released. The thought of going to jail, or worse, calling their folks, was unbearable.

After a long lecture on the vices and virtues of thieving and hard work, Ms. Johnnie Mae did something that was characteristic of her. She gave the boys a job working at the restaurant delivering food to customers and cleaning up.

Dirty Dick also put the boys to work. It had been his objective all along. They were a rough lot, tough enough to deliver and handle any problems that came with delivering his bottles of homemade hooch to the watering holes on Cedar Street, or wherever else a taste was needed.

Redd and Pumpsie, evermore the student, quickly picked up on the secret sauce for both trades. Years later after Ms. Johnnie Mae had gone to glory, her famous beef brisket and pork butt could be found in their corner-side concession stands at the rodeo, as well as Dirty Dick's cat piss.

The second floor of the Lodge consisted of several conference rooms and a lavish office space Lenny had assumed after Redd's murder. Prior to his death, he had risen to the sublime degree of Master Mason and Worshipful Master. Sitting on his throne had taken some adjusting to say the least for Lenny, who still had yet to get used to the position despite Old Man Blue's reassurances and insisting he give it some time to grow on him.

"Lenny, you family. And we both know Redd wouldn't have wanted it any other way," Blue reasoned as they sat in the office sipping on a cognac.

"I know… But it's just—"

"Besides…" Blue interrupted, "… with Pumpsie up state and my commitment to the rodeo and helping Sticky at the club, where on God's earth would I ever find the time or someone better than you to run this Lodge?"

Lenny sat in silence pondering the question. "I guess you have a point!" he finally said after a minute of reflection. "But it's a lot of responsibility."

"Ah hell Lenny, since when have you ran from responsibility? Look! Don't let it overwhelm you—"

"That's easy of you to say. Rodeo season is right around the corner. You know, if we don't get official recognition as a Master Lodge it's going to be bad for the rodeo… Bad for the stills… And bad for business!"

"I realize that! But for now, we just need you to take care of things around here until we get things squared away with the IRS."

"Okay, okay!" Lenny said, turning his glass bottoms up and slamming it down on the top of the desk. He then stepped from behind the desk and walked towards the office door. "Let me get back with you on that later. I'm certain those boys upstairs are about to tear up some shit."

Blue laughed and nodded in agreement as Lenny took to the stairway leading to the third floor.

"Bruh Secretary, are there any committee reports due?" King questioned solemnly with much ceremony. His feet swung back-and-forth under the throne of the Worshipful Master, which stood as a monument attesting the royalty of its mystical engravings. Several boys and he were role-playing, childishly imitating their elders in carrying out an order of Masonic business.

"Yes! There are two reports, Worshipful. One application for Mister Dre Trammell, and the application of Mister David "Big D" Cuzby." Slim smirked and responded in his best English, fighting back the urge to laugh as he jokingly mispronounced the boys' names.

"That's Mister Tramble and Busby!" King retorted, playing his role to the fullest, and chastising him for his lack of formality. "Now, is the chairman of those committees here as well?"

The boys knew the drill all too well. They had watched their Uncle Lenny and grandfather perform them a thousand times during the initiation of other Masons.

"Worshipful, I'm the chairman who referred both Dre, I mean, Mister Tramble and—" Big-D stammered.

"Boy! Get your ass off that chair!" Lenny's voice boomed as he suddenly appeared at the doorway.

King, startled, quickly jumped from his seat, acting as though it had been set ablaze.

The ground floor of King Solomon's Temple, the third floor of the Lodge, was a magnificent layout with finely crafted olive wood furnishings and gold ornaments, which sparsely decorated and ordained the temple's quarried stone floor and ornately carved cedar walls. The larger of the two rooms that made up the top floor had a transcending effect on Lenny each time he stepped into it.

"King Solomon recognized architecture is not neutral. It makes a statement!" he often recalled Redd saying. Certainly, each floor of the building reflected Redd's meticulous nature for detail. However, none more so than the third floor. No expense had been spared in its construction.

The second room, a small vestibule at the entrance of the stairway, held several large display cases filled with a fortune's worth of Creek Freedmen and Black Seminole Indian artifacts Redd had collected over the years.

At the center of the temple, engraved with a gold leaflet Masonic insignia, an altar stood. Three-gold plated candelabrums, similarly engraved, stood positioned with one in front, and one at each side. On top of the altar sat the book of all knowledge and wisdom, along with a compass with both points covered by a square. They were the *jewels* of the lodge, indicating the degree and order of business it was conducting at any given time. A compass with both its points covered symbolized a lodge of Entered Apprentices, First Degree Masons. One point elevated above the square, Second Degree Fellow Craft Masons and two points, Third Degree Master Masons.

It was there, on the third floor, that King and Slim had begun their studies into the mysterious Masonic order as Entered Apprentices. After Lenny's calling to order and having put an end to the boys' spirited charade, they settled in for their weekly lecture.

"What are the three immovable jewels of a Lodge?" Lenny questioned after making his way over to the throne and taking a seat.

There, he sat on an elevated platform some four feet high, 25 feet in length and width. Each time he sat there, it felt like his first. He marveled at the temple's beauty. Several platforms, smaller in stature, sat about the room decorated with thrones as well for each of the other Master Mason positions. In all, they provided the temple the appearance of a royal chamber.

"Well?" he asked again. "What are the three—"

"The square, level and plumb!" King quickly spoke up.

"What do they masonically teach us?"

King's thoughts raced like a Google search for the answer.

"The square teaches morality, the level, equality, and the plum teaches rectitude of life." Slim answered, beating King to the punch.

King smirked. He had known the answer all along.

"How should a lodge be situated?"

"I got this!" Big-D piped up. "Due east and west."

"Why so?" Silence fell on the temple as Lenny looked down at the small crowd of boys before him. They were the sons of fellow masons. Somewhere from the 'hood. Others, from the wealthy families of politicians and businessmen they had built relationships with over the years.

"Because..." a tall skinny white kid stood to say. Heath was one of a handful of white kids that attended the Lodge. Unlike the others, his father was not a member. He was King and Slim's "brotha from another mutha" as they always joked, who lived on a two house ranch about a half a mile down the road. Like King, he had lost his father at a young age, which made for common ground for the boys to bond. "Because," he continued, "After Moses had safely conducted the children of Israel through the Red Sea, by Divine Command, he erected a tabernacle to God, and placed it due east and west, which was to commemorate the miraculous east wind that wrought their mighty deliverance—this was an exact model of Solomon's Temple. Since, every well-regulated and governed Lodge is, or ought to be, so situated."

The temple erupted in applause as the boys stood and slapped him on the back.

"Roof, roof, roof..." they barked cheerfully.

"White Jesus! My brotha from another!" King yelled in the midst of the cheers and whistles.

"You square!" Slim laughed.

"Alright, alright! Now you boys settle down," Lenny said in admiration. "Let's get back to it."

After a few more whistles and remarks the boys settled down for the remainder of the lecture.

"Okay, now… To whom were the Lodges dedicated to in the ancient times?"

Again, silence fell on the room.

"King Solomon!" Dre finally spoke up.

"Why so?"

"Because it was said he was our most ancient Grand Master, or the founder of our present system," Dre again answered.

"And what or whom in modern times?"

"To St. John the Baptist and St. John the Evangelist, who were two eminent Christian patrons of Masonry. And since their time there is, or ought to be, represented in every regular and well-governed Lodge a certain 'point within a circle', the point representing an individual brother, the circle boundary-line of his conduct…," King went on to explain.

Inside Lenny was all smiles. He had achieved the impossible with these boys. Few Masons, not to mention those of the First Degree, could ever answer every inquiry. Not even to save their own lives. Not one in a hundred ever gets them perfect, none but a few inspiring members commit them to memory, and do so with such perfection as the boys had. They quickly picked up on the use of the three signs of recognition: sign, grip, and word. Studying the various sects of the Masonic order was also part of their apprenticeship. There was the Turkish, oriental version that was commonly referred to as Sufi Freemasons. It was described as a cult of mystics who claimed the ability to decipher the secrets concealed within the text of the Holy Quran. Legend had it that the prophet Muhammad had encoded a series of symbols throughout the text which were said to unleash the cosmic forces of the universe once decoded.

The Greeks and other European sects had their own version as well. However, they deferred to the parables and scriptures of the Holy Bible. From this, the Rosicrucian's would spring to become the spiritual backbone of America's founding fathers. The version of the science they practiced was then said to have lent itself to the Masonic order practiced by Native Americans.

However, the Freedmen had adopted the practices of Prince Hall, a student of Egyptian Pharaoh Amenhotep IV, who, in Masonic folklore, was said to have actually founded the first school of mysticism that taught to King Solomon.

Despite their studious display of attentiveness, to King and Slim, all this was nothing more than a twist on a Harry Potter flick, which better suited a campfire story than a way of life. They were, perhaps, mere boys, and the Masonic teachings, hype and adventure. It would be years before they truly realized or understood the significance of the Reed Temple and the instruction their uncle and grandfather had imparted to them.

For the time being, they did what all adventurous boys do when challenged by mystery—they went on a treasure hunt. The boys, along with the sons of other masons, would spend their summers searching the religious texts of the Holy Quran and Bible for clues to a treasure that, quite often, sent them deep into the forest, only to discover the occasional arrowhead or Native burial site.

Chapter 6

"Now I know you boys enjoy the turnout... the cars, the girls... and the competition. But it is the history you must not ever forget," Blue stressed to King and Slim as he looked up at the bleachers. The rodeo arena was filled to capacity. Thousands of rodeo goers gathered from as far as Nebraska, Houston, Atlanta, and from both the east and west coast.

Outside the arena, on Pecan Street, candy and pearl flip-flop splashed everything: donks, bubbles, slabs, Europeans, ATVs, and Harley-Davidsons—all of which set on 24 inch shoes or bigger as the sideshow filled the air with Vogue smoke.

Earlier in the day, several drill teams had stomped, as shorties gyrated, bouncing their asses to that down south bounce. Daisy Dukes exposed stretch marks and razor bumps as the crowd stood in awe of the elegant parade of thoroughbreds and whips that stretched as far as the eye could see.

For Blue, the Boley Rodeo was about so much more.

"This is one of the oldest, if not the first, black rodeo events to be held in the world," he explained to the boys. "It's a bridgeway, connecting a part of black history with its current progress."

For King and Slim, the events were not only a time for celebration; they were an opportunity for them to compete in the *Junior Pro Rodeo* event.

King jumped over the rail into the chute to steady himself on the back of a bull calf. "Why is it most of them are held in August?" he asked, pulling the rope of his rig tight around his hand and again applying rosin to strengthen his grip. Slim anxiously waited at the gate for a signal as King shifted about on the bulls back.

"He's got 20 seconds to get out of that chute or he's disqualified," a sports commentator said before continuing, "That's Javon Reed Jr., son of the late H.B.R.C. champion. He's rode 11 out of 12 of his last bulls. Let's see how he's going to fair today."

"Its tradition," Blue paused before continuing. "Years before this was a state, the Freedmen had held a number of these events to celebrate their freedom and emancipation from the Natives."

"And what of that lawyer fellow?" Slim asked, knowing it would draw his grandfather's attention.

"J.C. Johnson? Well..." Blue exclaimed, "He was a staunch advocate for the Freedmen over in—"

A sudden commotion interrupted him mid-sentence as the bull began kicking at the cage violently. It was if gunshots sounded off in the arena. The calf began acting erratically, gouging its horns at the gates.

"Looks like they're having a little trouble down in the chute," the commentator said.

"Those steel bucking chutes have no give," another announcer said.

"I tell you, there's not going to be an eight second ride with many of these bulls today," the other commentator chimed in. "This particular bull comes from top-end stock and has been perfect in his career."

Puzzled, Blue frantically tried to figure out what was wrong. Occasionally, a bull would get a bit aggressive while in the chute. But this was a bit more than the ordinary ruckus. The calf was violently striking at the cage.

As soon as he figured it out, King gave the nod, looked over at his grandfather and winked with a wry smile.

Slim jerked open the gate.

"Pull loose that goddamn flank!" Blue yelled. It was too late.

The gate flew open and out shot the calf in a frenzy of speed and chaos as King struggled to regain his position.

"Oh, it's pretty much over with when the bull beats you out the chute," one of the commenters said.

"I tell you, I don't know how he's going to be able to recover. Typically, if a bull beats you out of the chute, then it's over before it started. But this kid... I tell you, he's everything his father was and more," the other commentator added.

The bull bucked and twisted wildly with all his might to remove its rider, yet King's grip held firm as his free hand swung wildly over his head for a counterweight and he regained his position.

The second hand on Blue's watch ticked aimlessly as he looked on. The boys had intentionally distracted him so as to slip the flank around the bull's nuts. It was sure to be ruined, and King injured, if not killed.

"Somebody get that boy off that goddamn bull!" Blue shouted over to several rodeo clowns who were observing the ride.

However, before they could respond, King had counted his eight seconds and jumped from the bull to do his victory dance and wave his cowboy hat at the crowd of cheering fans. Before his feet hit the dirt, his grandfather and several of the ranch hands were down in the rodeo pit with their horses trying to tie the bull down so it could be examined.

"Well?!" Blue finally turned to King to ask.

King's face dropped to the ground as he nervously began kicking at the dirt beneath his feet.

Blue, however, wasn't looking for an explanation. The calf was fine. It was up on its feet and being ushered out the arena in no time. It was obvious to him that the boys had come to an age where they had begun to smell their piss. Even more, he knew their intentions had been innocent and done in the spirit of gaining a competitive edge.

"I ought to tie a rope around your nuts," he continued as the boys walked out of the arena.

Then, slowly, a broad smile swept across his face, exposing a gold crown as he broke out in a fit of laughter.

Confusion immediately swept across the boys' faces. Up until he started laughing, they had been kicking dirt with their faces hung low in anticipation of being punished. Everyone was now laughing, including the boys.

"Did you see how high that joker jumped?" King asked, excited.

"Man that was a perfect ride," Slim responded, looking over at the scoreboard.

"I know this much," Blue said, turning to look at the scoreboard card as the laughter died down. "You better not ever pull that shit again. And let's hope you don't get disqualified. Seriously, you could have ruined that bull with that little stunt. What if we lost business? Then what? That bull's nuts worth a hundred grand!" he sighed, relieved neither King nor the bull had been injured.

"A hundred grand? What?" Slim blinked in disbelief. The boys certainly understood money. There were money counters everywhere; the club, Lenny's office, at the rodeo grounds. Yet somehow they never thought to connect the dots between the coin and the bulls on the ranch. Up until then, they hadn't put much thought into it. Nor did they really understand how history, politics, and business were tied together to feed their grandfather's pockets.

For all his proclaiming the importance of black rodeo history, Blue never missed a beat with the business side of it either. Breeding rodeo bulls was lucrative. "History, politics and business are inseparable," he often stressed.

"Speaking of money..." Sticky appeared out of nowhere to interrupt their conversation. "Daddy, I need to speak with you about some things later on this evening."

"Sure thing baby girl! Let us wrap up the event and I'll meet you at the Lodge, say, in a few hours?"

"Sounds good," Sticky replied, as she turned to disappear into the crowd.

As the evening wound down, and the crew and the boys closed the rodeo arena for the night, Blue sat on the tailgate of his pickup truck sipping a pint of bumpy face, taking in the scene, and recalling how he had put it all on the line in a dice game. He couldn't help but to shake his head thinking of how he had won more in one day by losing at the gambling table than he would have had he actually won when the dice rolled.

"Pass the dice nigga!" Five grand hit the table as Blue reached down for the ivory that came tumbling across the green plush. He quickly scooped them up and began shaking them high above his head. "Shoot the five!"

Retirement had made life good on the ranch for Blue. His father, who had long since passed away, had left it, plus an old juke joint, for him to do with as he pleased. Occasionally, he got an itch for some action and frequented the bar to tell war stories and patronize a good dice game. On any given night, a quarter of a million dollars, if not more, set on the table. Ballers, from as far as Kansas City, Nebraska, and Arkansas often sought out the action.

"Bet! Shoot the five," a man across the table faded Blue.

"Bet five?" Blue threw five more on the table.

"Bet! Bet five?" Ten grand hit the table.

"Bet!"

Thirty grand sat on the table between Blue and the other man. The crowd gathered around and quickly placed side bets and anxiously awaited the dice to roll. All bets were down.

"Sevens come from way down yonder. This that cornfield money!" Blue threw the dice—seven—he won. "Shoot it all!" he yelled.

"Bet back!" the man he had just licked threw fifteen stacks on the table. Two other men at his side each pitched in $7,500 to cover the bet.

"Bet five!" The side bets again went around the table.

"Bet!" Blue threw another five stacks, as though it were a five-dollar bill, and seized the dice. His hands were so hot that the bits of bone felt like pieces of ice. The fever was on him. He spun around on the heels of his boots, did a double down and threw the dice.

"Seven!"

"Goddamn it!" his opponent cried. "Muthafucka!" The crowd around him erupted in a mixture of disappointment and bliss. In a matter of a few minutes Blue had won $70,000.

"Bet the club, old man?" a familiar voice pierced the stirring frenzy.

Blue knew the voice. He reached up with one hand and tilted the light hanging over the table, shifting the eclipse in the dim lit room to reveal enough light to draw sparkles from the platinum slugs and diamonds radiating from Redd's smile.

From jump, he had taken a liking to Daddy Redd. He was the type of hustler he could appreciate with a mean flip game washing street money stock trading cattle. The boy was onto something unlike a lot of cats in the streets. He'd flipped over $100,000 in livestock he had bought from Blue and was offering him a pretty penny for the club.

"Boy... You just don't know when to quit, do you?" Blue shook his head.

"Can't say that I do when I got my eye on something," Redd stepped to the table and sat down the gym bag he was carrying. At his flank stood Lenny and Pumpsie. It was better days. Pumpsie was still on his "G," sporting diamonds and furs.

"I tell you what! I'm going to assume you—"

"Cut the small talk old man!" Redd waved a handful of diamonds to cut him off. It was all business. He then reached down and opened the bag and began tossing bands on the table. One by one, he counted the money out loud as it stacked high on the table. "20, 40, 60, 80... that's $175,000? Three times what this joint is worth. Now take the bet!" Standing at the table, he was as sure as any gambler that Blue would take the bet. Of course, his confidence had little to do with the amount of money that was at stake, and more to do with ego.

For a moment Blue sat contemplating the odds. Recalling what his father always said about a fool and his money parting ways. The club had been in the red for the past five years. It wasn't worth but a quarter of what Redd had thrown down, given his cattle business, which Redd had also significantly contributed to, the odds were in his favor, win or lose.

"Them quite some plans you got there son," Blue finally said, breaking the silence.

He knew of Redd's plans to bring some exotic entertainment to the area. With the recent construction of an Indian casino out on Highway 270, it seemed like a good business move. Especially considering many of Redd's clients and friends already frequented Cedar Street to pick up track dragons and bops.

"Too bad I got to be the one to ruin them," Blue continued.

"What's with all the chatter? Bet or pass the dice nigga!" Redd insisted.

"Bet! These dice hitting sevens," Blue stated matter-of-factly. As predicted, he wasn't about to let the young buck walk into his establishment and put him on the spot without taking the fade. His ego had gotten the best of him as well and convinced him to put the deed up.

Again the chatter went up around the table as the other gamblers rushed to get their bets down. The cigar and tree smoke in the room quickly grow thick as the stakes rose to a quarter of a million dollars, the majority of which Redd had put up.

"Ugh, hmmmm…" Blue cleared his throat. "This the business youngsta. I'm going to fade you one time! One shot. One point. However the dice fall, that's it! No bet back. No getting your money back. You game?"

On the outside, Redd appeared dapper and calm. He sucked at his teeth, and brushed a diamond crusted hand across his heavily starched sleeves. Inside, however, his gut tightened with his prospects. It was every dime he had. *Risk it all?* He had been broke before and wasn't afraid of being broke again. Especially, if it meant losing an opportunity to take his hustle to another level. *Have heart, have money!*

"Game? Humph! Let the dice roll nigga!" he spat with a certain confidence that told nothing of his uneasiness. "Then pack your shit!"

"Pack! Pack what? Them bands you put on the table?" Blue shot back, lips twisted, frowning. He then schooled the dice and said, "Now let's cash out and send them back to the trap house." The dice flew.

Redd's diamonds flashed across the table as his hand quickly swooped up the dice before they caught a point. "Slow your roll O.G.!" He banked the dice off the table and caught a point just to check to see if they were loaded.

Blue grinned, then said, "What you catching the dice for? Let the muthafuckas roll! Then you can go back to chasing lunch money!"

Redd tossed the dice back to Blue one by one before responding, "Lunch money! I got your lunch money right over there," he pointed to three dimes standing next to Pumpsie, and then continued, "We're going to build a stage, stripper poles and all, and give you a front-row seat."

"And I'm going to make it rain with your lunch money?"

Suddenly, the crowd broke into a fit of laughter as Blue again took up the dice, redoubled his contortions, and threw them.

"Fo'!" the houseman called the point. Everybody in the crowd, including Blue and Redd, knew it was a hard point to make.

"Little Joe!" Blue exclaimed. A bead of sweat raced down the side of his face as he reached down to pick up the dice and begin shaking them. "Three an' a po' one, little Joe… Little Joe, op!" he grunted and the dice rolled.

Landing with a bounce, they stumbled and bounced again and again. The room stood on the edge, watching them as though they were moving in slow motion. Redd's stomach turned as his grip tightened around the rail of the pool table. Blue nervously wiped at the sweat that was now pouring from his forehead as the dice came to an abrupt halt.

"SEVEN!" the houseman called the point.

"Goddammit!" Blue cried. The crowd around the table simultaneously erupted into a fit of disappointment. Blue had lost and they couldn't believe it. Neither could he.

As soon as the dice jumped seven, Redd's fist shot up in the air like a kid on Christmas morning. Immediately, he started jumping up and down and shouting to the top of his lungs, "That's what I'm talkin' about shorty!" He was the hero of the moment, and was soon surrounded by cheap admirers and parasites expressing their admiration for his nerve, predicting for him a bright future as the club's new owner.

Thereafter, the guilt associated with having lost his father's establishment in a dice game would trouble Blue for weeks. He made desperate attempts to reason to himself it was the memories the club held that were important. *Boards and nails, that's all it was.* Still, the guilt consumed him, and inevitably drove him to focus more on the family stock contracting business.

One day, after signing over the deed to Redd, Blue discovered that many of the rodeo events his father's bulls had been contracted for had been left to chance, or to family with good intentions, but poor management.

"Blue... The problem is a lot bigger than you realize," Redd said.

Blue had stopped by the club to drop off some paperwork and retrieve the remainder of his personal effects.

"Yeah?" Blue responded as he looked around. In just a month's time, Redd had already drawn up the floor plan and hired a construction crew to remodel the joint.

"Yeah! It is. I was jus' talking with Cole. You know Cole don't you? He runs that event over in Slick—"

"Oh yeah! I remember him. Now... what's this you talkin about?"

"So anyway... Cole was telling me about how he was thinking of retiring and, ah... His boys, well, he isn't for sure if they can keep the event going."

Blue rubbed his chin and began to realizing there was an opportunity in what Redd was telling him.

"Yeah I heard a while back one of his boys, I think it was his oldest, had gotten himself in a fix."

"It was a bit more than a fix. The damn boy got himself ran over and paralyzed from the waist down trying to steal somebody's goddamn cows," Redd said, stopping for a moment to entertain the conversation.

"Hummmp!" Blue shook his head in disbelief, and then said, "Imagine that! Here it is we live in the twenty-first century and these dudes still out here stealing live stock. I guess it's just as profitable today as it was a hundred years ago."

"Damn right it is! Hell, I know an outfit down in Texas that's getting that butter man. I'm talking about these boys making *dope boy magic.* Big rims, F450 trucks, and the whole nine, cattle rustling! They stealing them tractor trailers too. Getting big money! Something to the tune of $25,000 a pop on the black market!"

Blue let out a long whistle and said, "Damn! And to think... People leaving that kind of equipment sitting around in the field?" He shook his head again before continuing, "I think we in the wrong business Redd."

"Hell, we ain't doing all that bad!"

"Guess not. Anyway, now about this here problem. I heard you say Okmulgee and Claremore having the same problem?"

"Shit Blue... They all are. If it wasn't for me stepping in and taking over Boley, and you running the Wewoka Rodeo, they would be in the thick of it too! Anyway, we opening in a few days. So, make sure you saving your lunch money." Redd grinned and turned to disappear out the door.

Learning about the problems facing many families who had inherited the rights to these events struck a chord in Blue. Knowing numerous black rodeos were struggling to remain afloat gave him an overwhelming sense of urgency to assist in keeping the events going. Blue left that day with his thoughts on something grand. For months thereafter, he struggled to find a solution. He felt as though his family's legacy was at stake if he didn't come up with something.

After six months of consulting with business associates, and the families who held the rights to a number of the rodeo events throughout the state, it finally hit him— his grand idea was born—the Historical Black Rodeo Commission.

Never in Blue's wildest dreams, would he have imagined that the H.B.R.C. would have reached the point it had. He took a hard pull on a bottle of bumpy face and took it all in as the alcohol burned at his insides, providing a warm sensation against the cold September breeze. Redd had done it all, gave everything, including his life, to put him in the driver's seat as the commission's chairman.

An hour later, Sticky, Lenny and Blue sat in the office at the Lodge discussing the turnout for the rodeo.

"Things definitely improved this year," Blue said with little optimism.

"Yeah, but the turnout needs to increase by some 40% before we are in the clear and profiting from our investment," Sticky countered.

"Hell... We brought in a little over $75,000 with the admissions, merchandising, concessions, and sponsorship," Lenny said, wrapping a rubber band around a ten stack before throwing the last stack of big faces in the money counter. The machine spit like a rapid machine gun running through three grand in cash in less than a second. "$78,282.10 to be exact," he continued.

"That's good... But in terms of profit, all we did was break even. Which is cool considering how, up until this point, we were in the red. Still, we have to clear at least $97,500 to $105,000 just to see a 30 to 40% return. That's $22,500, $30,000 on a principal investment of $75,000!" Sticky reiterated, crunching the numbers for clarity.

"So where does this leave us in terms of the IRS?" Blue asked, reluctantly.

"The good news is, finally, after all this litigation with the courts, we won. I just received word from our attorney yesterday. The bad news is, in order to keep all this going and to get Uncle Sam off our backs, we're going to have to shoot for a 67% return on the principal. That's a little over a $50,000 profit. So, while we brought in close to $80,000, again, we're at the break-even point, which does nothing to help our tax situation."

"Well shiiit!" Blue said, throwing his hands to the air. "Just how is it we're ever to get ahead in the game with the government breathing on us like this?"

"It's not going to be easy! But then, nothing has been since Senior was killed," Sticky responded. "Now, thinking in terms of expanding our earning potential, we're going to have to restructure some of our other business assets. Namely, the club and liquor—"

"Shit Sticky! We've been losing money with that hole-in-the-wall titty bar for years," Lenny protested. "And that bootleg scratch ain't the same ever since the ATF came knocking. Hell, people scared... You know that type of heat ain't good... Ain't been for years."

"How about you focus on getting money instead of looking at how we losing it!?!" Sticky shot back. "That's why I said we're going to restructure, redevelop, and remodel our business strategy."

"And about the taxes, what were the terms negotiated for repayment?" Blue asked.

"$20,000 a month—"

"Shit!" Lenny exclaimed. "That's not much of a victory. Where in the hell are we going to get that kind of money, legitimately?"

"—$20,000 a month for the next ten years," Sticky continued. "We're selling all of those raggedy ass houses Redd owned over in Wewoka. Plus his cars and investment holdings with the exception of the club, the old Hayes Axle building in Seminole, and his truck and Impala. This will get us by for 12 to 18 months. After that, we best pray things pick up with these rodeo events, the club and liquor business."

Not one to leave things to chance, Sticky and her attorney had already begun mapping out a business plan to increase the turnout for the Boley and Wewoka rodeos, and to remodel and develop the club. Also in the works was a business plan to determine whether or not they could obtain a distillery permit to legitimize Redd's old bootlegging operation. However, given the raid, the fate of those licenses rested in the hands of the state liquor control agency—the ATF.

Chapter 7

Shortly after Slim's 13th birthday, Regina decided it was time for them to spend some quality time together. Up until that point, they had crisscrossed the sky, flying back and forth to visit one another during the summers and holidays. Life in the big city was a lot less complicated these days. She upped her game in the streets and now operated an upscale escort service, which had removed her and her camp from the gutter life into a life of gated communities, executive suites, and elegant dinner dates at expensive restaurants and hotels. Without question, it was a far cry from the slum hotels and ghettos that lined MacArthur Boulevard and the trap houses in East Oakland.

"But I don't want to go!" Slim protested, fighting back tears. Since learning that he was going to move to

California, both he and King had been trying everything in their power to dissuade their grandparents.

"I don't like it no more than you," Blue explained. "But..., your mom's need you little man," he added, knowing it was only right.

Betty-Jean had opted out of the matter. Regina was her stepdaughter and things between the two had been distant since the day she and Blue married. That pretty much left it up to him to break the bad news and be the bad guy in denying the boys' pleas.

It was difficult to say the least. He enjoyed his time with his grandboys. In a way, it was redeeming, given the time he had missed during Regina's childhood, depriving her of a father.

Ultimately, Blue knew Slim needed to be with his mother and that she needed to share in his childhood. The decision had been made and there wasn't much he could do.

King looked out across the park with puppy eyes and a heavy heart. It hadn't been a week since Slim had left for California. Still, without him, King felt like his world had ended. His best friend was gone and nothing was the same. He tried hunting. He tried swimming and fishing. But it just wasn't the same.

"What's wrong with you?" a familiar voice popped up out of nowhere to ask as he aimlessly picked at the underbrush that grew around the park bench where he was sitting.

King's frown began to climb upwards. Standing beside him was his girl, or so he liked to believe, Kay-Kay. She stood there with her hands on her skinny little hips and a sassy look on her face that told nothing of her attraction to him.

"Nothing now," King smiled, thinking of the day they first met.

Kay-Kay had come down from Tulsa with her parents a couple summers ago. King and her first met at the park when Kay-Kay's mother Sonya, dropped her off. Together they played hide-and-go-get-it.

"17, 18, 19, 20! Here I come," King yelled after counting to 20. The whole time, he'd been peeping between his fingers and watching as 'Ms. New Booty' disappeared behind the community center to hide. He quickly made his way over to the building and found her hiding behind an AC unit.

"Unh uh! You cheated!" she complained when he found her. They began rolling in the grass as King attempted to dry-hump her.

"Ain't nobody cheating!" he retorted sourly. "I got the cookie fair and square. Now you know what you signed up for. Let me see it!" he demanded, breathing with childlike wonder as he slipped a hand under her skirt.

That's when it hit him. For the first time in his life, he felt that tingle in his loins that mannish boys experience when they begin to smell their piss. Awe, wonder, joy, and insecurity came crashing over him strongly, and all at once, in a single phenomenon. The innocence of his childish ways quickly vanished the moment he pulled back and smelled his fingers. Boy met girl. Girl met boy. Boy wanted *some*! Girl's mother had taught her to play hard to get.

"Yes you did! Now get off me!" Kay-Kay protested. "I ain't letting you see nothing. Now get off me before I tell my daddy!"

The two struggled for a few minutes before King relented and finally came to his senses. They quickly jumped to their feet and began dusting off just as Slim found them.

"Ain't no fun if the homies can't have none—" Slim started to sing.

"An' I rock hard and tough with my afro puffs," Kay-Kay said, chicken necking, then dissed them with a freestyle. "My milkshake brought two boys to the yard/but getting this cookie go be hard/first grade/and You Ain't Getting no play/no time today!" She ended strong, striking a classic Run DMC pose, arms crossed, head tilted, mean mugging. She then turned and ran back to the park to play with the other kids.

Both King and Slim stood speechless. Ms. New Booty was not Disney or Barbie. She had that star appeal and attitude like Cardi B, giving her a certain edge that left them hypnotized.

Suddenly, King was struck by Slick Rick's "Teenage Love." She was definitely a challenge. Nevertheless, he was as determined as a pup in heat to make her his girl.

"So why you sitting here all puppy eyed as if you just lost your best friend or something!" Kay-Kay asked.

"I did," King replied softly, then told her about Slim moving to California.

"Cali? I'm from California," she responded.

"I thought you were from Tulsa?"

" No! I was born in California," she replied, then asked, "So where did he move to?"

"Richmond."

"Richmond! That's hella ghetto. My daddy say them niggas hella hella grimmy. It's up North, by Oakland."

"I don't think he is living in Richmond. But it's somewhere close to it," King said as weariness swept across his face and he began to wonder how his cousin was doing. Despite the fact they spoke daily, he still worried. And it was for good reason.

"Say Cuddy! What size them J's you got on?" a chubby, Doughboy looking kid asked Slim as he walked out of the corner store a few blocks from where his mother and he now lived.

Bouncing from rural Oklahoma to the inner city was like throwing Slim from the frying pan into the fire. While Regina's living arrangement was situated in one of the nicer gated communities in the East Bay Area, it wasn't but a hop, skip and jump away from the Northside of Richmond, California. Population 105,020, Richmond was one of the most dangerous cities in Northern California. Dubbed the "Killing Zone," the media often reported on the extensive drug wars and gang violence that had torn its social fabric to shreds. Once a stronghold for the Black Panther Party, it now stood in shambles. Pimps, junkies, dilapidated homes boarded up and tagged with graffiti littered every block. Like chalk on a chalkboard, yellow tape and makeshift memorials marked off corners with signs of tribal warfare.

"Damnit! I hate California. Why in the fuck did I have to move here," Slim cursed under his breath. It hadn't been a month since he'd arrived and already things were taking a turn for the worse.

He did a once-over of the kid and quickly concluded that he must have been the leader of the pack, as two other boys had now jumped off the building's façade and we're standing at his side. All three boys stood within inches of Slim and were threatening his space. They were a rough-looking bunch of mop-heads. Filthy, to the point you couldn't tell if the t-shirts they wore were cream-colored or simply covered with filth from being on the grind for days.

"What you say?" Doughboy got all up in Slim's face all aggressive as he reached up to wipe snot from his nose with the back of his hand.

"Where you from?" another asked.

Slim glanced at the bottle of Snapple fruit juice in his hand. Regina had sent him to the store thinking it would be a good idea to get him out of the house and to make some friends.

So much for making friends, he thought to himself. In spite of his better judgment, which was telling him to run, he stood firm. His frustration with the whole move to California finally reached its peak and his pride weighed on his feet like a ton of bricks. If he ran, he would be running from then on. It was about to jump off and Slim knew he had to get off first. This much he had learned from the all the skirmishes King and he had, locking up like pit bulls, fighting the other boys whose mothers worked at the strip club.

"Your size, nigga!" Slim finally snapped just as Doughboy stepped into his strike zone.

"POW!"

Before Doughboy realized it, the Snapple came crashing down across his face, opening up a gusher, as the bottle shattered into a million shards. With a loud thud, he hit the pavement hard, and was out cold.

It all happened so fast, Doughboy's partners didn't have a chance to respond. Seeing him sprawled out on the ground, bleeding profusely with his wig split to the white meat, fear swept over them and they froze instantly. They turned to run, almost tripping on one another to get away.

"Wooop waaaah!" Slim jumped up an down, hollering to the top of his lungs like a madman. He was doing his best Jackie Chan impression. It was some Richard Pryor shit he had picked up from an old movie. "Yeah! That's right... Run nigga, run! I'm crazy!" he screamed, drop-kicking one of the boys in the ass as he fled.

❝❝I'm sure Slim is fine," Kay-Kay said in an attempt to put King's mind at ease. "Here, check out my new song," she added as she pulled out her iPhone and began searching for the MP3 file before pressing play.

King smiled. He admired her ambition. Ever since they were kids, she had always bragged and boasted of someday being a famous entertainer. To an extent, he was jealous. He was jealous of the fact that she had a father who supported her in every way he could to make her dreams come true.

She quickly set the phone on the bench next to him and began her number, beating a beat with hand to chest rhythms and snapping her fingers to the music as the song started to play. She started singing the hook and rapping on cue, "Some girls like bad boys/like toys/we grow up/we come up/rip pockets like jack boys/we bubble/flip dunks on 8's/trap weight between states/rob niggaz on dates/this *sweet* top rate—"

"Girrrrrrl, you's a damn fool. Stupid!" King laughed, and then said, "That shit dope! Let me get that."

"Nawl, nawl now! I spit this shit to eat, not fame. Respect my hustle," Kay-Kay said, confident in her ability as she struck her signature pose. "I'm going to send you the link to iTunes so you can support that!"

"Nigga you stupid!" King replied as his phone began ringing 2 Chainz. It was Slim. "What's good cousin!?!" he answered with a sigh of relief. Before he could get another word in, Slim was explaining everything that just happened.

Word quickly got around the neighborhood that there was a crazy out-of-state kid who cut up Doughboy and put a country ass whooping on his crew. It wouldn't take long before everybody in North Richmond figured out who that kid was.

For the remainder of the summer, Slim caught 'oooh weee' knots defending his rep. Every time he stepped off the porch, there were other boys, older boys, and even a few tomboys, who wanted a shot at his crown. Like a true champ, he remained firm, representing his soil. The South had raised a king from its red clay. Fighting was in his blood. Whether he won or lost, he stood firm and soon gained the respect of his peers.

Chapter 8

King sat up on his bed, restless. The image of his father lying in a casket ran vividly through his mind as he desperately searched his memory for something more. He needed something, anything, to remind him of better times with his father. His absence had created a void in his life, leaving only the memory of that tragic moment of pain and confusion when he touched Redd's corpse.

Nothing! His mind drew a blank as he aimlessly stared into the neon lights of the alarm clock, 3:45 a.m. It had been 11 years since his father had been murdered. Sadly, all he could remember was the eerie feeling of Redd's corpse, which haunted and deprived him of the joy his mother often spoke of when reflecting on his father.

"King Cowboy," she'd smile, remnants of Senior's profound effect gleaming in the cloudiness of her pain spoken eyes. "Your daddy, I tell you! He was one hell of a man. A proud man! That's all you ever wanted… To be a cowboy like your daddy."

King smiled, reaching for the picture of his father and him that sat on the nightstand next to his bed. He held it to the light of the clock for a minute. There, they sat atop Big Red, fitted with Stetson cowboy hats and Tony Lama boots. Two dandies, dressed alike.

As he stared at the picture, a stark realization suddenly came over him. His father's spirit was alive and well within him. His eyes teared up with feelings of joy and pain. The pain stemmed from the sense of betrayal of having outgrown his passion for boots and horses, and failing to connect with them the more favorable times he had with his father.

Since Slim left for California, he'd begun to outgrow the whole cowboy thing. Little by little, that aspect of Redd's influence had vanished. Memories of his love for all things cowboy quickly flooded his memory.

"I want cowboy boots!" he'd pout as a child, arms folded in dissatisfaction.

"But what about when your little feet start hurting?" Sticky would ask in a motherly tone, hoping he understood.

"I want cowboy boots!"

"Baby, you can't wear them. You have a high arch in your foot. That's why they—"

"I want cowboy boots!"

King shook his head, recalling how adamant he was to wear boots in rain, sleet or snow, with or without socks, and in gym shorts.

Up until that point in his life, he paid dearly for his love of boots. His feet often grew sore to the touch of a boot before he finally gave up on the notion of wearing them.

He then looked over at the trophies that sat on the shelf. He was a junior pro rodeo champion. But things just were not the same without Slim.

Reaching under his bed, King pulled out a shoebox. Inside, were his father's Tony Lamas, bearing the familiar Masonic insignia. They were a symbol of legacy. A legacy his father had worked hard to re-establish.

Unlike most kids his age, he knew the history. Even more, he recognized its tenets, which were at the heart of his father's legacy. It was becoming more and more evident by the day, since his mother and grandfather reopened the Lodge.

Inside the box was another picture. One of King, sitting atop Big Red, that had been taken shortly after Slim had left, and within months of the tragic accident that resulted in the horse being put down.

The heat kissed the sun scorched red clay as Ole Man Blue and King rode their horses down a back road leading into town. It was humid. Heat licked at their shoulders like a fire breathing dragon.

"Be careful now!" Blue warned as they made their way across a tattered bridge. It was a relic, constructed from wood that creeped and cracked and slumped under the weight of whatever crossed it.

"I got it," King replied, confident of his ability to handle a horse.

Dirt and gravel shifted through several holes in the bridge where the wooden planks had rotted.

Suddenly, there was a loud splintering sound. A plank broke.

Big Red, startled, high stepped several paces before rearing up in an attempt to save footing. It was too late. The horse's hind quarter suddenly went crashing through the bridge, sending it falling to a sure death.

King flew through the air and hit the ground with a loud thud as Big Red landed under the bridge with an even louder snapping sound like branches breaking on a tree.

King hastily regained his composure and quickly made his way down under the bridge with his grandfather to check on the horse.

There, Big Red lay laboring and suffering from what Blue realized was a broken back. "Run up yonder and get that there rifle!" he snapped, not wanting to see the horse suffer.

King's eyes cue balled as he blurted out, "You ain't killing my horse!"

"No! You are! Now get that goddamn rifle like I told you!"

King stood reluctant to retrieve the gun as the horse squealed in obvious pain. He could see blood rushing from several huge puncture wounds. Several planks had splintered and stood upright on the ground the moment the bridge collapsed.

Tormented with the task before him, he quickly turned to retrieve the rifle.

"Do we have to... Isn't there something else we can do?" he plead, hoping somehow the horse's fate had changed in that brief moment it took for him to return.

"Yes... you do," Blue responded without emotion.

King braced himself. Before him lay his father's prized possession, which he now was being forced to free of its suffering. No one else could do it. Not his grandfather, mother, or God, or they would bear the guilt. And they would never forgive him for that. He had to take it upon himself to kill Big Red.

It was in that instant, his adrenaline kicked in and a sense of emptiness swept over him. Ironically, he was overwhelmed with a sense of power to give or take life the moment his finger wrapped around the cold steel of the trigger.

"BOOM!" the rifle kicked. A tear ran from the corner of his eye.

The loss of Big Red would add to the list of life altering events that eventually hardened King's soul. With his father's murder, and now his prized possession lying dead under a bridge, something inside of him cut off.

"I don't know what's gotten into that boy. He's mad all the time," Sticky shook her head, puzzled.

"Ahhhhhh, it's just he's coming of age and trying to figure some things out. Then too... You know it ain't easy... His father gone and all," Betty-Jean said wistfully as she looked over at the wall clock, 7:38 a.m.

"I know Mama. I know. It's just..." Sticky paused for a moment, and then said, "I worry about him. All this anger... Nothing good can come of it. And I'm afraid he's looking for someone to blame for his father's death."

"So whatever came of that visit with Pumpsie?" Betty-Jean jumped at the opportunity to pry. Deep down inside, she knew what was troubling her grandson. There was a festering in him. And anger, a thirst for blood that was building in him after learning of his uncle's involvement with his father's murder. For years they had done everything they could to keep it a secret. Now it was all rushing back to haunt them in the most disturbing way.

"How did you find out about that?!" Sticky asked, surprised.

"Blue. He and King were talking about it after he found Pumpsie's letter. You need to talk to that boy. He wants answers. People talking... You know?"

Chapter 9

*D*ear Sticky, greetings. I know this letter comes as a surprise and likely unwanted. Yet there's some things I need to get off my chest. You blame me for Redd's death. I get that! It's something I'll have to live with for the rest of my life. But understand we both hurting. And I had nothing to do with that. I know you still have a lot of unanswered questions after all these years. Unfortunately, I can't get into all that on paper. But we need to talk. Visiting hours are from 8 a.m. to 2 p.m. Saturdays and Sundays...."

Agent Sisco took a hard pull on a fifth of whiskey, holding Pumpsie's letter as though it was a winning lotto ticket. Here was a long-awaited break in the case. For years, he had been monitoring every inch of Pumpsie's life in prison.

A decade later, it still made him hot under the collar that the son-of-a-bitch had slipped through the cracks of justice with some slick lawyer. It wasn't enough he'd been sentenced to 15 years for attempted murder. In his mind, the nigger deserved to be on death row. But, somehow, the murder and kidnapping charges had wound up in the cold case files.

Over the years, he'd almost drunk himself to death fighting with the O.S.B.I. supervisors to keep the case active. In the end he'd lost and lost big. It was now a one-man show. He lost his family and came close to losing his job after running up the tab for unauthorized investigative fees surrounding the case. His colleagues regarded him as a has-been, a Festus Haggen in comparison to the Marshal Matt Dillon he believed himself to be.

Still, after all these years, he couldn't quite put a finger on why it was Blue Williams had retained Jack Butler as Pumpsie's attorney. Everybody in the office knew Butler was connected. He was the epitome of corruption and had been under investigation several times by federal authorities. And to top it off, every judge, prosecutor, and police force in Seminole County was in his pocket, protecting him for decades. He used every trick in the book to extort their favor, from child porn to bribes. The political machine in Wewoka was corrupt and Sisco knew the Freemasons over in Boley had a lot to do with it.

"Looks like we finally got something coming," Sisco said out loud to himself as he sat Pumpsie's letter down and reached for his phone. He began dialing the number to the Criminal Investigation Unit at OSP.

Agent Sisco stared at the letter in deep thought as the phone rang several times. *Jackson's paroling in 36 months. Shit! I got to get something on this motherfucker before he reaches the gate or he's going to get away with the whole fucking thing.*

"Hmmmmm," he sighed.

"Hello... hello...." Lieutenant Riley repeated, finally getting his attention.

"Oh, excuse me. Lieutenant Riley?"

"Yeah..."

"Greetings... This is agent Sisco over at the O.S.B.I."

"What can I do for you?" Riley asked somewhat irritated. Agent Sisco didn't know when to quit. Over the years he had become somewhat of an annoyance to the department with his repeated requests and obsession to indict Pumpsie.

"I just received a faxed copy from the C.I.U. of Jackson's letter to Miss Williams, I would like to set up some surveillance in the event she pays him a visit."

"We may have to get a warrant to listen in on a civilian's conversation," Riley stated enthusiastically.

"I'm one step ahead of you. I already got it!" Sisco said.

"Well... what do you have in mind?" The lieutenant asked with a drawl heavier than syrup.

"You remember that case about fifteen or twenty years back, the joint operation between the FBI and the Illinois Department of Corrections?"

Riley paused for a moment to reflect, then said, "Oh! You talking about the one where they took down that Larry Hoover fella?" He knew the case. It had been well-publicized throughout correctional departments nationwide.

"Yelp! That's the one. I plan on taking a clue from the FBI's playbook."

"Gotcha! Let us know what you need in terms of logistics and resources and we'll get right on it," Riley lied, then thought to himself, *I hope this idiot don't think we're actually going to go through with this shit.*

"Thanks." Agent Sisco hung up the phone and leaned back in his office chair to kick up his boots on the desk. He sat there, fingers interlocked behind his head, satisfied that if and when Sticky visited Pumpsie, he'd get the drop on them and get some answers, if not evidence enough for an indictment.

"Jackson, 118. Visit!" The PA system cracked just as Pumpsie's cell door opened. It had been a few months since he'd written Sticky. But he knew she would come.

Sticky sat in the visiting room, nervously looking about, waiting for Pumpsie to come out. It was her first time in a prison. Clipped to her chest was a bright neon-green visitation pass. Not that she was trying to impress him or anyone for that matter, but it clashed terribly with the baby blue Armani pant suit she was wearing.

She could see that most of the guards who worked there were racist, backwood Hillbillies who acted more like plantation overseers than correctional officers to the prison's predominately black population.

Without question, being a successful black woman made her the focus of their attention. From the very moment she stepped onto the compound, she was under constant harassment.

"Excuse me Miss, do you mind if we inspect your vehicle? Our dog has indicated the possibility of narcotics in the truck," a fat, freckle face guard eagerly stood behind her as she closed the Escalade's rear door. At his side was a pitiful looking specimen.

The dog was simply a mutt. Its ribcage told of exposure and starvation, and it seemed more focused on fleas and ticks on its ass as it violently scratched and bit at his rear end, than it seemed concerned about drugs.

"Drugs!" Sticky laughed. "Oh, okay. I see where we're going with this. No, I don't mind, as long as you don't mind me video recording you searching my truck?" she asked, pulling out her cell phone to turn on the camera.

The guard paused with a puzzled look on his face, which turned beet red. He had never been put on the spot like that before. "Well… it appears Rocky hit on the car next to yours," he replied just as the dog lifted its leg and pissed on the tire of the car next to where she had parked.

Sticky had called the guard's bluff. He knew if he proceeded to search the vehicle on the false premise of suspecting drugs, he would be facing a civil lawsuit for discrimination or harassment, if not both. And a video would most definitely prove it.

Once inside, Sticky was told all the rules—

"No excessive touching…one kiss and hug," a tall thin manly looking female guard spat, putting extra emphasis on Sticky wearing the ugly visitation pass. "You must wear this at all times! You take it off, you leave," she added, hoping to incite Sticky so she would have reason to terminate her visit.

After waiting close to an hour, Pumpsie finally peered from behind a small window in the dressing room where he and other prisoners were stripped searched before and after their visit.

The moment their eyes met he found himself uneasy, dripping with sweat as the door leading to the guard station popped open. Sticky's stare was cold, calculating.

As Pumpsie walked out, Sticky couldn't help but notice he had put on some weight. His build reminded her of an action figure doll with bulging veins and humongous arms that measured every last bit of 20 inches in diameter. His barrel chest hung over a tight waistline, giving him a V12 stature that made his state issue bust at the seams.

As with Redd, Pumpsie had inherited their mother's native lineage. Despite a beautiful bronze complexion, it was evident they had different fathers. Pumpsie was amazingly unattractive. Large craters and potholes covered his face from years of drug use.

Nevertheless, he strutted over to the guard station with an air of confidence and placed his inmate ID on the table, then said, "Ms. James, good morning." He intentionally flirted with his eyes as he picked up the pink visiting pass she slid across the table to him.

For months, he had been chipping at Officer James, trying to get her to break some laws and taste that *sweet*. Officer James was a big booty white girl, his type. However, on the streets she was a four on a scale to ten. In prison, she was a dime to him. Of course, once he paroled she would be a four again but still, "She could get it," he always bragged.

"Jackson," James acknowledged.

"Finally got the old lady back online," Pumpsie smiled, missing teeth and all. "You know how it be when you get short to the house. They all of the sudden back on the team ready to play ball. But hey, she still mad about me fucking around on her with you. So don't panic if she slap the shit out of me," he added, feeding her some of his outdated game.

"Guess you have that coming," she laughed, shaking her head before adding, "Wouldn't be the first time it happened in here."

"Yeah?!" Pumpsie replied before turning to walk into a landmine.

"Smaccckkkk!"

"Damn! Did she just slap him?" Agent Sisco asked as he looked over at Lieutenant Riley in disbelief.

"I think so."

"You no good piece of—" Sticky's voice could be heard struggling.

"I didn't do it—"

Agent Sisco snapped to attention at the sound of Pumpsie's voice.

"Please, please… Chill… Tissues are over here," his voice was fading in and out. Suddenly, there was a great deal of static and distortion before the wire went dead.

"Shit!" Agent Sisco spat angrily as he and several officers scourged about the office trying to fix the equipment. "The fucking bug malfunctioned."

Lieutenant Riley and Agent Sisco sat in the C.I.U. office defeated. Their attempt to eavesdrop on Sticky and Pumpsie's visit had failed.

"Well, don't just sit there. Get out there and terminate that fucking visit!" Riley barked at the officers.

As predicted, Sticky slapped Pumpsie, slapped him hard the very moment he walked up to greet her. Officer James was in stitches as several other visitors joined in the laughter while others looked on in awe.

"You no good piece of shit," Sticky managed to get in before Pumpsie grabbed her in his arms to shield her blows.

"I-I-I didn't do it. Please, please. Just hear me out—" he whispered between clenched teeth as his massive arms held her against his chest.

Sticky put up a brief struggle before eventually relenting to his hold. Despite the time that had elapsed, seeing Pumpsie brought back all the pain of losing Redd. Tears immediately filled her eyes as she belted out, "How, how… Could you take him away from us?" With each word, her fist pounded his chest.

"Come on!" he said, taking her by the arm and leading her to the microwave and several vending machines situated along the wall of the visiting room. "The tissues are over here," he added, handing her several tissues as he waited for Officer James to turn her attention elsewhere.

"Twelve o' clock outline. Johnson, Hernandez, James—visit is over!" Officer James rattled off over the intercom. Several prisoners and their families stood to hug and kiss.

Pumpsie seized the moment as the officer and cameras zoomed in on the departing inmates and their families. It was a common practice for them to make their move at this time. Some simply wanted to get their fingers wet. Others, hooped contraband.

With a slight of the hand, Pumpsie quickly removed both visiting passes and tossed them into the microwave. Within seconds of turning it on, a small explosion lit up inside and fried the microscopic bugs embedded in them.

"Figured as much," he said under his breath.

"What in the hell was that?" she asked.

"A wiretap. Now look, we don't have much time before the goons bust up this visit. So hear me out!"

Sticky reluctantly nodded her head. She was at a loss and stood speechless. Pumpsie was on his game, and she was impressed. Red always said his brother had taught him everything he knew about it. A part of her wanted to resist, but deep down inside she knew she needed to hear what he had to say. It was a long-awaited moment. Truth was finally at her doorstep.

"Jay-5 killed Redd—" Pumpsie started to explain.

"But, the police found him bound in duct tape," she interrupted.

"Look we don't have time for this. Listen!" Pumpsie took a firm hold on her arm before continuing, "I don't expect you to trust me. But if you want to see that bitch nigga bleed, you going to have to." He then slid a small piece of paper into the palm of her hand and stepped back just as the goons busted into the visiting room.

Chapter 10

Sticky sat in the parking lot of the prison, carefully unwrapping the small piece of paper, which turned out to be an actual letter, written in the tiniest print. She strained to make out the message within the clutter of words that Pumpsie wanted her to pass on. Apparently it was to her chief of security, Lenny.

After Redd was killed, Lenny had proved reliable in more ways than she could ever have imagined. He was a true friend; trustworthy, and more importantly, loyal. All that, however, was about to be put to the test.

As she continued to read over the letter, she recalled the many private meetings Redd and Lenny had had over the years. Though she was not privy to the nature of their business, that did not stop her from prying.

"There's some things you just do not need to know— for your own good," Redd often stressed, as though his reasoning should suffice to cure her curiosity.

It was all coming together now. Lenny was Redd's 'go to' guy when he needed something more than muscle at the door of the club. He was Redd's hitman.

She had always suspected he had someone to do his dirty work. However, the thought of all the meetings they had over the years, and the fact that in the letter, Pumpsie had instructed him to give her the rest of the ransom money, sent a chill running up her spine. *Was Lenny in on this? Not even!* She quickly dismissed the notion.

Pondering, she slowly pulled out of the prison compound, realizing now that there had been a war going on around her all these years that she had been oblivious to. There was more, however. That, she knew, she would have to get from Lenny.

In no time the Escalade was turning off Highway 270 onto 48 towards Boley.

Lenny peered from the second-story window of the Lodge just as the Escalade came to a screeching halt in the parking lot. As soon as she stopped, Sticky swung the driver side door open and was marching toward the building. In no time, the click-clack sound of her red bottoms could be heard as she scaled the marble stairway leading to his office.

"Dammmnit Lenny!" she exploded, bursting through the door and throwing Pumpsie's kite on the desk.

Lenny's mouth opened to speak, but quickly closed as he picked up the kite and begin to look it over.

"How could you? How could you not tell me about this shit?" she demanded.

"Now hold up! What's this all about?" He looked on with surprise like he didn't understand what she was talking about.

"Don't play crazy with me nigga. Read the muthafucking letter!"

The moment Lenny picked it up he knew who it was from. *She must have visited Pumpsie in prison*, he thought. The format was something he was familiar with, having made several trips himself over the years.

"Okay, okay, calm down, damnit," he demanded, getting up from his chair and walking over to close the office door.

"Calm down! What? How the fuck you expect me to calm after reading that shit?" she snapped.

"Look—"

"Look my ass! I want some fucking answers!"

"Okay, okay! Just give me a minute to look at this."

After taking a few minutes to look over the kite he sat her down and began to explain everything. Nothing was mentioned in the kite about the day Redd was killed, so he started there first before explaining to her the fact that he had been strapped with the task of her and King's safety after Pumpsie was sent to prison.

"We came in within seconds of Pumpsie having shot Jay-5. He was dead—so we thought. There was nothing we could do for Redd...," he paused, then after taking a few deep breaths to calm himself, continued, "I sat there while Pumpsie held him in his arms. He made him promise... promise to look after King and you."

There was a great sense of loss in Lenny's voice as he spoke. Sticky stood there listening with a stern look on her face as her heart raced with emotions. She had cried enough. Yet she could not help but appreciate and love Redd, who with his dying words, thought only of her and King's safety.

"But why? I don't understand," she began to cry.

"Jay-5 had been trying to extort Redd ever since he set up shop in Wewoka. And Redd knew about his plan to shake him down in the weeks prior to Pumpsie's kidnapping—"

"So you telling me Pumpsie didn't have nothing to do with this, absolutely nothing?" she interrupted.

"No! Absolutely nothing," he responded, then he went on to explain. "After Pumpsie was arrested, he had informed me not to retaliate, that it was personal and that he would handle it. That's been the hardest thing in my life to respect. You know how much I loved Redd. Him and Pumpsie are brothers to me, and I definitely wanted to see this bitch nigga Jay-5 dead. So to put him at ease, we've been singing his tune for years now. We've been using the ransom money to pay a small tax on your business so that he thinks he's won the war. 'The money,' Pumpsie explained 'meant nothing in exchange for exacting vengeance for Redd.'"

"But why did Jay-5 testify?" Sticky asked, confused.

"The nigga is a bitch! Everybody know Pumpsie was stealing from Redd. So by the time Jay-5 woke up in the hospital, he had cooked up the whole scheme about Pumpsie being the mastermind behind the kidnapping. He then played the victim, which wasn't a hard sell to the district attorney."

"So basically he used the court to handle his business by putting Pumpsie on the shelf for a while?" Sticky asked.

"That's what bitch niggas do. They testify in court and get real niggas locked up so they don't have to look over their shoulders in the streets. And that's not all. He has been cooperating with the police long before he arrived in Wewoka. *Tell on three, get away free*, that's what they say where he's from. How do you think he's managed to stay out of prison all these years? The courthouse got transcripts stacked to the ceiling, filled with his testimony and reports in a number of cases from Oakland all the way to Oklahoma," Lenny explained.

Sticky quickly put two and two together. It all made sense now. It was Jay-5 and his goons that had attempted to rob Redd in the months prior to the kidnapping. Two of his goons had been found dead at Clove 9 at Lake Seminole during that time frame. *Lenny must have killed them*, she concluded.

After handing over the remainder of the money, minus enough to continue to pay the tax until Pumpsie was paroled, Lenny instructed Sticky to continue with her daily activities so as not to raise any suspicions with Jay-5.

"We've worked hard over the years to put him to sleep and get him comfortable with his surroundings," he said as she stood to leave. "Trust, everything is under control. We'll take care of everything as soon as Pumpsie comes home."

News of the O.S.B.I. raid at the prison was supercharged on the prison's grapevine like CNN reporting on the cell block. The most trivial of events could now be recorded and uploaded to the internet within seconds for the world to view. And it wasn't just the inmates who were posting content. The guards and other staff set up fake accounts and posted videos of the fights that they staged between prisoners from rival gangs, riots, stabbings, and just about anything they could film that would increase their followers and likes.

Within minutes of the raid, a video surfaced on YouTube. Someone on the compound had filmed Agent Sisco storming the visiting room, and the link to the video eventually made its way to Jay-5.

The minute he saw it, he recognized Pumpsie's face, despite it having been some 12 years since he sat in court and testified against him. It was a face that had been forever singed into his memory with repeated nightmares— Pumpsie towering over him with Redd's Llama spitting fire.

The burn and sizzle of flesh and the gym lighting up with a flash all came rushing back as Jay-5 reached up to massage the scar on his face, his fingertips tingling. Pumpsie had put the fear of God in him, something not even his mother could do. This enraged him! Pumpsie was a dope fiend, a nobody! Disgrace quickly consumed him as he reflected on the fact that he had been lead checked by a hophead. Only his arrogance would vindicate Jay-5. He was confident prison had made Pumpsie more of what he was before he went in.

Over the years, he had attempted to keep tabs on Pumpsie's situation behind the walls. Word was he was strung out, snorting psych meds just to keep the gorilla off his back. *The nigga is damaged goods, broken and defeated*, he thought. He was all too confident that Pumpsie would quickly resort back to his old tricks once he touched down. But as he watched the video, Jay-5 began to realize that he had made his biggest mistake by leaving loose ends untied.

"Daddy," Kay-Kay said as she walked into her father's man cave, disrupting his thoughts.

"What's up baby girl?" Jay-5 asked a bit startled as she walked over, sat on the arm of his chair and leaned in to hug and kiss him. "What's all that for?"

"Now what? I can't hug and kiss my own father?" she asked with a telling smile that indicated she was up to something before reluctantly pulling away.

"Knock it off girl. You too much, just like your damn mother. I know when you're up to something. Now what is it you want?" he asked again, knowing he could deny her nothing.

Like many fathers, Jay-5 doted on his baby girl. Kay-Kay meant the world to him. Unlike his father, he spoiled her with affection, and was always kind and gentle with her. Even more, Sonya and he had gone to great lengths in an attempt to shield her from his lifestyle. And living in the suburbs of Tulsa, some 100 miles away from Wewoka, somewhat assured this.

But Kay-Kay had long since known of her father's activities. The only thing the seclusion had afforded them was anonymity. But the controversy surrounding Redd's murder threatened that, and forced them deeper into seclusion. Agent Sisco had held true to his word and worked overtime to keep Jay-5's name and face out of the press, which allowed Sonya and him to settle into a relatively quiet suburban area.

To their neighbors, they were a happily married couple with a talented daughter who was musically inclined. Sonya was now working as a counselor at the Tulsa County Jail and Jay-5 had recently opened two custom auto detail shops and a small recording studio that was mostly used by Kay-Kay. Indeed, they had adjusted.

Despite appearances, Jay-5 remained knee-deep in the *game*. The anonymity he had enjoyed at the expense of the taxpayers proved longevity in the streets was possible. Years of grinding from block-to-block and state-to-state had taught him that while the *game* was the same in most places, the method for putting the hustle down could be as different as day and night. Some niggas set up trap houses. Others kept jobs as a front, and some used churches as stash houses. Then there were those who simply posted on the block with a mouth full of spittas.

Before moving to Oklahoma, he had never worked an honest day in his life. That was some square shit that was not part of the script fed to him in the streets of Oakland where life was fast and niggas said fuck Mickey D's and posted on the block to stack geez. However, in the Heartland, the *game* was to keep a front. Whether it was a job or a business, niggas in the south kept a front so as to keep the alphabet boys at bay.

The shops were a front. Each location concealed his chop shop and drug smuggling operation. They had been strategically located. *367 Customs* was located in North Tulsa and served as a drug trafficking hub for Northeast Oklahoma—Tulsa, Muskogee, Miami—and the cars stolen from the South Central Area—OKC, Wewoka, Shawnee— were disassembled and vice-versa for those stolen in the northeastern region. Between the two shops, Jay-5 was able to keep the streets of Oklahoma flooded with enough dope to make El Chapo look like a middleman.

"Well, spit it out!" Jay-5 demanded of Kay-Kay, who of course had ulterior motives for her display of affection.

"I'm not up to nothing," she plead innocently before continuing, "I just want to go to Wewoka this weekend. Mama said I can help her around the shop," she lied, striking a defensive pose with her arms crossed at the elbow.

He paused to reflect before finally responding, "I don't think that's a good idea." For obvious reasons he did not want her around the shop. *Now she lying to me. Sonya ain't said shit.* This much he knew. And she definitely did not need to be spending time in Wewoka. This, he strongly felt, was on account of who she spent time with.

Chapter 11

Sticky played her part and did as Lenny instructed. Inside, she struggled to keep it together and do everything in her will to keep from going ballistic. She was on the verge of a mental breakdown. The stress of the court proceedings, raising money to pay back the taxes, and now, the pain of learning that Redd was killed for nothing, had taken its toll. If not for the distraction of her work and wanting Jay-5 dead, she would have lost it and not been able to push it all to the back of her mind and set the stage to carry out their plan.

"Ms. Williams..." Sticky's doctor paused to choose his words carefully before continuing, "I recommend you visit a psychiatrist and take a—"

"Psychiatrist! What?" she snapped, "I'm fine. I just have a lot on my plate and can be absent minded at times."

"Your lapse in memory and the lethargy concern me. I could be wrong, but—"

"It's nothing!"

"Could be… But let's play it safe. I ordered a CT scan and it wouldn't hurt to get a second opinion."

Despite the doctor warning her that she was exhibiting early signs of dementia and that she needed to take a break, she left the office with intentions of doing neither—taking a break or seeking a second opinion. The thought of her possibly suffering from such an illness was ridiculous. As far as she knew there was no family history of anyone suffering from mental illness, and she was too young to be losing her mind.

With the completion of the Lodge, and years of negotiation, the broadcasting rights covering the *Cowboys of Color Rodeo* event were finally extended to cover the Boley Rodeo. Both Sticky and her attorney were sitting in his office recalling how they had desperately hoped that plan would improve the turnout for the event.

"I can't believe it's been ten years already," Sticky said sitting across from his desk dressed in a Versace sheath dress and lace-up boots with a wool shawl draped across her shoulders. While stress had aged her considerably, the contours of her beauty remained intact and she still retained her voluptuous figure.

"I know. Everything seems to have worked out as planned," the lawyer said, elated about the fact that their plan had turned out successful.

In the years since opening the Lodge, the broadcasting coverage had made it a magnet for entrepreneur seminars. *Black Enterprise*, *Jet*, Bishop TD Jakes, and a number of other prominent magazines and organizations all booked events during the rodeo season. Hundred-mile BBQ runs had once again become the usual thing. Some 100,000 patrons were now descending on the small town annually just to enjoy the festivities and Johnnie Mae's favorite beef brisket and pork butt.

Stage two of their plan had called for the transition of Redd's bootlegging operation into a legitimate business. The operation had previously consisted of several distillery factories he had scattered about the Tri-County area. As a testament to the sure size and scale of the operation, each facility produced some 1000 barrels of whiskey per week.

For years, a sizable contribution to the local D.A.'s office had kept the operation running smooth with little interference by the local authorities. After Redd's murder, however, the district attorney had gotten cold feet and in no certain terms, let Blue and the family know they best start considering a distillery permit if they wanted to stay in business.

After several years of filing and waiting for licensing and manufacturing permits, J. M. Spirits was finally set to be distributed nationally to wholesale liquor chains. Going legit meant a significant cut of the profits would now go to Uncle Sam. Still, with national distribution, the business would see five times more in profits, which made up for any loss.

"Indeed..." Sticky finally said after briefly reflecting on just how far they had come. The visit to the doctor's office kept nagging at her.

"Now, about the club," her attorney started to say but stopped abruptly after noting her offish behavior. She was not her usual self. Sticky was one of his most dependable clients. She had overseen and worked with his law firm every step of the way to restore her late fiancé's estate. Over the years, he had grown to know her well enough to know when something was troubling her.

"Are you okay?" he asked, "Excuse me... Ms. Williams—"

"Oh…ah, me? Forgive me. You were saying, the club," she responded, ignoring the question. She had a zoned out and began questioning whether or not she was actually losing her mind. She admitted to herself that she was slipping. A couple of times she forgot to lock up the club and misplaced her car keys. *Nothing,* she thought before continuing, "Here's the papers you asked me to look over and sign."

Sensing whatever was troubling her must be personal, her attorney let it go. "Thank you," he said, reaching for the papers she extended over the desk.

Finally, after a little over a decade, they had reached the last stage of their plan, which entailed a complete makeover of the club. Up until that point, it's standing in the community had been one known to bottom feeders, who conjured sexual demons and threw wild orgies until the wee hours of the morning.

With the exception of Thursday nights, phat boobs wobbled from table-to-table and phat asses with stretch marks swallowed poles on stage. Girls kissed girls and the other amateur acts mostly consisted of strippers placing foreign objects, like champagne glasses, between their ass cheeks while someone placed a straw in them to drink.

After taking a few minutes to look over the paperwork, Sticky's attorney finally said, "Well… looks like everything is in order. I'll get down to the courthouse in Wewoka and file them tomorrow. Is there anything else I can help you with?"

"No." she said flatly, distracted, and stood, indicating the meeting was over.

When Redd's silent partner initially learned of the tax problems the club faced, his attorneys immediately filed a motion with the court claiming his limited liability in the business. As a silent partner, he had remained out of the picture and had hoped he would be absolved of any tax obligations. For several years the court entertained the motion. By the time a ruling was made, his attorneys had struck a backroom deal with Sticky's attorney, who orchestrated a buyout of his ownership in the business. King was now the club's sole proprietor.

After having her attorney draw up the paperwork transferring ownership and promptly filing them, she quickly went to work renovating and reinventing the club's image. Within months, the old disco ball and wall-to-wall mirror scene Redd had constructed was replaced with contemporary furnishings and several VIP lounges that gave both the office and club a touch of class.

Despite the casino out on Highway 270, the club's gambling business had not been affected and remained a steady source of cash flow. It now held a members-only gamblers den, outfitted with several Vegas-style dice, roulette and blackjack tables. Overhead, hung three cage enclosures equipped with stripper poles and strippers.

Pooches was now a real gentlemen's club, geared toward and upscale, high-end clientele. Particularly, local judges, politicians, and businessmen. To attract them, Sticky ultimately decided to get rid of Redd's more ratchet dancers and bring in a more upscale class of entertainers.

After realizing her shortcomings in this area, she quickly concluded that there were no two better people for the task than her brother and Regina.

Chapter 12

Child... now you know Redd rolling in his grave at the very thought of this," Dekoven said in a pretentious effeminate voice. He was sitting in an office chair across from Sticky's desk dressed casually in a Marc Jacobs leisure suit and wearing Lacoste loafers.

"I know..." Sticky laughed, "but I can't think of a better person for the job. These girls really need a makeover and—"

"Now you know these bitches need more than that! They need some NA, AA and Dr. Phil too, before I could ever do anything with them."

Sticky and Dekoven both broke out into a fit of laughter. What he had just said was so true. Most of the girls that work in the club had battled addiction of some sort or another and had daddy issues. How Redd, or even Sticky for that matter, kept the place running was beyond anyone's guess. Every night there was a problem; the till got clipped, someone went to jail, the police raided. All sorts of underhanded schemes seemed to unfold under the roof of Pooches. Despite it all, Sticky was determined to make it a first-class joint, and she knew she had to start with the girls.

"Besides…" Dekoven continued, "You know Redd wouldn't want me in charge of nothing that had anything to do with this business. Let alone being put in charge of talent development."

Sticky sat quietly thinking of how Redd never really accepted her brother. Dekoven was simply too much for him to process. Often, and especially on Thursday nights, he would show up at the club as his alter-ego in drag—Ms. Gina—who dressed in six inch heels and made more of a fashion statement than any other woman in the joint, including his sister.

He was so convincing in his appearance as a woman, with such remarkable grace, it never failed that some unsuspecting patron or male stripper new to the club would cozy up to him, and after things heated up, slip a hand under his skirt, only to discover his gumdrops. A fight would promptly break out, and all hell would unravel as the unfortunate soul would make his second mistake, thinking gay meant Punk.

Boo bop boo! Dekoven would transform into a Marvel hero defending gay rights. He would go from one extreme to another, drag queen to brawler, and quickly deliver a set of mixes and counterpunches, whipping most who thought that, just because he was a fag, he could not or would not fight.

"I never quite understood that boy," Blue often said of him. Betty-Jean and he always fought about how Dekoven would play with Sticky's dolls when they were children. "Just don't understand it," Blue would shake his head and feel guilty, believing his lack of presence in the boy's childhood had somehow contributed to him being gay.

With exception of his father's absence and the dolls, Dekoven's childhood was as normal as any boy's. He had girlfriends. All the girls wanted to date him, be his girl and kiss on him, even the older ones, but kissing them didn't feel right. He competed in some of the toughest bronc busting events. He fought with the other boys and won most of the time. However, by the time he reached his late teens he knew he was gay. He would go on to graduate at the top of his class as a hairstylist and develop an acquired taste for fashion that eventually built him a considerable Hollywood clientele. Often, he would fly out to L.A. or New York for one event or another to have some model or actor showcase his skills. He became a professional in his own right, which ultimately made his father proud.

"To each is own... to each his own," were always Blue's final words.

For King, growing up with such a flamboyant uncle was surprisingly the least bit of a hassle. From time to time some kid would crack a joke about his *sweet* ass uncle. He would often dismiss it without much fuss, and as time went on, and they came to recognize he was unaffected by their banter, the jokes all together came to an end.

Inside, however, he was affected. His uncle being gay had given him character beyond his years. Long before homosexuality was acceptable in popular culture, and state courts and legislators debated gay rights, Dekoven was the one person in King's life who taught him to be himself and never try to live up to someone else's standards.

Naturally, they did everything that uncles and nephews were supposed to do. They went fishing and hunting together, rode horses and bulls, and Dekoven even showed him how to fight. As a testament to his character, he always carried himself like a man while in his nephew's presence.

After taking a few seconds to think about Dekoven's comments, Sticky finally said, "I know, that's why I spoke to Regina about recruiting some girls to work the club—"

"And what that bitch say?" Dekoven interrupted, still somewhat reluctant to accept the position.

"She would work on it. So what…, you in or what?"

"Well… I'm going to need about six months to clear my schedule. And—"

"So you're in? I knew I could count on you," Sticky smiled in excitement.

"Yeah, but I am… it's only part-time. And Regina is going to have to deliver."

"Now girl…," Sticky said, knowing she was playing up to his alter ego, "You know she is. And when she bring them city hoes up in here these country niggaz go get to acting up."

"Child… You ain't never lied! Most of these niggaz grew up staring at the rear end of a cow or pig. And seeing them top-notch hoes Regina got, along with what I bring, definitely go get them chafe in the pants."

They both fell out in a fit of laughter knowing what he had just said was so true. Life was but a stage for him in which performances played out in his mind like a XXX flick. With Regina's girls and his talents and imagination, putting together a new stable of entertainers would be a piece of cake.

Over the years, Regina had grown into a thick, rich, dark chocolate honey. Her almond-shaped eyes were the greenest of emerald, and her high cheekbones and silky jet black hair betrayed her African lineage. Still, all of Africa was represented in her full figure. Standing 5' 11", she had all the curves in the right places which had an intoxicating effect on both women and men, making it easier for her to eat from both sides of the plate.

Yet she bore the scars of rape.

"Come here you little bitch!" her stepfather yelled, clawing at her undergarments.

Spring found little Regina lying in her bed dreaming of beautiful flowers and butterflies. It was a peaceful dream only to be interrupted by the heavy hand of Papa Joe. He'd gone bust at the crap house. Cedar Street seemed his only hope to escape the dreaded poverty that stole away his dreams of living the good life. Disgusted with himself, he had attempted to drown his troubles at the bottom of a bottle after snorting a few lines of powder cocaine. The mixture of the two had him on diesel ready to fight and fuck.

"Come here you little bitch," he shouted, then slapped and positioned himself between Regina's struggling legs.

"Please Papa Joe, please daddy...." she cried. She had grown numb to the abuse and her cries fell on deaf ears as his shaft penetrated her tight virgin womb.

Flesh tore, gouged by the thickness of his dick. His thrusts came hard and fast as his bull nuts begin to bounce up and down on her asshole. The look in his eyes went from wild to exhausted, as sweat poured profusely from his forehead before he cried out in relief and collapsed on top of her.

Regina quickly fought to get out from underneath him. Her gown, soaked with blood and semen, added to the smell of sex in the air. Her body convulsed with agony as his manhood slid out of her.

Shadows danced in the night as the scented candles on her nightstand lit up the room. Arms thrashing in an effort to free herself, Regina knocked one of them to the floor. A flame caught the sheet and the bed went up in flames. The sickening scent of Papa Joe's burning flesh filled the air as the flames grew, rapidly consuming more and more of the room.

Regina gasped in horror as Papa Joe's flesh sizzled like bacon in a frying pan. She quickly pulled herself together and fled the house. It would not be until she was standing in the yard that she thought of her mother's whereabouts. It was too late!

Helpless, she could only stare into the flames as the blaze tore through the house like a matchbox. The thought of her mother being burned alive caused her eyes to swell with tears, but, the violence her step-father had imposed on her would not allow those tears to fall.

Both the rape and Regina's experience in Oakland practically made her a sex therapist by virtue of misfortune. They provided her an ability to easily spot the damaged girls and boys. Within the first five minutes of a conversation she could pick up on whether or not they were cut out for the business.

Things in Oakland were good. Nevertheless, Regina was homesick, and had been contemplating a trip back East for quite some time. *A vacation to the country would be good for Slim and me.* Little did she realize, the nature of her business would force her decision.

Chapter 13

Shortly after Slim left for California, King discovered that their little hobby, cultivating the marijuana seeds they swiped from the club, was profitable. All the kids at school were experimenting with something: Molly, OxyContin, alcohol, syrup, and of course, the gateway drug, which was the most popular and cheapest. Even King himself had developed a taste for it.

He had taken to hanging out with Heath, whose uncle Danny, a classic Hells Angel type, didn't mind partying with the boys. It had become their ritual to camp out on the weekends and get high.

"You know the first rule of hustling?" King asked Heath and Danny as they sat beside a blazing campfire.

"No run it!" Heath responded, looking to his uncle expecting an answer.

Danny sat quietly rolling a blunt.

"You create your own product. It's that simple. See...," King paused. "We have a good thing here. But well, let me put it to you like this. My mom's ran my pops bootleg business since I was a toddler. She think I don't know what's up. But I've been peeped *game*. She won because pops had that secret sauce, that A1 recipe. He did it the best and for the cheapest price."

"Okay, so where you going with this?" Heath asked after taking a hard pull on the blunt Danny had fired up and passed.

"Man... We have to step it up. Go big! In this backyard boogie..." King looked at the blunt as he held it up in one hand, a cup of orange soda and syrup in the other, and then said, "This is tennis shoe money. We want that big wheel money. You know... that 420. And the only way we go get it is by coming with the best product for the cheapest price."

"You have a point young buck," Danny said thoughtfully. "But you realize it's more to it than just product and price?"

Danny knew the game. It would take a major indoor-grow to produce not only a quality product, but also enough quantity to put them in the wholesale business. It was either that or they would have to locate specific areas throughout the county where the soil was good for cultivating and a major water source was nearby in order to build an irrigation system. In either case, it meant work, and a lot of it. Not to mention, dodging the authorities.

"Look! I already know what you thinking," King replied, reading Danny's mind. He then looked down into his cup and began making twirling motions to create a tiny tornado in the sippy cup he held. It was beginning to take effect. He nodded and grew numb.

With every ounce he consumed of the opiate-based substance, his body grew more and more addicted. It was liquid heroin. His stomach cramped. Occasionally, he got the shits and chills and scratched at himself to relieve the feeling of a thousand mosquito bites. He knew he was flirting with destruction. Heroin had been his Uncle Pumpsie's downfall—it drove his addiction, ultimately causing the murder of his brother, King's father. This much he had learned from his grandfather, which had also been his mother's reasoning for blaming Pumpsie for Redd's murder.

"It wasn't your uncle's fault," Blue told King.

Still, he was old enough to draw his own conclusions. And like his mother, rage and hatred were eating at his better judgment. They consumed him. He was now becoming something, someone, he had vowed to never become as a result of his illogical thinking, which led him to believe his "use" wasn't quite the same as his uncle's.

I got this, King repeatedly told himself as he stared into the cup. *It's not what you do... But how you do it,* he'd convinced himself. *I'm no junkie, I only do it every now and then... To take the edge off, like medicine to rid myself of all these feelings. Yeah, its medicine,* he thought as he slipped into a deep nod.

Before long, Danny was showing King how to better cultivate the soil and prune and cure his plants so that they would reach their full potential. King was now venturing deep into the woods around the countryside to find discrete locations that would be suitable to plant his cash crop. Eventually, he settled on several secluded areas that ran along the bank of the Canadian River. Much of the land surrounding the river was ideal for outdoor-grow operations due to the sandy composition of the soil and its high nitrogen content.

After spending several months building irrigation canals and balancing the nitrogen levels in the soil, the results were impressive. King had produced some 150 plants that were blooming with six-inch buds frosted with sticky green leaves.

"Bro... This shit gas! For reals," Heath choked after taking a pull on a blunt. "And the head change... whoa!" he coughed. "This gas bro. This gas!" He was stuck and high as a kite.

The THC levels of King's product had skyrocketed to produce a strain of pot that was more than deserving of an honorable mention in *High Times Magazine.*

"Hey, that's it!" King snapped in excitement. "I've been trying to think of a name for it for weeks now... We going to call it 'HEAD CHANGE'".

As the word spread about HEAD CHANGE, money started to pour in hand over fist. Heath was now treking over to Seminole to sell nickel packs to the white kids who hung out on the strip, and Danny was dumping it by the boatloads to his biker buddies. Even Slim was in on it.

"You get the Christmas present I sent?" King messaged Slim on Facebook.

A thumbs up emoji popped up, and within seconds King's cell phone began to vibrate.

"What's good cousin?" King answered.

"Shit!" Slim replied.

"I know... I've been jumping from toilet to toilet all day. So what's good?"

"Christmas trees and presents... Christmas trees and presents," Slim sung with a lilt in his voice. "I'll be putting something in the mail for you in a couple days."

"Bet!" King replied, a big smile sweeping across his face.

The boys continued to make small talk, speaking of the holidays. Yet they secretly confirmed to one another the package had hit.

King's Christmas present was 25 pounds of HEAD CHANGE, vacuum sealed and shipped, via UPS Priority Mail to a hotel room Slim had rented under an alias. Since the harvest, it had become a weekly routine.

A week later Slim's present arrived.

"Thirty bands... 30 bands, $30,000!" Kings voice lit up with excitement with each stack he counted. A small stuffed animal lay on the bed ripped apart sitting next to three, $10,000 bundles that were tightly wrapped with a rubber band.

Things had taken off so fast he hadn't slowed down enough to count all the money they were pulling in, which for him, meant nothing next to the sense of accomplishment he gained from making something out of nothing.

Before long, King's name was ringing amongst his classmates as he drove into the school parking lot in his father's *SS*. He had flipped it, dipped it in a candy cobalt blue with ghost flames and matching cocaine white guts. The undercarriage had been powder coated white, and a chrome suspension and eight inch lift kit stood over 28" Fogiato rims with white insets.

Dre, and he were now living out the "Trap or Die" track off Young Jeezy's album *Let's Get It: Thug Motivation 101*.

There they were, teenagers, working the door at the school bathroom like a trap house.

"Yo Bama, let me get a Nickel pack!"

King spun on a dime and looked up to see the school security guard walking into the bathroom just as he handed three bundles of 20 nickel packs to one of his bundle boys. The kid had snitched—he had been arrested for selling HEAD CHANGE in the school parking lot and had been turned.

Dre quickly sprang into action, rushing the guard like a tackle sled on a football field, hurling him into the wall with a crash.

King read the play and broke wide for a bathroom stall after snatching the bundles from the kid and tearing them open to flush.

Ms. Williams, Javon and the other young man are looking at some pretty serious charges. I have a staff member with three broken ribs and, apparently, a drug operation that was being run from my school bathroom. Now what in God's name am I supposed to do with that?" the principal asked..

"DRUG OPERATION!" Sticky exclaimed. "We're talking about a few bags of weed... Don't you think that's a little bit of a stretch?"

"Absolutely not! We have another young man who's informed the authorities that he's been dealing for your son for quite some time now."

Sticky didn't want to believe her ears. As much as she wanted to think otherwise and dismiss the charges as hyperbole, she dared not, knowing her son was too much like his father to doubt it.

"Okay, so where do we go from here?" she asked, certain the principal was going to call the police.

"Well... I'm sorry Ms. Williams, but my hands are tied on this. There's not too much I can do with so much happening in school these days. Here it is: I have a staff member who's been assaulted...," the principal said, pausing for effect before continuing and leaving Sticky with little doubt as to his next move. "I'm afraid both boys will be permanently suspended and I have to call the authorities."

Not long afterward, it began circulating around the club that King was the man.

Sticky and Dre's mother, who happened to be employed at Pooches, stood in the police station waiting for their sons' release.

Fortunately, for King, Chief Brown was a regular at the club, which went a long ways in eventually getting his charges dropped. Dre, on the other hand, because of his record, would be sentenced to a 90-day boot camp after pleading guilty to interfering with a police officer's duty and an assault.

"I didn't raise you to become a fucking drug dealer," Sticky snapped at King. She had been grilling him for the past two days since they left the police station.

"What you mean you didn't raise me? Hello, did you forget you practically brought me up in a strip club?" he shot back defiantly before continuing. "Mama, please! You know I got my daddy's blood running through my veins. Hustlin' is in my DNA!"

Tears swelled in Sticky's eyes, knowing what he had just said was so true. Still, it was something she wasn't ready to quite accept or deal with. Her baby was growing into a man and had chosen to follow in his father's footsteps.

"Oh... Okay, so you are your daddy now?" she finally asked after pulling herself together. "Okay smartass... You hustling? So that was your money I found stashed away? So what's your next move hustla?"

King's eyes lit up at the mention of his stash. All in all, he had stacked a little over $35,000 off HEAD CHANGE.

"You see what it is... stack money like Mark Zuckerberg!"

Sticky was shocked. At first she thought the money was Redd's. Over the years she occasionally stumbled across one or two of his stash spots. Now, all of a sudden, she was being forced to dismiss that notion and deal with the fact that her son was becoming a factor in the streets.

"And how the hell you going to account for all that money to the IRS!" she spat, thinking of nothing else to say, for nothing else seemed appropriate at the time that would get him to thinking.

"Run it through the club just like you and Daddy!" King responded.

"Boy! You don't know a damn thing about business or laundering money. What in the world ever gave you that idea?"

"Look... I'm no fool, moms. I know that's how my pop's and you cleaned up that bootleg scratch. You want me to go on?" King folded his arms in defiance as surprise swept across his mother's face.

It was in that moment she realized how irresponsible she had been in allowing him to work at the club. At first it seemed like a good idea. It would allow for him to gain some work experience in the family business. Now, it had proven not to be her brightest idea. *What was I thinking?* she questioned herself.

"Okay... So you want to talk about money!?! Let me tell you something about your daddy." What she was about to say would be one of the most difficult things she had done since burying Senior. Nevertheless, the boy needed to hear it. He needed to know the truth. "Your father, for all the things he was... your father well he..." she paused to search for the strength to force the words from her mouth. "Your father... well, he knew how to hustle and get block money. But as much as I love and respect him, he didn't know a damn thing about how to make money make money, or clean it up as you say. It wasn't until your grandfather took him up underneath his wing that he was able to take it to another level!"

Tears were now raining down Sticky's face as she stared at her son and saw Redd in his face and actions. It was inevitable. As much as she had prayed that this day would never come, she was now being forced to reckon with the fact he was his father's son. Redd's spirit had begun to fester within him.

King had grown up under the auspices of a legend. He had spent most of his life, since being knee high to a pool table, listening to the stories about Daddy Redd the Hustla... Daddy Redd the ho getta. And now her greatest fear was materializing. Daddy Redd had gone out, guns blazing, and she was afraid that her son would too.

" Son... there isn't nothing in those streets but cutthroats, court dates, crooked cops, and caskets. I'm not going to let you die in those streets like your daddy," she uttered softly.

"Mama," King took his mother by the shoulders and looked her square in the eyes before and saying, "Mama... I'm not going anywhere. The streets, they'll never take me from you. I love you and promise, I'm not going anywhere!"

For the first time, King thought about what he was getting into and how much it had affected her and others. Her words were powerful and came down on him like a ton of bricks. And while he didn't like what she had said about his father, it weighed on the *real*. He never thought of the role his T-Jones and grandfather had played in his daddy's rise from the streets. So much he had taken for granted.

"Look! There is something I… I need you to understand," Sticky said firmly. "Those streets…" she took a deep breath. "Those streets, they break promises. I know because your father made the same promises. I don't want you to have to go through that. I don't want to bury you or see you in prison like… like your—"

"Uncle Pumpsie?" King interrupted, ready to press.

"Yes. Pumpsie."

As much as he wanted to press the issue about his uncle's involvement in his father's death, he could see that the mere mention of his name had his mother literally shaking, barely able to get her words out. He decided against it, knowing the answers would come in time. The past few days had been difficult enough for them both. Seeing her smile for a change was a relief.

"Look moms…" King finally said, "we in this together. Ever since I can remember, you've been grinding away and stacking everything to make sure I'm good. I'm good. But it's time for me to start looking out for you."

Sticky threw her arms around him and said, "I know baby, I know. But look… Don't let those streets hijack your head. You ain't going to be no two-bit hustla slanging dope."

King sat in silence with his mother's head in his chest. He knew being a two-bit hustla was the last thing he'd ever be. He'd been blessed in the *game* with an advantage and he was about to use it for everything it was worth.

Chapter 14

"What's going on with you boy? Your grandmother tells me you have gotten yourself kicked out of school. She want you back at the Lodge when we get done here. And your mother tells me you trying to be Nino Brown. What's up with all that?" Blue shifted about in his saddle and asked, looking down at King.

King rode alongside him on a Yamaha YFZ450 ATV. Several ranch hands had fanned out around them, either on horseback or ATVs, as they drove a large herd of cattle towards a makeshift stockade. Summer was around the corner, which meant the herd had to be rounded up and vaccinated.

As a kid, King loved the roundup. Racing back-and-forth around the herd on his ATV was an adrenaline rush. The thrill of a stampede and the danger that accompanied it broke the monotony of life on a cattle ranch. However, he was no longer a kid, and after getting a taste of the *life*, he now dreaded the work, any work, that didn't involve stuffing packs and getting money. Like all things cowboy, the cattle business no longer appealed to him.

"Well?" Blue insisted, looking to King for an answer.

"It's nothing," King responded, then attempted to change the subject by asking, "Why is everybody so tight-lipped about what happened with Uncle Pumpsie and my pops? I mean… It's not like I—"

"What? Don't have a right to know?" Blue finished King's sentence. "You do! But—"

"But what!?! Why ain't nobody trying to tell me what happened? Uncle Lenny told me about everything that led up to it. I know my daddy was a factor in them streets. I know that. And I know what comes with it. But, what I want to know is who, who killed my father and not all this about how everybody feeling about it or who's to blame or not to blame!" he demanded, forcefully.

Blue looked out across the field in silence. A slight east wind blew the heady smell of fresh-cut grass in his direction delivering its serenity. In the distance, he could see one of the John Deere 9330 tractors he recently purchased as it made its first cut of alfalfa hay. It was a beauty. A farm boy's Bentley, costing almost a half a million dollars. Its tires were more than five feet tall, and despite one of his ranchers sitting at the wheel of its air conditioned cab, every movement was entirely automated: the tractor's course predetermined, self-correcting, and precise within an inch, guided by two dozen signals from the Global Positioning System and the Russian Global Orbiting Navigation Satellite System. It was a marvel of efficiency.

After spending several tours in the war torn fields of Afghanistan, Blue had grown to appreciate the peace and quiet of life on the ranch. Still, he knew war. Wars grew from old wounds. And in this case, where his grandson was pressing him for details about his father's murder, were closure had been waiting in a prison cell for over a decade. He thought long and carefully before responding.

"Well... truth is, don't nobody really know but your Uncle Pumpsie." Blue lied. As much as he felt it was the boy's right to know who killed his father, he reasoned it was best he not know, fearing he would lash out in retaliation. He knew his grandson. He had known his father. And there was little to distinguish between the two. They both were hot heads. "Y-Your Uncle P was one of the... I mean the only person there," he added, attempting to clean up the blunder. "He was the last person that seen your father alive."

King's eyebrow arched with disbelief as his lip twisted sourly. It was the same old bullshit. He knew his grandfather wasn't keeping it one hundred with him. All the secrecy surrounding his father's murder was causing him to grow distrustful of his family. There was more to the story than what he was being told. He could feel it in his bones. It was as if his father had reached out from the grave to tell him there was more to the story than what he had been led to believe.

"So which one is it?" he finally asked.

"W-W-What do you mean?" Blue stammered nervously. He had slipped.

"You said my Uncle Pumpsie was 'one of,' meaning there were other people there when—"

"I-I-I meant to say the last, the last goddamn it!" Blue fumbled with his words trying to get them out. "I don't know. Anyway, what's this shit I hear about you selling dope?"

Like his mother, King recognized when his grandfather was trying to avoid something. "It wasn't but a few bags of weed," he responded.

"A few bags of weed..." Blue smirked, and then said, "Trap Money! Boy what the fuck you trying to prove? What... You want to walk in your daddy's shoes? Those streets will burn you and leave blisters on everyone in your circle. Just like they did with—"

"I ain't trying to prove nothing to nobody!"

"So what's all this about? You want to get money? Look around you," Blue pointed to the tractor, then the roller crimper, vertical tillage aerator, air seeder, and said, "When I look at that equipment, that's money! That tractor cost half a ticket. Look around you. That's over one thousand acres covered with a thousand head of cattle. Now do the math son! That's one thousand times $1,000 per acre. That's a thousand times a thousand dollar's worth of beef. And that's not to say nothing about that 'coin' those cornfields bringing in. See..." he paused for effect, then said, "While them city boys waste their money on luxury cars, gaudy jewelry and designer clothes, your father invested his in land and equipment to turn a profit. This here... This is a real machine. It is generating money every season. And there's a premium on everything it produces. Think about that! Here it is some 12 or 13 years after your father was killed and it is still producing. Those cows multiply! Those fields... guaranteed money. All you have to do is plant the seed each season."

As much as King respected and could appreciate what his father had accomplished, he had begun to recognize the fact that it meant nothing in the face of dying in vain. He wanted answers, not lectures. His grandfather, like his mother, only sought to avoid providing them.

However, he had another piece to the puzzle now and knew what he had long suspected: There were other people besides his uncle that were present when his father was killed. How many, and who, remained unknown. He rested assured time would tell.

"When your father placed that crown on your head, he portrayed his hope and vision for the man he wanted to see you grow into. You cannot become that man if you don't understand the world you live in, how it works, and where you from, particularly your history. And you can't become that man selling drugs either," Betty-Jean said.

She and King sat at a conference room table located on the second floor of the Lodge.

"For years I taught African American history and cultural studies in several universities throughout Chicago. Your grandfather would always say I was one of those NOI types who was extremely passionate and motivated when it came to the progress of black folk. Now... since you were a child, I have worked hard to instill in you the value of education and my most regarded principal to never half-ass do anything. Always do your best or don't do it at all."

"I get all that Grandma. I do. And I understand what you mean about education," King said. "But I wonder sometime, where do we come from? I mean... I know Africa. But what part, what tribe?" he asked, trying to ignore his grandmother's comment about drugs and hoping to change the subject. A can of orange soda rested in his hand.

"We're descendants of the Gullah speaking people of West Africa, Sierra Leone to be exact. Our ancestors were captured and transported from Banana Island to America and enslaved on the plantations of Georgia and the Carolinas. Thereafter, many escaped into the disease filled wilderness of the Florida Everglades where their masters dare not venture. There, we were welcomed by the Natives who grew to appreciate our fierce fighting spirit. For decades, we mixed our culture and bloodline, eventually producing a hybrid people, the Black Seminoles, Seminole meaning 'runaway'."

"Black Seminoles? Like you and Grandpa Blue?" King asked enthusiastically, intrigued with the story.

"Yes. Our ancestors were a force to be reckoned with," Betty-Jean responded, prideful of the fact. "There are many great warriors, both black and Native American: King Payne, Bowlegs, Nero, Abraham 'the Prophet', John Caesar, Osceola, and, most notably, John Horse, Wewoka's founder, all of whom led the First and Second Seminole Wars against the United States military prior to the Civil War.

King sat quietly thinking about how the history he had been taught in school had omitted this. Not even the Native American kids he knew were aware of it.

"What is this?" he asked as his grandmother handed him a thick hardcover book with an image of several black soldiers dressed in early 20th century military garb.

"It's a documented account of both U.S. military records and the oral history of the Black Seminole War parties that resisted the incursions of the U.S. government and slave catchers between 1812 and 1842."

King took the book into his hands and began to flip through its pages. He was immediately stirred by the stoic portraits of his ancestors. Their hardened faces and dark eyes exposed the fierceness they possessed. They bore the characteristics of two continents bound by slavery and war and blackened by the African blood that ran through their veins.

As Betty-Jean continued to recount the history, King nodded off into a daydream.

Suddenly, he was wandering about the Georgia plains. For miles, trees and mountains stretched before him, never ending as he seemed to run in place. The forest flew by him like a Spike Lee flick. He desperately sought freedom. He ran for his life. Fear gripped at his heart as he suddenly came to an abrupt halt and his eyes frantically searched about the trees for signs of danger. There, under the dim light of the moon, he stood bearing the scars of rebellion on his back. His ears were his eyes and the sounds of an owl and crickets reassured him that they were alone and safe.

"Quickly! We must join our brothers and sisters in the swamps," King heard himself call out in Gullah. He then signaled to a small band of runaway slaves that the coast was clear. "There, we will fight and find freedom with the natives of this land."

At that moment, he envisioned Nat Turner, Kunta Kinta, and Harriet Tubman leaping forward with their glistening faces sweating profusely. They had their crude weapons drawn, ready to kill.

There, in the disease filled swamps of stagnant waters where marsh marigold and deadwood trees were home to pits of poisonous snakes and man eating alligators, they would join the ranks of those who had come before them to fight alongside the Natives. For centuries prior to encountering the Africans, these areas were uninhibited by the Native Americans. King's thoughts drifted to the notion that his band of warriors and he would find the terrain advantageous and ideal to execute guerrilla warfare.

"Javon, Javon! Boy are you paying attention?" Betty-Jean reached over and shook King, waking him from the nod. "Jo—"

"Whoa uh, yeah," he finaly responded. Realizing there was somewhere he needed to be, he said, "Yeah…, say, Grandma, let's finish this later. I gotta b-up… To see moms," he lied.

This boy must think I was born last night, Betty-Jean thought to herself. She knew she couldn't force the history on him. He would have to take it upon himself to discover its importance and the impact on his life. *In time, in time…* she figured, and then said, "Well, you take that book and read it. And work on your damn grammar. All that 'dims' and 'gotta b's'—"

"I gotcha… I mean, okay Grandma," he smiled as he stood to kiss her on the cheek and turned to leave. "Love you!" he added before hitting the stairs.

"Love you too. And be safe."

The lessons King's grandparents sought to instill would take some time to come full circle. He quickly disappeared out the door with only one thing on his mind—trapping!

The history of Wewoka had been interesting. However the streets were calling and he needed to get his weight up. So the books got tossed to the wayside. And little did he realize he was about to learn why they called it "trap money!"

Chapter 15

W hat's good cousin?" King asked as he whipped the *SS* out of the Lodge parking lot onto Pecan Street and drove toward the intersection leading to Highway 48. He was on the cell phone talking to Big-D.

"It's lovely cuz," Big-D replied, referring to the lick he had just recently put King up on.

Despite being King's younger cousin, Big-D had grown into an exceptionally talented athlete. A husky kid, with an NBA reach that had him ducking doorways, he was a bit mischievous too. On several occasions he had earned himself a suspension from school and eventually a permanent assignment at continuation school for repeatedly hacking the navigation and computer systems of several teachers' cars, causing everything from the windshield wipers to the engine to go haywire.

Having spent the first ten years of his life in foster care, he had been forced to live by the code "survival of the fittest." It had been hell on him to say the least. By age ten, he had grown to be a heartless tough who learned to steal to eat, to clothe himself and put a few measly dollars in his lint filled pockets. Fortunately, his mother's half-sister eventually found him in the system and after a long drawn-out legal battle, he was placed in her care and now lived with her and her children, five boys and a girl in Bristow, a small suburb 20 minutes west of Tulsa.

Naturally, there was a power struggle amongst the children when David joined the camp. War was declared, but his foster care experience had provided him with an advantage. After a few skirmishes and unsuccessful attempts to rat pack him, "Big'D", as they would call him, had earned their respect and was deemed the leader of the pack.

"Auntie, here take this," he said, surprising her one day as he placed a band in her hand and gave her a hug and a kiss. He had long since recognized her struggle and loved her dearly for rescuing him from foster care and providing him a home and family.

To help, he began hustling again. At first it was an honest grind. He did what most kids do to make a few dollars. He collected cans, bottles, mowed lawns, and did a number of odd jobs around town. However, as he and his cousins approached their teens, he reverted back to his old ways. He had since gave up the shenanigans at school for a more suitable profitable hustle for his talents, stealing cars!

"Look I'm coming out of Boley now. I'm about to hit 48 to the B-town. I'll be there in 20," King hung up the phone and reached down to turn up the music before hitting the gas to sail down the highway.

"It's simple, you see..." Big-D explained to King as he circled the parking lot at the Woodland Mall on the eastside of Tulsa. After picking David up in Bristow, they had jumped on the Turner Turnpike and headed to "Thug Town" to hit a lick. It was late by the time they reached the mall and the sun was already setting.

"These new cars are like smartphones on wheels, giant rolling cages of software code controlling everything from the brakes to the ignition," Big-D continued.

"So you telling me you can hack a car like a computer?" King asked in disbelief as he spotted an empty parking space next to a new Escalade and whipped in to park.

"Even easier!"

"How so?"

"See..." Big-D said, "the people making them haven't really came to grips with the whole cybersecurity aspect of the technology they putting in these cars. There's like over 100 microcomputers built into these muthafuckas that makes them vulnerable."

"Kind of like back in the day when the PC first hit and everybody shit was getting hacked?" King asked.

"Hell, they still getting hacked! But yeah, to make it simple, the auto industry ain't caught up and that's making it easy for us, nuh mean?"

"Hmmmmm..." King sighed, stroking at the tuffs of his chin, then said, "Somewhat. Now explain that whole Wi-Fi, UCONNECT thing again."

"Okay so here's the deal. With these new whips, most of them come with cellular or Wi-Fi technology hardwired into their GPS and music or video streaming systems. Other systems, such as UNCONNECT, are wirelessly linked to the car. Kind of like OnStar, for example. Now with all this wireless technology hooked to the car, the computers are controlling it and those same computers can easily be controlled by someone else, nuh mean?"

"I get it. But how?" King asked, still somewhat confused.

"With an app! Do I have to spell it out to you? See, I can upload a virus to the car's entertainment or GPS system through an app, which will then allow me to access the microcomputers controlling it. Once I connect my Bluetooth to the Wi-Fi or UCONNECT, I can send a command, any command, to the car's control panel."

King sat quietly at the wheel of the *SS* and tentatively observed as Big-D's fingers went to work on his laptop like a piano player. A few minutes later, a digital control panel popped up on the screen signaling he had accessed the Escalade's computer system.

"Wala!" Big-D lifted his head and grinned. "Genius!" He quickly sat the laptop on the console and jumped out of the car after giving the parking lot a once-over.

"Now hit the enter button and let's get this money!" he said, turning to the truck.

Big-D reached out to grab the door handle, and King pushed the button. The Escalade's doors unlocked and the engine roared to life.

Out on Old Vic's Road, *257 Customs* seemed closed for business as King, Dre, and Big-D drove up and parked in front of the garage door in a jewel green BMW sports coupe on 22" chrome rims with mirror tints. Dre quickly parked the *SS* and walked up to the other car as he looked around. The area surrounding the shop was dimly lit by a light loosely fixed to a telephone pole some 30 or so yards from the building. It was late. Stars flickered in the sky like dance hall lights. To the side of the building, partially assembled cars and car parts lay scattered about the yard, which was fenced off with a 6-foot security fence and razor wire. Three American Short Nose Pitbulls struck at the fence fiercely, barking and biting at it as King waved at the surveillance camera mounted above the garage door.

"Bruh, leave them damn dogs alone!" King snapped as he hit Big-D on the shoulder with a backhand in an effort to stop him from throwing ice at the dogs. This only enticed him further as he reached into his cup and threw several more pieces of ice at the dogs.

"And put that shit out!" King continued as he turned to address Dre, who was standing outside the car, toking at a blunt he had just put a flame to as they waited for the garage door to open.

"Cousin, you need to relax," Dre said as he took a hard pull on the tree and started choking violently. "Besides… I'm going back to H-Town in a few days. So let's celebrate stacking this paper all summer, smell me?" He took another pull of the tree and again started choking as he attempted to pass the blunt to King, who waved it away before it was offered to Big-D.

"C mon' man! You know I get tested for football season next week," Big-D smirked as he took the blunt, put it to his lips and took a hard pull, filling his lungs with dank smoke. "Good thing I got those Golden Seals," he added between attempts to hold the smoke in and talk before Dre and he busted out laughing.

King shook his head. Secretly, he envied their carefree attitudes. Here it was: he was almost seventeen and felt like he was going on 30. His boyhood had been sucked into the vacuum of his father's legacy. He had to man up, keep the torch lit, and the money coming. It was in that moment he thought about the love and admiration he felt for his crew. It was overwhelming. They had assisted in putting him on top and expanded his hustle without even knowing it.

Slim had 71st and Hamilton in East Oakland on lock with HEAD CHANGE. Danny and Heath were bringing in bigger crops. *And this lick with these cars,* he couldn't believe it. In just a few months, he had almost tripled his stack from the cars they stole. "See cousin!" he recalled Big-D boasting as he handed him his cut from the Escalade. It was two bands and a nickel, $2,500, the easiest money he had ever made. Dollar signs began popping up in his head like an emoji as he slapped Big-D on the back and recalled saying, "Boy you is a fucking genius if I ever knew one. A few more licks like this and I'm going to be in the *game* for reals!"

As King sat there taking it all in, he also thought about an offer Jay-5 had made him shortly after they started to take him cars. Jay-5 offered to put him in charge of the region's Young Money Click. King knew a lot of the youngstas who had clicked up with them. Most of them he had grown up with. But then the offer came with a hook. Jay-5 would front him the dope and he was to supply all the schools in the region.

If there was one thing King had learned in his short career in the *game*, it was to owe nothing to it or anyone in it. He was no bundle-boy. He knew his worth and quickly recognized Jay-5 was trying to strap him with a debt he would spend the rest of his life, if not die, trying to repay.

Inside the shop, several goons were hard at work disassembling a handful of cars that had been brought in the previous night. Sparks from a cutting torch lit up the windows on the garage door as sounds of a grinder and air compressed tools could be heard grinding away. Jay-5 sat in his office with two grizzly looking bikers.

Ironically, the interior design of the office radiated class. State-of-the-art computer and surveillance systems sat on a mahogany desk along with two Tiffany lamps. The walls of the room were lined with bookshelves filled with neatly arranged books, many of which were old, leather-bound tomes. On the other hand, the 20 foot saltwater fish tank, which held two baby sharks, was in stark contrast to the intellectual feel of the room. So too did the inexpensive sports memorabilia and amateur boxing trophies that spoke of a boy's dreams never fulfilled.

"There's 50 pounds of 'Gorilla Glue' in those bags," Jay-5 said as he looked at the two bikers sitting in front of him. He then nodded towards a green duffel bag sitting in the corner of the office.

One of the bikers leaned forward, sat a brown paper bag on the desk and said, "It's always good doing business with you Jay."

Jay-5 nodded approvingly as the other biker got up and walked over to the bag and unzipped it to remove a brick. He then reached into his soiled pants pocket, retrieved a knife, and with a flick of the wrist, exposed the blade and jabbed it into the package.

"Its top-notch grass, boss," the biker said, nodding to his partner.

"My product is always the best. The best! Only from the Bay!" Jay-5 replied, somewhat offended as he glanced over at the surveillance monitor and saw King waving. A sinister grin flickered across his face. The boy was clueless as to who really killed his father, thinking his Uncle Pumpsie did it. Pumpsie didn't even know that his nephew was in cahoots with him. It was Jay-5's dirty little secret. *Keep your enemies close*, he thought.

"Get the door for the youngsta!"

One of his goons spun on a dime and headed for the garage door.

A few minutes after King's entourage had parked, the garage door opened and the beemer disappeared through its doors.

"What's good folks!" King said as he parked and got out of the Benz. "Where is Jay?"

"Wait over there," the goon who opened the garage door said, pointing to a bench beside Jay-5's office door.

Dre and Big-D quickly made their way over to an old Pac-Man video game that sat in the corner of the shop, dropping a few quarters in it and taking bets from the other goons.

King did as instructed and took a seat. As he waited for Jay-5, he could see there were two Hells Angel's inside the office that he knew from somewhere. While he didn't place them immediately, it eventually dawned on him when he noted their club jackets, which bore the insignia of a local chapter of the organization that just so happened to be run by Danny.

"Come on in young buck!" Jay-5 said as he noticed King sitting outside the office door.

From the moment King walked into the office, it was clear to everyone he possessed character beyond his years. He stood poised, dressed in a black leather jacket, fitted Tom Ford jeans, with black Adidas Adi Quilt boots on his feet. A black beanie hung from his right back pocket. He did an once-over of the office, a security check, and noted everything was on point.

"What's good Jay?" he asked. It was all business. It was obvious to him that the bikers had grown uncomfortable the minute he stepped into the office. He had placed them. They were Danny's boys. *Now what's this about?* He wondered to himself. *Are they making side deals? If so, they will be taxed for crossing game.*

"I need to rap with you," King continued.

"Fellas, this my young protégé," Jay-5 motioned towards King with the slight of the hand. "A real chip getta! His little crew good for a few cars a week, plus they're moving product. Y'all ain't going to believe this. I tell this lil' muthafucka I'm going to drop a hundred pounds on him. And, you know what he tell me?"

The two bikers looked at Jay-5 clueless as to what to say.

"The little muthafucka dropped 30 bands on the table and say, 'That front shit, punk shit!' Now tell me that ain't boss!"

King nodded at the bikers in acknowledgement, and then gave a slight shift of the head, which indicated to Jay-5 that he wanted to talk in private.

Jay-5 picked up on the signal. "Excuse me fellas." He stood, reached for the paper bag on the desk and pulled out several stacks before following King into the garage.

"So what's this next job?" King turned just as Jay-5 walked out of the office. There was a tinge of aggression in his voice. He wasn't feeling Jay-5 for putting his business out there like that.

"It's a special order," Jay-5 replied, ignoring King's tone as he handed over a picture of the car and the payment for the BMW.

"What's this? Some Batman shit?" King asked after looking at the picture Jay-5 handed him.

Jay-5 gave a slight laugh, and then said, "No. It's a customized AMG S65 Cabriolet Benz."

"Special order, huh?"

"Yeah. I know we have an arrangement, but this won't be a problem will it?" Jay-5 asked.

King's lip twisted sideways, indicating he wasn't feeling it. Not their arrangement, which was his crew and he would locate the cars at random, and Jay-5 only provided the make and model, but the whole biker thing and putting them in his mix rubbed him the wrong way. He was on the verge of telling Jay-5 it was a no-go. But he quickly changed his mind. He recognized the fact that he couldn't allow his emotions to interfere with his getting paper.

"This shit gon' hit you in the pocket for a little extra bruh!" King finally said.

"Name your price," Jay-5 responded without hesitating.

King paused a second to think. He knew the blue book value on the Beemer had to be somewhere around $100,000 but wasn't sure. However, the one thing he was certain about was the fact that even a fraction of a hundred grand would definitely put a nice lump in his knot.

"Twenty bands," King shot back, confident that his number was within the ballpark of the price the car would sell for on the black market.

"No problem!" Jay-5 said, knowing that the parts alone would fetch five times that. "I'll see you in a few days. We good?"

"We good," King responded as he pocketed the money Jay-5 had given him, and turned to leave.

Big D and Dre sat in the *SS* as lookouts while King was across the street hacking the Benz's computer system. Sweat poured profusely from his forehead as he worked the laptop's keyboard and wondered if he was doing it right. He had insisted that he do the job. After walking him through the process several times, Big-D had relented. It was show time.

After taking a few minutes to upload a virus to the Benz's UCONNECT system, King eagerly pressed the enter key on the laptop. Right away the car's doors unlocked and its engine roared to life. He quickly jumped in, pumped the clutch and shifted into first gear. By the time he pulled along the side of the *SS*, Michael Jackson's song "Smooth Criminal" was playing from the stereo.

"Bruh, we about to get tore off some real scratch for this one," Big-D said, looking down at the car and nodding his head in approval as King drove up.

"Real talk!" If Jay-5 broke off five racks for that beemer, imagine what we're going to get for this muthafucka!" Dre chimed in as he jumped out of the *SS* and got in the car with King.

"Already!" King shot back. He threw up the two fingers split and hit the gas, causing the Benz to dip sideways as he sped onto the expressway leading to I-40 East, Wewoka bound.

Forty-five minutes later, King's caravan turned off on 1st Street headed towards *257 Customs*. A small crowd of teenagers could be seen gathered up the block in the parking lot of the old Ben's BBQ restaurant, which sat boarded up and tagged with graffiti.

As they made their way up the street, King made a left on Seminole Street, which ran adjacent to the parking lot. The Benz slowed to a roll and Dre hung out the window and threw up 5th Ward.

"What that Young Money like?" he shouted at the crowd of onlookers.

"Get Rich Gang!" Ziff shot back and threw up GRG.

King smiled. GRG was his clique. He noticed the homies Ziff and G-Wayne posted in the crowd with Kay-Kay. She was the main attraction and reason why he had bent the corner after spotting her car from a block away.

Over the years, Kay-Kay had sprouted in every way. She had that whole Nicki Minaj thing going on when it came to her smile and lips. Her figure was banging out of this world with hips and thighs that seemed to have a mind of their own each time they stretched a pair of designer jeans.

By the time King had reached puberty, he was getting more ass than a toilet seat. All the girls, including a few strippers at the club, was throwing pussy his way. Kay-Kay however, was one piece of ass that he was missing. She was still playing hard to get.

Look at this nigga, Big-D thought to himself as he whipped the *SS* into the parking lot and parked. *Shorty bustin' corners hotter than a street light trying to show out for some pussy.*

"Hey David," Kay-Kay said, as she greeted him along with several of her girlfriends.

"What's good?" he replied, hopping out of the car and making his way through the crowd to embrace his homegirls: Casey, DD, Shelly, Trina, and Shara. He knew them all from Bristow. They were the "Hill Hoes" and everybody knew that if you wanted to knock a bad bitch in the B-town, then Trina's house on the hill was where you would go to find them. All the shorties from the hood hung out there and most niggas from GRG stayed on the hill trying to *cut* something. Occasionally, Trina and Shara would dance at the club on the weekends to make a few extra bucks and afterwards, they would hang out at the park with King and the rest of his crew.

As the Benz drove past the crowd, King leaned into the console trying to impress Kay-Kay. He made a U-turn at the end of the block, and as the car turned back to face the crowd, he slammed his foot down hard on the gas pedal.

Immediately, the 600 horsepower roared to life as the Batmobile spun out of control and King struggled to swing it into a series of donuts. Round and around and around it spun. Tire smoke quickly filled the air and concealed the car within a thick fog. When it cleared, police lights flashed in the distance and quickly approached.

"Aye yo! Five-O!" King panicked as he looked up in the rearview mirror and saw the police lights coming down on them.

A siren blurped in the distance as the police cruiser sped in their direction.

"Hit the gas bruh! The gas!" Dre screamed, slapping King on the shoulder in an attempt to snap him out of it.

King reacted right away, smashing his foot down on the accelerator as he shifted into first gear. The car's tires dug deep into the asphalt like a drag car on a green light, and the chase was on.

The Batmobile flew past the parking lot, hitting second, then third gear as they darted across 1st Street and across traffic. Several cars swerved in the oncoming traffic to avoid a collision. Tires were screeching. Horns blared as everyone in the crowd disappeared.

"Make a right up there!" Dre pointed towards Cedar Street. "No, no… I mean a left! Make a left!" he shouted as his hand gripped the passenger side door handle, and he anxiously awaited the opportunity to bail and run.

They flew past the turn before King could even consider it and quickly approached the intersection of Seminole and Park Street. That's when he was forced to make a sharp right to avoid a head-on collision with an oncoming car. The Benz spun out of control, jumped a curb and stalled out.

Dre's feet hit the ground like a happy cat on a hot tin roof as he jumped a fence and disappeared into a nearby residential area.

King frantically pulled at the door handle to avoid getting caught. It was jammed!

"Freeeeze!"

It was all over just as quickly as it started. The police had the car surrounded, and to King's dismay, an officer was towering over him with a Glock 17 pointing at his dome.

Chapter 16

"**W**hat!?!" Sticky couldn't believe her ears. Chief Brown stood outside of the Wewoka Police Department on his cell phone inquiring as to why she and the family hadn't been present at King's hearing.

"He was arrested around 1 a.m. for GTA and avoiding arrest two days ago. I just came out of the courtroom. He's being transferred to Cojac as we speak. Didn't anyone notify you about this?" Brown asked after informing her of the situation and noting her surprise.

"No... I, can't you do something until I get there? I should have been notified. He's a juvenile." Sticky shouted into the phone, panicking. She grabbed her keys off the mantel and ran out of the house to the car.

"No. Not on this one," he replied, reluctantly. He had yet to tell her the worst of it. "Olsen is on this one. He's all over it—"

"Olsen! What?" Sticky snapped. It was a name she had grown to despise over the years. He was the source of her strife. Redd's too.

"—Yeah, Olsen! Before I even got in this morning, he already issued a no bail order and signed off on the transfer. There's more…" Brown sighed, then said, "They're charging King as an adult."

Sticky stopped dead in her tracks. She looked down at her feet and realized she had run out of the house barefoot.

"Where are my shoes?" she wondered out loud.

"What?" Chief Brown asked, confused.

"My shoes… Where are my fucking shoes," she screamed into the phone like a mad woman.

Brown realized she was in shock. He had been trained to recognize the symptoms. It was part of the job that unfortunately, he had encountered one too many times.

"Sticky… Get it together baby girl," he finally said as he began to talk her back to the situation at hand. "Calm the fuck down… I'm sure your lawyers will have him out in no time!"

"No bail! What?" Sticky was mentally all over the place. From the moment she picked up the phone her maternal instincts had kicked in. Hearing of King's arrest overwhelmed her emotionally. She had to protect her baby. No mother wanted to see her son on lock. At once, she began to question herself as a parent. *What did I do wrong?* Deep down inside, she was beginning to doubt if she could raise a man. *He needs his father. A strong role model. Daddy? Yeah, call Daddy… he'll fix it.*

After gathering her senses, and Chief Brown's assurances that he would do everything he could to help the family, Sticky hung up the phone and quickly dialed the one person she thought could help her and King the most. He was their only hope.

Judge Jim Olson sat in his chambers with a look of scorn on his face. He flipped through the defendant's probation report. With the exception of a prior charge of distribution of marijuana, which had been dismissed, the boy had a clean record. Yet he knew all too well the ties the young man's family had with the prosecutor's office. Even more, as a former U.S. attorney, he had sought to indict the boy's father years ago.

"Alllll riiiiise!" the bailiff announced as Judge Olsen stepped into the courtroom.

King stood nervous. He was wearing an OJ, bright orange jumpsuit. Three months had passed since his arrest and he was being held without bail in the Central Oklahoma Juvenile Adjustment Center, also known as Cojac, which was located in Tecumseh. Cojac was known throughout the state as one of the toughest and most violent maximum-security juvenile lockup units. Olsen had personally seen to King's placement in the facility. He knew prison, the juvenile justice system for that much, would begin the process of conditioning him to live life on lockdown, just where he planned to see the boy would do hard time.

The following morning after King was being booked into the facility, he woke with an uncontrollable bowel movement. He had the shits, along with the feeling of his guts being literally ripped out by the bare hands of a thousand pound gorilla. For most of the day, he remained balled up in a fetal position in his cell, weak and fiendish, craving for an ounce of *lean*. By the second day he could no longer bear the pain and decided to throw in the towel. His feeble efforts to kick cold turkey were overpowered by the extent of his addiction. For the first time, he contemplated whether or not he had let his *use* get the best of him. He had been using daily, and now it had caught up with him in the worst way.

"You may be seated," the bailiff said after Judge Olsen was seated at the bench.

"In the case of people of the State of Oklahoma versus Javon Michael Reed, Jr...." the court clerk began reading off King's charges.

Sticky and her parents sat uneasy in the courtroom. As with Pumpsie, Blue had called in the big guns to represent his grandson. Problem was, however, Scott Butner didn't have any pull with Olsen. He was an outsider who Butner never had the chance to get some dirt on. Therefore, there was a good chance he wouldn't go with the sentence recommendation made by the probation officer for probation and time served. A motion to withdraw the plea had been filed. So too had a motion for recusal of the judge. Both motions were denied, which pretty much informed everybody of what to expect.

"Son you have entered a guilty plea to grand theft of an automobile, destruction of private property, and evading arrest," Judge Olson stated with a stern look on his face. "These are some very serious charges. Is there anything you would like to say to the court before it pronounces judgment?"

"Your Honor—" Butner stood and began to speak.

The judge quickly indicated for him to take a seat.

"No!" King stood, pulling his shoulders back. In that moment he thought of that scene out of *Dutch*, where Angel's crew jumped up in the courtroom and sparked the judge and the police.

"Very well. I hereby sentence you to a year at the R. E. D. Adult Correctional Camp in McAlester. Upon completion of the initial 90-day program, you will return to this court for consideration of a suspended sentence and probation. In addition, I order you to obtain a GED and attend NA."

Sticky broke down crying as her body rocked back and forth. Her hands quickly covered her mouth in an effort to muffle her anguish.

Shortly after King was locked up, the counselors at Cojac had notified her of his addiction to opiates. After seeking medical treatment for the withdrawal symptoms, they had to contact her for permission to start him on methadone. She was devastated. The thought of her son being addicted to the liquid equivalent of heroin sent chills down her spine. She could not help but reflect on everything Pumpsie had put the family through as a result of his addiction. Now she feared the possibility of having to watch it all play out again with King. It was just too much.

Three weeks later, a company size group of ununiformed young men, including King, stood in a loose military formation on the sun-scorched field of Camp R. E. D. as a bullhorn wielding officer was addressing them from a reviewing stand. He was the type that thought his dick grew an inch every time he put his uniform on.

"If there is anything, anything…" the officer stressed before continuing, "… you sissies will learn while at Camp R. E. D., it is the fact that I am not your friend! I am not your homeboy, yo mama, daddy, or anyone else that gives a rat's ass about you. Rule number one…" He then began barking off a series of rules as long as the Bible.

The sun beamed bright, temporarily blinding King as he struggled to assess the situation. The officer was a middle-aged, overbearing white man dressed in black fatigues, a utility belt holding of a pair of handcuffs, a baton, and a large canister of tear gas strapped to his thigh.

The wards that accompanied him were a wild and tough-looking bunch, culturally lost, morally disinherited, candidates bound for the morgue, a lifetime in prison, and the death chamber, which sat up the hill at Big Mac. Despite their youth, the result of hard drugs and a harder life, gave them a worn look far beyond their years.

Scattered about the campus grounds, surrounded by a 15 foot perimeter fence and razor wire, were several small cottages, a chow hall, gymnasium, chapel, barracks, and a building with big, bright yellow letters that spelled out "School."

A Concentration Camp! King quickly concluded.

The weeks and months dragged by as King attempted to make the best of a bad situation. The camp was a rigorous torture device of control. Not just control of the body, but control of the mind. All day he was made to sit in a classroom where he was being subjected to the rudimentary teaching methods of testing and sorting, and the indoctrination of someone else's truth by the sort of instructor his grandmother had warned him of that stagnated black progress for years with an outdated model of pedagogy, classism, and colonial hierarchies in American society.

"You must study them nonetheless," Betty-Jean would insist. "It's the only way you will understand their pathology and false ideologies of what it means to be educated and what have you...." After King had been permanently suspended from school, she had done her best to drive home the point that the classroom was a jail of another people's interest.

"The library was open, unending, free...." she encouraged.

Now that he was incarcerated, Betty-Jean would make good of a bad situation. Fortunately, she knew enough about prison to know it was a place where time was spent idly in most cases. However, she also knew it had the potential to become a university, a place where, if encouraged, a person could potentially grow in perspective and come to see more of the world through a narrow prison window than most people walking around outside. This much she had learned from the example set by Malcolm X, who she would often quote; "I have often reflected upon the new vistas that reading opened to me...."

She had tried, with little success, to encourage the boy to read. She constantly preached to King, "It's only through reading that you will be exposed to the information you will someday need to inherit the true blessings of your father's legacy."

King sat quietly thinking of his grandmother's words. He couldn't help but appreciate that, in the months since being at the camp, she had gone out of her way to make sure he had plenty of literature to read. There were novels, magazines and books of every subject and genre. Bored, with time on his hands, he eagerly consumed them, and to his surprise, soon developed a passion for reading.

He especially loved the urban novels she sent; not realizing his grandmother had purposefully sent them to captivate him with cheap thrills long enough to get him in the habit of reading.

Gradually, she had increased the depth of the subject matter, and within a relatively short amount of time, he was reading everything from Ashley & Jaquavis to Ta-Nehisi Coates.

Suddenly, King's thoughts were interrupted.

"Mr. Reed. Mr. Reed, Mr. Reed... Do you hear me? Are you paying attention?"

"Whoa... ah, what's that?" King finally responded.

Frustrated, the instructor repeated the question. "What role did President Washington play in shaping America?"

"What role did President Washington play in shaping America... hummmmm," King repeated, giving it some thought, before saying, "Well... I think he was a goon! He enslaved, stole, and swindled Britain out of the American investment!"

The instructor stood speechless. Before he could respond, King added:

"That investment was then put to his personal fortune and used to fund a Turf War—THE AMERICAN REVOLUTION! And if it wasn't for his sheisty ass ways—"

"Reed!" the teacher snapped, while turning beet red. "Drop and give me 50!" he added before going into a tirade about how the remarks were slanderous and untrue.

King dropped to the floor and began to count the push-ups out loud. He had grown accustomed to the workout. His rebellious nature had blossomed and often landed him a discipline, if not a few days in the brig.

"You beefy son!" lil' Jay poked fun at King as he returned to his seat. James Taylor, Jr., also known as lil' Jay, was a square from Bristow. An "A" student. His two favorite subjects in school were computer engineering and chemistry. The latter of which had landed him a stent in R. E. D. after getting caught on campus with a quarter pound of methamphetamine. He had cooked up the dope himself, using a recipe downloaded off the Internet, and tried to pawn it off on the same kid that had landed Dre and King in jail.

Naturally, his knack for whipping up synthetic drugs made for a common ground for the boys to bond with. The two connected immediately, and despite the situation, kept it light with each other by playing the dozens and capping on each other constantly.

"Oh! We got jokes?" King laughed at the pun. "Okay! Just so you know... I'm getting strong so I can lift your mama fat ass cheeks—"

"Mr. Reed!" the instructor yelled. "Would Mr. Taylor and you like to share with the class what is so funny?"

"Huh, it's nothing. I was just saying I—"

"Save it Reed, save it! Now take a seat and be quiet!"

"Yo mama," King turned to lil' Jay and whispered before kissing his biceps for effect and taking a seat.

For the remainder of the class, lil' Jay and he shot spit wads at each other and mimicked the teacher when his back was turned. Together, they were like the Mike Epps and Kevin Hart combination of laughter, gimmick and fool.

Chapter 17

Later that evening, King lay restless, tossing and turning on his cot. With the exception of a few grunts here and there, the barracks were relatively quiet. After staring at the ceiling for hours, he finally reached over and turned on a small reading lamp and picked up one of two letters he had received earlier that day. He had read them three times already, but couldn't get them off his mind.

Dear Javon,

Surprised? I bet you are! I saw your cousin David the other day and he gave me your address after telling me about how you got caught up. Stupid! SMDH. How is it a kid with everything winds up in your situation? I don't get it. I don't get you sometimes. I mean, since we were kids, you always showing out trying to impress somebody instead of just being yourself. Why can't you just be yourself. You know… Javon. No! You think you a King.

Well, you will never be my King:(Why? It's like my mama always say, "You can't have somebody who goes from Xbox to your box to the next girl's box." You don't get to push my button like a video game and run up your playa points. Playa! I need love, LL Cool J. (LOL.)

Seriously, I know you're probably reading this like, yeah, yeah, love is overrated! But remember this, love penned this letter! What we have is special. We grew up together from the sandbox. And you know you the only one that ever got to second base with me. So while you running around being a playa and living out your gangsta fairytale, here's one about love I wrote especially for you. Maybe you can figure it out before you come home?

King held the letter in his hand for a few moments as he thought about how he had taken love for granted. Not just with her, but also with his mother who he missed dearly, and for some reason, hadn't shown up at the past few visits. Up until then, she had visited him regularly. Figuring she must be busy with work and everything else she managed, he quickly disregarded the worrisome thoughts in his mind and continued to read the letter.

Once upon a time, there was an island where all feelings lived. Happiness, Sadness, Knowledge, and all the others, including Love. One day it was announced to the feelings that the island would sink. So they all prepared their boats and begin to leave. Love was the only one that decided to stay. Love wanted to persevere until the last possible moment.

When the island was almost sinking, Love finally decided it was best to leave as well and asked for help. Richness was passing by Love in a grand boat.

"Richness, can you take me with?" Love asked.

"No, I can't! There is a lot of gold and silver in my boat. There is no place for you," Richness answered

Love decided to ask Vanity, who was also passing by in a beautiful vessel. "Vanity, please help me!"

"I can't help you, Love. You are all wet and might damage my boat," Vanity replied.

Sadness was close by so Love began to beg for help. "Sadness, please, please let me go with you."

"Oh love... I'm so sad that I need to be by myself."

Happiness passed by Love too. But she was so happy she didn't even hear when Love called out to her.

Suddenly, there was a voice. "Come Love, I'll take you." It was an elder of Love.

Love felt so blessed and overjoyed that he forgot to ask the Elder her name. When they arrived at dry land, the Elder went her way. Love, realizing how much he owed the Elder, then asked Knowledge, "Who helped me?"

"It was Time," Knowledge answered.

"Time?" asked Love. "But why did Time help me?"

Knowledge smiled with deep wisdom and answered, "Because only with Time and Wisdom are you capable of understanding how great love is.

--Love, Kay-Kay

King smiled at the thought of how Kay-Kay had a way with words. She was always the poetic type who expressed herself through poems, music and short stories. Despite growing up in two completely different worlds, they understood each other. It didn't take long for him to figure out the meaning of the fairytale; love was deeper than money or beauty. Those who thought otherwise lived to discover wealth only brought sadness, and disappointment came from lust. Only time and wisdom would tell. This much, he had already come to realize after considering that, out of all the girls that were on his jock when he was in the streets shining, she was the only one who had reached out to brighten his spirits.

Still, he was deeply conflicted over their relationship. Jay-5, her father, had left him hanging after he had gotten caught up and charged with GTA. He cursed himself a thousand times, feeling like he had been played like a sucker for allowing her father to persuade him to violate the arrangement he had set in place when it came to scoping out the cars they stole. It was his safety net. For that, he had to accept responsibility. He got himself caught up by breaking his own rules.

However, the fact that Jay-5 hadn't even attempted to reach out to him or bless him with some commissary or something, didn't sit well with him. Not that he was hurting for anything. His family saw to that. However, it was a matter of principle that he felt he was obligated to look out. The fact that Jay-5 had so easily disregarded him, tossing him to the wayside without even the slightest consideration after all the paper he had spent with him, and the money he had made off the cars he and his crew had delivered, not to mention, the favor he called himself doing by taking the job in the first place, enraged him. *The nigga is a real bitch for that.*

After taking a few minutes to reflect, King carefully folded up Kay-Kay's letter and placed it back in the envelope before picking up the other one. As much as her letter had lifted his spirits, the second one pissed him off. Every time he read it, his rage grew more and more intense. *Cowboy,*

I got your letter and was surprised to hear from you. Boy! I haven't seen you since you were a baby. So, I imagine this correspondence is just as awkward for you as it is for me. Anyway, the warden approved my correspondence with you. So you can mail your letters directly to me from now on. Also, being that you right across the street, I'm sending something your way that should make your time a little bit smoother.

Now, your grandfather tells me you done got yourself caught up in some B.S. Yeah, I know I'm the last person to be criticizing or giving advice. But seriously... What you a car thief now? C' mon, look around you! By now I'm sure you realize you are way ahead of the game and in a league of your own? But hey, who am I to judge?

About that there letter you wrote. Shorty, there ain't no words I can write to you... No words I can say to you, that would change or atone for the choices made that led to your father being killed, my baby brother. That's been, and always will be, something I'll have to live with for the rest of my life. He paid the ultimate price for my mistakes. I slipped big time! But as much as it may seem I'm at fault, peep this.

You asked why he's dead and I'm still here? I can't go into detail about all of that, at least not now, not in this letter. But let me say this: both your pops and me, we're blessed into them streets. Understand what that means, prison or death! Usually a person has to die before the vultures start circling. But out there, in those streets, it's the ones that smoke blunts with you, want to be in the picture with you, that grab guns and come get you. That's how raw it is out there nephew! Them streets ain't for everybody... That's why they got sidewalks.

See, everybody think I was hating to see your pops winning. To see him happy with a family and all. Not! I love my baby brother more than anything in the world and couldn't have wanted anything more than his happiness and success. Hell... I was his number one coach and cheerleader. But, truth is, I lost his respect. Once I fell off and got strung out on that dog food, he made the mistake of

*judging the messenger and not listening to the message.
Don't make that mistake!*

*I used to tell your father all the time, you can't stay
relevant unless you're pushing yourself out there on the
razor's edge of life on a regular basis. Once you become
comfortable, you become complacent. If you become
complacent, then you don't want to throw yourself into the
icy cold water. You just want to sit in the sun. That's what
happened with your father. After getting with your mother,
he got soft and exposed himself, you and her to the streets.
What I'm trying to say here is, we all were a distraction to
him. He lost focus... loving and looking out for us all.*

*That said, I ain't never going to be one to sugarcoat
nothing. So miss me with all that... sounding like your
mama! Women forget all those things they don't want to
remember, and remember everything they don't want to
forget. I'm still your uncle, so respect my gangsta. It's
because of me that yawl been living drama-free considering
all the hyenas that was chipping at your daddy's plate
before and after he was killed.*

*I'm going to be at you soon. In the meantime, if you
decide you want to continue to write, be mindful of how you
get at me on paper. I ain't got to tell you your mail is being
monitored.*

--Unk

King saw nothing but red as he stared at the letter in
his hand. His anger and frustration had accumulated and
reached its pinnacle by the time he had finished reading it.
Enraged, he immediately ripped the thing to shreds and
threw it in the trash. He couldn't bear to read it again. He
hadn't written Pumpsie to receive a lecture about the
streets. He wanted answers, who and what, not lame-ass
excuses and mentoring! He knew the consequences of the
game. He had been living with them since the day the

doctor slapped him on the ass. It was clear at this point he
had lived a life paying the price for other people's
decisions. "No... No more," he quietly vowed between
clenched teeth. His Uncle Pumpsie was one of those
people, and no matter how he tried to explain it, he had lit
the fuse that was about to blow the door off Pandora's Box.

Although King's anger and frustration had prevented
him from reading between the lines of Pumpsie's
letter, Agent Sisco clearly got the message. He had spent
over 20 years on the force decoding phone and other
electronic communications between drug dealers, hackers
and government officials. It didn't make one bit of
difference how slick they thought they were or how
intricate the communication, whether it was digital or an
outdated handwritten letter, there was always a sequence of
exchanges, Apple crates=kilos, oranges=pounds, etc., that
left a trail of incriminating evidence.

A week later King was unexpectedly summoned into
the captain's office. As he sat outside waiting to be
seen, he was consumed with worry. The only time an
inmate was called to the captain's office was to receive bad
news. Usually the captain would be waiting along with an
officer to inform them of a loved one who had gone to
Glory. He feared the worst. Months had passed since his
mother had visited. And to make things worse, his letters
and phone calls went unanswered. *Something is wrong.* He
braced himself for the news as worry washed over him and
his muscles grew tight.

"Reed!" a feminine voice boomed from the office. It
was soft but firm.

King snapped out of his thoughts upon hearing his
name. Slowly, he rose and walked into the office.

Immediately, he noted that there was no chaplain awaiting him. The tension in his body eased a bit. Captain Jennifer Barreatto was sitting alone at her desk overlooking a pile of paperwork.

Barreatto, 51, was a woman of extraordinary beauty. 5'4" and 140 pounds, she was an Irish bombshell with luscious lips, fire red hair and more curves than the average sister. Her tight uniform gripped her assets like Harlem Globetrotter's gripped basketballs, and it hugged her cookie like camel-toe. A 20-year vet, she was the first female captain in the department's history. The male-dominated prison system had reluctantly begun permitting females to work in adult male prisons, and had begun placing them in positions of leadership. Despite her beauty, she was tough as nails. Stabbings, murders, rapes, riots, she had seen it all.

"Have a seat Reed," she said, pointing to the chair in front of her desk.

King tightened at the site of the imposing woman in front of him. Prison had taught him to act decisively and cautiously with both prisoner and staff alike. *Maybe the chaplain is running late,* he worried to himself. The confusion of the situation was eating at him and again his muscles grew tight as he took a seat and said, "Thank you. What's going on, cap'?"

"I'd like to discuss with you the prospect of you participating in the upcoming OSP Rodeo," she said.

"Pheeeeeeww!" he sighed with relief. He was so psyched out thinking the worst, the upcoming rodeo never crossed his mind.

Rarely was it that the public found anything entertaining about a person who was convicted of a crime and sent to prison. However, both King and the captain knew this was not the case with a prison rodeo, which people from all over the United States and even other countries eagerly attended.

The Oklahoma State Penitentiary Rodeo event was one of the Department's major attractions. Annually, it pulled in some five million dollars, making it a big draw for the local economy in McAlester. Founded in 1941, the OSP Rodeo began as entertainment for prisoners and guards at Big Mac. Two years later, the event opened to the public with a 4500 seat arena, and a new stadium completed in 2000. It now held 10,000 thanks to a joint venture between ODOC and the Historical Black Rodeo Commission, founded by none other than Blue Williams.

King sat atop a ton of pure rage as he pulled tight the rig and wrapped a gloved-hand with the rope to secure his grip. Psycho, the bull he had just mounted, racked its horns against the chute violently and gored at the gate. The crowd rumbled loudly, thirsting for blood. No doubt, the OSP Rodeo was a blood sport in every aspect of the meaning and very much the same as those held in the Coliseums of Ancient Rome. He knew that come the end of the day, many inmates would lay seriously injured, or worse, gored to death.

Growing up, he had heard his grandfather always talking about how the inmates that participated in the rodeo had received no training and how the event had been purposefully designed to appeal solely to the audiences' blood lust. He definitely was intent on not becoming the next victim for the sake of their entertainment. Still, the possibility remained, and after some serious persuasion on behalf of Captain Barreatto, he reluctantly accepted the offer, which had its perks.

As he prepared to launch from the chute, he shook his head in disbelief and recalled how it felt when she had latched on his dick and convinced him to ride again.

"Out of all the prisoners in this compound, why me?" King recalled asking after he was summoned to the office and Barreatto requested of him to partake in the event. Naturally, he assumed her interest in him had something to do with his grandfather's contract with the state. However, he was about to learn otherwise.

"Your Uncle Pumpsie," Barreatto explained, then added, "I used to work behind the *Walls*. And well... let's just say your uncle and I have a good rapport with one another. He was always talking about you and how you were an up-and-coming rodeo champion like your father. I recently saw him on 'The Rockpile' and he asked me this favor. That's why."

King's eyes quickly turned to ice at the mention of his uncle's name. Then suddenly, as if the name had never been mentioned, they softened and grew warm after he noted the way her eyes lit up when she mentioned his father. It was the same look he had seen in his mother's eyes when she spoke of him. He could tell right off there was some history between the two. The tension in the room quickly vanished and before he realized what was happening, Barreatto was on him like 99 on a hundred, acting like a mad woman grabbing at his crotch.

Immediately, his dick grew hard as he thought to himself, *this bitch crazy!*

To be sure, Barreatto was a freak; a cougar. Her hardened shell was a façade. And from the moment King stepped foot on the compound, she stalked him like she once did his father, but now it was Junior's dick in her mouth.

"Damn! You taste like your daddy," she said, licking his dick before swallowing him.

Within seconds, the sensation of her warm, tight jaw game, had him pinned against the wall singing E40 and Too Short's song "Sliding Down the Pole" before he exploded in her mouth.

"The shit a nigga do for some pussy," King shook his head and nodded to release the chute. Eight seconds later, he stood in the center of the arena and did his signature victory dance before walking out and heading to the captain's office for his prize.

Chapter 18

The cool breeze of the bay found Regina's girl, Peaches, entertaining a client. They had met at Jack London Square in downtown Oakland to have a few drinks before retiring to a room at the Hilton off Broadway Boulevard.

As they stumbled into the room, Peaches began to undress and dance seductively, revealing a flaming red Provocateur Denver lace corset and garter attached to a pair of fishnet stockings. She was simply stunning, standing at 5' 7", weighing 130 pounds with curves like a video vixen. Her smooth fair skin looked as though it had been dipped in a pot of honey. Both her complexion and the model like European features stood in contrast of the rich color of her negligee and made for the most mesmerizing appearance hypnotizing her client like a snake charmer.

"Boom bada boom! How you like it Daddy? Rough?" she flirted as her hands caressed her curvaceous body, stopping to expose her firm breasts. Holding one to her mouth, she gently began suckling at it as her tongue circled the tip of her brown areola.

"Oh yeah baby... I likey," a middle-aged Asian man grunted in pure delight at the site of the beauty standing before him. He quickly began fidgeting at his belt to get his pants off.

Just as his pants hit his ankles, Peaches consumed his rising manhood, which was now diving at her tonsils.

In the midst of sucking his dick, she attempted to lift his wallet. It was some low-budget shit Regina often had a hard time breaking the girls of who she had pulled from the streets. Things quickly went left from there as her trick was not as liquored-up as Peaches thought.

"What the fuck!" he spat before sending a fist smashing into her face. Right away he recognized her play and commenced to beat the dog shit out of her.

Fortunately, Slim had been making his rounds. Now 17, he had been forced to grow up fast in the murderous streets of the Bay Area. When they called, he had answered with a growing body count, pimping and HEAD CHANGE. No longer the innocent farm boy, he stood 6'2" with urban art tattooed across a well sculptured and muscular torso, arms, and thick neck. A platinum grill, encrusted with yellow diamonds and rubies, spelled out "Taliban"—his adopted turf in East Oakland—across the front, top and bottom teeth.

As he approached the hotel door, he could hear the commotion coming from inside the room.

"You dumb nigger bitch! I'll teach your ass..." the Asian man shouted, enraged, as he continued to beat Peaches.

Slim quickly responded, reaching into his Burberry Brit pea coat for Roscoe, a 17 shot HK 9 mm.

Words quickly became grunts and the sounds of fists striking flesh suddenly found their owner as Slim sent an Air Force One crashing through the door and caught a glimpse of the mayhem Peaches was entangled with.

It was horrifying. She lay sprawled out across the floor with her face covered in blood as the trick held her by the throat, smashing a fist repeatedly into her face.

Slim could see in the dimly-lit room he was up against a bolo built Asian, who stood a bit shorter than him, yet was every last bit of 50 pounds heavier and rock solid.

The sound of the door crashing open caught Bolo's attention and he spun around to be greeted with the butt of the HK. Dazed, he quickly regained his composure and launched himself at Slim as he drew back for another swing, catching it in midair. As the two cannonballed into a violent struggle, the Asian latched onto Slim's arm and delivered a knee into his midsection. The force from the blow caused Slim to instantly drop the pistol as they both fell to the ground and began wresting.

In a moment of sure desperation, Peaches struggled to her feet and instinctively moved in for the kill like a wild jungle cat launching at its pray. With great skill and agility she grabbed Bolo by the ponytail and pulled his head back. Before he could react, she slit his throat from ear-to-ear with a straight razor. Blood sprayed as if a water sprinkler. Reflexes kicked in and Bolo grabbed at his neck, gasping for air.

The tables had turned.

Infuriated, having been handled like a bitch, Slim was instantly on his feet, furiously kicking Bolo in the ass. He kicked, and stamped for what seemed like an eternity. Only the sound of police sirens in the distance deterred him.

Peaches stood bent in a corner, exhausted, blood dripping from her razor. After taking a few deep breaths, she spotted the wallet lying on the floor and retrieved it.

"Ooooooh shit!" She held the wallet up, displaying a police badge. Bolo was an undercover detective, Kim Li.

"Ayeeee! We gots to b-up blood," Slim panicked, grabbing his pistol.

"I'll get the car, wipe down the room," Peaches instructed before disappearing out the door.

Police sirens grew louder and louder as Slim frantically cleaned the room and quickly stumbled down a short corridor to the rear exit where Peaches awaited. A few minutes later, with the sirens receding in the distance as they sped away, they were able to contemplate their predicament.

"Bruh, you shittin' on yourself?" Peaches asked, covering her nose and rolling down a window.

"Nawl!" Slim replied, hitting the interior light in the car and inspecting himself.

"Aw Fuck!" He had literally stomped the shit out of Bolo. His Air Force Ones were covered with do-do.

In that moment they both looked at each other, realizing the chances of the cop surviving were slim. They had to act and act fast.

"Get your shit together and do it quick," Regina snapped handing Peaches and Slim two, one way plane tickets to Oklahoma the following morning.

It had been a week since they left and the streets of Oakland were buzzing with police activity. Twenty-seven agencies, ranging from the OPD to the ATF, were out in full force, shaking down prostitutes and Johns, junkies and drug dealers, and whoever else they thought could provide a lead in Officer Li's homicide.

Fortunately for Peaches and Slim, it turned up the identities and addresses of two deceased senior citizens, compliments of his identity theft operation, which had provided them false aliases.

Then again, Regina realized it would only be a matter of time before the police ID-ed them and came searching for her and the rest of her crew. It was time for the gang and her to pull a disappearing act.

It had been a while since she had been home. The timing could not have been better for a trip. A year had almost passed and she had built up a nice stable trafficking girls south for Dekoven to manage. She definitely needed to put some distance between her and the heat.

Eighteen hours later, Regina's caravan of Benz's, box Chevy's and Cadillac coupes pulled up in Wewoka like a presidential procession.

Askari, one of Regina's henchmen, sat at the wheel of Slim's green '85 Jolly Rancher Caprice Classic that sat on 28" rims with a Euro-clip and coke-white interior. At first, he didn't think much of the town. There wasn't but a few apartment complexes and old shotgun shacks as he turned off 1st Street to make a right on Cedar Street. Then, out of nowhere, it seemed as though they descended into a valley of vibrant life. It was like driving into little Vegas.

Things were flashy on this side of town. Neon signs lit up the block like Christmas ornaments: *Sam's Pussy Palace, Dolly's* and several others. One sign in particular stood out amongst them all, *Pooches Gentlemen's Club.* Askari had heard a lot about it from Regina and Slim, and next to Atlanta's *Magic City*, it was one of the most popular strip clubs in the nation.

As he drove down Cedar Street, he could see crowds gathered everywhere, dressed to the nine, sporting name brand everything from Burberry to Gucci with square toe slides and six inch heels on their feet. Even the country boys, despite their overalls, wore wide brim cowboy hats and ostrich skin boots that radiated mad scratch. A number of candy-coated whips lined the street. Everything from Lexus Coupes to '55 Chevy trucks sat on Vogues and fat white walls. As Regina and the rest of the entourage made their way into Pooches, Askari quickly docked the Caprice and jumped out in order to follow suit.

Inside, the club was buzzing like Wall Street. Peaches and another girl Regina had flown in were on stage performing a seductive number, ass clapping. The local ballers were more than appreciative of the new talent. Hundred dollar bills shot up on the stage like they were fresh off the U.S. Mint.

From the moment they stepped through the door, Regina was taken by surprise when she saw what Sticky and Dekoven had done with the place. Over the years, she had grown accustomed to Redd's old disco ball and wall-to-wall mirror scene. She wasn't aware they had renovated the establishment since she last visited. She looked on approvingly as she took in the new scenery and found it fitting to her taste. It seemed they had walked into an entirely different world compared to the one that existed right outside the club doors.

Contemporary white leather sectionals lined the interior walls, forming a number of semi-private booths. At each table, chilling on ice, was a bottle of Moet or other expensive champagne. The cheap, shoestring stripper outfits that once ran the stage had been replaced with see-through gowns, corsets, negligees, and extravagant costumes. The girls were polished from head to toe. Tattoos, stretch marks and bullet wounds were now covered with Mac makeup and manicures, pedicures and

$1,300 Christian Louboutin studded stilettos. No expense had been spared in transforming the place into a first class joint.

Even the entertainment had been upgraded. There were now themes assigned by the day and girl performing: Monday's Mardi Gras, Tuesday's S&M bondage, Wednesday's Big Body and so on and so forth the themes played out and occasionally changed. It was "Role Play Friday" and the number Peaches and the other girl were performing was one of many exotic skits Dekoven had concocted. The girls were but a work of fiction to him and the roles they played were but fantasy to his audience. With the exception of the captain's hat Peaches wore atop her head, and the stewardess' vest the other girl had on, they both were completely naked, fully displaying their Brazilian waxes, which were trimmed like a landing strip to guide the audience's attention right into their sweet spot, while their curvaceous figures gyrated to the music.

With exception of a few D-boys, the entire atmosphere of the club had changed overnight from street, to sophisticated. From looking around, Regina could see the majority of the club's patrons were middle-aged white men with deep pockets who made their living by extorting Wewoka's political machine and the county's oil reserves.

"R-Regina... Regina!" a familiar voice called. "Now girl, I know that ain't my kinfolk just walk up in here?"

Regina turned and a warm smile immediately spread across her face. Dekoven stood a short distance behind her and, as always, was dressed casually in a black Salvatore Ferragamo suit jacket, white polo T-shirt, Tom Ford jeans, and Cole Haan shoes. They embraced for an affectionate hug. Then Regina introduced him to her crew.

"Now, I just love what you guys did with the place," she finally said after introducing everybody. "And the girls... I mean, look at them. Damn!"

"Girl, now you know when Ms. Gina put it down, she put it down!" Dekoven snapped his fingers and placed a hand on his hips before throwing a mischievous grin at Askari.

"No homo, man!" Askari protested as he shook his head and held up a hand signaling he was cool.

"Well..." Dekoven hissed in disappointment as his mind quickly conjured up a few fantasies Askari and he could work out that involved rim shots. "....you never know what you like until you try," he again snapped.

"Imma try out this bar," Askari shot back, and then turned towards the bar and left Regina and Dekoven to catch up with everything that was going on.

"Now that sure is a fine piece of dark meat you got," Dekoven said eyeing Askari as he walked off.

"You ho!" Regina laughed as Dekoven quickly joined her. "Now what's going on with my cousin? And where's that boy of mine?" she asked, anxiously, speaking of Sticky and Slim.

Before he could respond, there was a sudden disturbance in one of the gambling rooms as a loud crash and breaking noise ended the music. That's when they heard the shouting.

"Muthafucka, don't you ever, ever, speak on my mama like that," a threatening voice pierced the crowd as Dekoven and Regina rushed into the gambling den with a fleet of security.

"Goddamn it! I knew this nigga was going to be a problem soon as he stepped his funky ass in the door," Dekoven spat angrily.

Jay-5 stood over a small time dope dealer named Po' T, putting hands and feet on him like a soccer ball. He had obviously gotten the best of him as Po' T's jumpsuit and dreads were now being used to mop the floor.

"J-J-Jay! I'm sorry man!" Po' T pled. "I didn't mean no disrespect by—"

His words were abruptly cut off as Jay-5 delivered several jaw breaking punches to Po' T's face. Blood and drool sprayed everywhere as his pleas fell on deaf ears. Jay-5 was in a zone, looking like a wild beast on the nature show *When Animals Attack.*

"I got a big face that Jay knock him out in less than a minute," an on-looker said as he surveyed the crowd for a sucker bet.

No one bit. Po' T was out cold within seconds. Jay-5 put a two-piece combo on him that stood him on his toes before rocking him to sleep with a left uppercut. Po' T hit the floor hard before security could even react. Jay-5 then rifled through his victim's pockets, and with a sinister grin, rose to pump his fist into the air to reveal the money he had lost.

"Dog ass nigga!"

Jay-5 spun around like a wild jungle cat. Standing before him, with his hands and arms crossed and folded at the elbow, was Dekoven.

He stood before Jay-5 enraged. He wanted to go big on him. Mixed images of violence ran through his mind like fast vanishing sand. He was at his wit's end, tired of playing the role and ignoring what Jay-5 had done to his family. In that moment he wanted to slap the dog shit out of him as Ms. Gina, crush him as Dekoven, and fuck him in the ass like the bitch he was. *I have to get a hold of myself... Calm down, calm down and play your part,* he convinced himself.

Seeing Dekoven flustered tickled Jay-5. "Miss Thang," he said as he broke into a wide smile.

"You foul fuck!" Dekoven spat, struggling to maintain his composure. "I don't have to tell you to hit the door," he pointed at the club's entry as several bouncers rushed over to Jay-5 and attempted to seize him by the collar.

"You niggaz must be crazy or something... You better get your muthafucking hands off me!" he snapped and quickly drew back his shoulders as several of his goons stepped up, ready to jump off. "This how you treat a nigga? All the money me and my team spent up in this raggedy-ass ratchet muthafucka!"

"Nigga Fuck you!" Dekoven snapped.

"Nawl fuck your sister! That bitch got all these stupid hoes and faggets up in here, lying on their back to feed her, but she ain't selling no pussy. Fuck you... ole sweet booty fuck-boy!"

Despite the mounting anger and frustration boiling in him, Dekoven knew he had to turn-down and maintain appearances. He had to give the performance of his life. He too was in on the charade of rocking Jay-5 to sleep. It was only a matter of time before the walls came crashing down on his world, and now wasn't the time to fuck off years of careful planning and getting Jay-5 comfortable, just for Dekoven to throw it all away by losing his temper. *Lord, if there ever was a time you wanted to bless me with your calm and guiding hand... Now would be that time,* Dekoven prayed.

"Now Jay... You really sounding as if you hating right now," he finally said after realizing he had to sacrifice his pride for his ego.

"Hating! What? Nigga please!" Jay-5 countered after noting Dekoven's change in demeanor. "Allow me to explain something to you. See, I don't blame a bitch for breaking a ho. I blame a ho for being stupid enough to pay a bitch who, like her, got a pussy and feel like she too good to sell it when she eating off the next bitch selling hers. Now… I'll gladly see myself out this raggedy muthafucka," he barked before turning to the bouncers and making his way out the door.

By now, Po' T had regained consciousness and was being helped to his feet. He had been severely beaten. Everybody in the club could see his head had been bashed up, like a smashed pumpkin.

"Help him to his car," Dekoven said as he shook his head in disbelief. No matter how many times he had seen it, the fighting, robberies, beatings, he still felt sorry for Po' T and others like him who fell victim to the wrath of a sore loser. *Gots to be more careful,* he thought to himself before yelling over at Po' T, "Hey Po' T—"

The two bouncers who were helping him stopped at the doorway. Po' T turned to look over his shoulder and then gave a nod, appearing to say, "What's up?"

"—there'll be a $5,000 credit waiting for you once you get back up on your feet. Be easy man and take care of yourself," Dekoven continued, realizing it was the least he could do to compensate for the money Jay-5 had stripped from the man's pockets. He then turned to answer the tap on his shoulder, "What!"

From the outset, the moment Regina laid eyes on Jay-5, he struck her as oddly familiar. At first she discarded the notion that she knew him, after mistaking him for a local. Still, his face had been stuck somewhere in her memory. It wasn't until she overheard him talking shit to Dekoven that she had recognized his distinctive West Coast accent, and upon hearing someone call his name, she quickly put one and two together.

Though he had aged and his face appeared to bear the marks of gin and the razor, it was definitely him. She couldn't believe it as she pulled out her cell phone and Googled the story: "KINGPIN RUNS DRUG RING FROM CAMBODIA TO LOS ANGELES... OAKLAND DRUG DEALER TIED TO CHAN SYNDICATE... TURNS GOVERNMENT WITNESS AND PLACED IN WITNESS PROTECTION PROGRAM AFTER DEATH THREATS...."

Ja'Monte Weaver! Regina couldn't believe it. She stood there shocked in disbelief of the fact that the rat bastard who had turned snitch, who had ratted out the Chan family, and a good friend of hers from Richmond, was literally standing right in front of her.

She quickly made her way over to Dekoven and tapped him on the shoulder.

Chapter 19

A lot had changed in a year. Judge Olsen had personally seen to it that King would not have a chance for early release. After calling in a favor to the warden, Olsen had arranged for King to be expelled from R.E.D.'s GED program. Given King and lil' Jay's antics, it seemed the appropriate action to curb the boys' disruptive behavior. Only Olsen and the warden truly knew the real motive behind their expulsion.

Thereafter, Judge Olsen would issue an order that summarily denied King's 90-day probation consideration hearing, citing failure to adhere to the court's requirements that he obtain a GED. He then sentenced him to "max out," which meant nine more months of rigorous physical and mental training. Olsen was intent on breaking King, who was learning some hard truths about how the system really worked.

"It's a white man's game…" King recalled lil' Jay explaining shortly after he had received the denial. Despite the bad news, the two kept it lit, never ceasing to have a dull moment between them.

Lil' Jay and King sat in the chow hall eating breakfast. It was a bittersweet moment. Lil' Jay was paroling the following morning. Despite their differences, James being a square and King being the more 'street' of the two, they had grown to be good friends in a short of period of time.

"Yo! You sure there ain't nothing you need me to do when I touch down?" lil' Jay asked, feeling a bit of guilt that he was leaving King behind.

"Nawl man… I'm short. Just stay up and I'll catch up with you in a few," King replied, and then added, "So about this game—"

Sensing King's reluctance to talk about the streets, lil' Jay went with the play. "Yeah, the game… it's like, man… them politicians like them boppers you tell me about that work at your Mom's club," he continued.

"Now, how those ho's fit into all of this?" King asked, knowing lil' Jay always had a way of drawing on his life to explain such things. Any time there was something in a book or a subject King didn't quite understand, he could always count on lil' Jay to compare it to something in his life to explain it.

"See… You once told me a bop, that is, a good ho, the best boppers are the ones that know how to pretend they like a trick while she playing him, getting his money, shaking that ass or fucking him—"

"Just like a politician?! I get it!" King laughed.

"—So recognize game… It's what your G-pa and Uncle Lenny been teaching you all along over at that Lodge. The white man's game… See, them white folks been doing this for a long time. They put they politicians in

office, and it don't matter too much what color they is…
They put them there to play ball, regardless. Once us dumb
niggaz fall into the trap, the judge just part of the machine.
He go max that ass out with some Buck Rodger years so
the politicians can keep singing that tune—You know,
'tough on crime,' then tax the 'hood and everybody else for
locking your dumb ass up. I don't know about you, but I'm
done being a dumb nigga in the *game*, losing while they
winning."

    … *dumb nigga, losing while they're winning*, King
reflected on lil' Jay's words and thought about how they
had motivated him to hit the books as he stood in the
courtroom, dressed in a casual Sean John dress out. He had
spent the last year absorbing four libraries full of books and
dissecting what he had been exposed to at the Lodge.

    Organization wise, many of the kids he had attended
class with at the J.M. Reed Masonic Temple were now
headed off to college to pursue political careers as attorneys
and businessmen. Thanks to his grandparents, what they
were to gain from sitting in a classroom he had already
absorbed, and learned more from in the books and lessons
he received on the farm and at the club. Even more, he
learned of all the great Native American and African poets,
writers, inventors, kings and queens, wars, and how their
civilizations were built and eventually destroyed. Of all the
subjects he had studied on history, the one that struck him
most was the history of Boley.

    Boley, King learned, had been founded by Abigail
Barnette, a descendant of the Creek Freedmen. It had been
named after J. B. Boley, a white railroad official of the Fort
Smith & Western Railway, who was one of three men,
white and black, who joined forces to give black Americans
the fair opportunity for self-governance. The railroad
station and agriculture business that eventually sprung up in

the surrounding 160-acre plot that made up the countryside, would make Boley the largest and most wealthy black city in the world.

When King first learned of this, it was simply too profound to believe. With the exception of the Lodge and rodeo, Boley was a ghost town. Adversity and racism had put the squeeze on its once thriving social and economic prosperity. For almost a century, the townspeople had battled with vice and misfortune. They had fought the good fight, even subduing the notorious Pretty Boy Floyd and his gang, who on November 23, 1932, had been run off in a hail of gunshots and bullets after a botched bank robbery attempt. It seemed that all that was left of Boley were the gangs and drugs that flowed through its streets and backroads.

Still, it was the place his father had been born and raised and had rebuilt the Masonic Lodge. King had grown up knowing that before Redd was killed, he had sought to rebuild the Temple as a symbol to preserve Boley's prestigious history. What he didn't know however, was his father had purposely rebuilt the Lodge because the families, his included, were deeply rooted in the town's history, and despite the fact that many of them had long since migrated elsewhere, they were forever connected, forming a national network that would extend its reach no matter where he went or set up shop.

In addition to the history books, Betty-Jean had also sent him a number of legal and business books, along with books on psychology, sociology, and other social sciences. She was a firm believer in the fact that black folks had to educate their own children because the schools would not. This was a simple truth she had observed far too often with the students that walked into her classroom. She had also arranged for King to obtain his GED through a correspondence program offered at Seminole State College.

Unlike many who got locked up, King's incarceration had worked in the most unorthodox manner. He quickly picked up on the game at hand and made it work for him. He had gone above and beyond the court's requirements. His bout with addiction, along with everything else he had gone through over the course of the past 12 months, had been a wake-up call. Though the urge to use would always be with him, the gorilla was not beating his chest as hard. He felt confident he had licked it and could manage without ever again touching another drug.

Despite having maxed out, his original plea arrangement carried a one to five-year tail, which meant he had to appear before the judge for a final consideration of the probation term before he could be released.

"Mr. Reed, I see you have obtained your GED and your conduct reports have significantly improved," Judge Olsen stated matter-of-factly as he peered over the frame of his glasses at King. His face was stoic, emotionless. However he was hot under the collar. He had intended to stretch the boy's probation five years, hoping he would land in trouble again and he could sentence him to five years of hard prison time.

However, his campaign manager had recently informed him that several of his major contributors had threatened to withdraw their support on a count of Blue William's influence. Election season was right around the corner and Olsen knew he couldn't afford to lose their support. It would cost him the bench.

"Yes sir! I mean, Your Honor!" King stammered. He had learned an invaluable lesson in humility, and moreover, how to play the submissive role with people like Olsen who, like most people in positions of authority, fed on fear and control. He quickly glanced around the courtroom and smiled at the sight of his family turning out to support him. They were all in attendance. His grandparents, Uncle Dekoven, Lenny, Regina, and Slim, were sitting in a pew directly behind him. Yet he quickly recognized his mother was absent. *Why isn't she here?* He hadn't seen her in months. Initially when she had not shown up to visit, he did not think much of it. She had previously informed him of her crazy schedule. She had been working overtime. This, he knew, had been causing her a tremendous amount of stress, the extent of which he was about to find out.

"Relax son," the judge said, noting King's uneasiness.

Certainly, King stood anxious. He was trying to process everything. Sticky's absence had sent up a red flag. At the same time, he was trying to gauge the judge's demeanor. His thoughts were everywhere. Olsen sat cold and unrevealing. King drew a blank.

Olsen was also trying to gauge the young man standing before him. He wondered if the boy knew of the influence his grandfather wielded. The fix was in. He knew he was walking on thin ice. Still, he wanted to see the boy sweat a bit. He fancied himself with the notion that he had broken King's spirit.

For all his years as a prosecutor, and now a judge, it would be one of the few times Olsen's intuition failed him. What he thought was pure reverence for the law, particularly himself, was mistaken.

King despised Olsen. He had since learned the judge had played a role in bringing down his father, and that it had been the reason he had received such a stiff sentence. What Olsen mistook as reverence and being nervous was anything but. King was plotting his revenge and was anxious to hit the bricks to check his traps and execute his plan, which included getting back at Jay-5 and his Uncle Pumpsie, who was soon to parole.

"Mr. Reed..." Olsen paused with a stern look on his face, and then said, "Not too many people come before my court and receive a second chance—"

King took a deep breath and held it in expecting the worst. While he had done the hard part already, he knew a five-year tail would easily result in a five year prison sentence.

"—but," Olsen continued, "Against my better judgment, I hereby sentence you to a year of unsupervised probation. Upon successful completion of the probation, your criminal record will be expunged." The judge stood to slam the gavel and leave, then suddenly turned to say, "Oh... and I wish your mother a speedy recovery!" before turning to retreat to his chambers.

... wish your mother a speedy recovery. What the fuck? King wondered as he turned to look at his family for an answer. Something was wrong. It was written all over their faces. His grandfather's face shifted and filled with guilt. King stood confused. The burden that was lifted from the relief he felt with the judge's words was soon replaced with another burden.

After several excruciating hours of waiting to be released from the Seminole County Jail, King eagerly greeted his family at the gates. He was finally free after having spent the past 12 months in a hell hole. As the gates closed behind him, he energetically began jumping up and down in excitement as he ran from one family member to another kissing and hugging them acting like he had just won an NBA championship. Slim and King playfully wrestled and took rib shots at each other before he finally turned to his grandfather and asked about his mother.

"Where's ma?" King asked. "And what's this the judge talking about? Is she sick? She fell off a horse or something?" he added, making light of the situation. However, his gut warned him otherwise. Whatever it was, it was the reason she hadn't been to see him in months.

"Ah, I… I don't know how to explain this son," Blue answered as they walked over to his truck and got in. A look of sadness clouded his face. Blue sat for a second thinking of how his grandson had already lost one parent, and now to some degree, had lost another.

Choosing his words carefully he said, "Your mother has had some recent health problems." He started up the truck and began explaining best he could as they drove home.

At first the family believed it was the grief and stress caused by Redd's murder that was at the root of Sticky's brief lapse of memory. Nobody thought much of it. The tasks that lay before her after he was killed had been difficult to say the least. She had fought the Feds, IRS… the courts. Then Pumpsie and Lenny dropped a bombshell on her that shook her to the core. Jay-5 killed Redd. He had gotten away with murdering the love of her life. And to add insult to injury, Lenny had been paying him protection money. The gravity of learning of all of this had been devastating. It had hit Sticky in the gut, just as if Mike Tyson himself had hit her with an uppercut. She was crushed beyond words, speechless and terrified.

After several stressful bouts with depression and coming to grips with the fact that her memory lapses were causing her to forget more than just her car keys, she had finally consented to her doctor's advice and underwent a CT scan for an accurate diagnosis. In the months shortly after King was sentenced to Camp R.E.D., a neurologist had confirmed her worst fears; she was diagnosed with Early-onset Alzheimer's. It was a rare form of the disease that affected its victims in their prime.

At 39, Sticky's memory was afflicted by a hideous disease that would cause her mental health to deteriorate rapidly. She quickly went from misplacing her car keys, to putting her clothes on backwards, to forgetting the names of her entire family. She no longer could speak coherently and struggled to communicate with others.

"Ma... You good?" King asked, as he knelt by her side and gently placed a hand on her forearm. Fighting back tears, he blinked rapidly in an attempt to keep them from flowing down his face. His grandfather had explained his mother's health complications and he now struggled with all his power not to lash out at the world. Sticky sat quietly with an empty gaze in her eyes as she sway slowly back-and-forth in a rocking chair on her parents' porch. Upon feeling King's hand, she stopped and looked over at him.

"Redd..." she said, staring into King's eyes.

When their eyes met, King could see the fatigue, the loneliness. She looked to have aged 20 years since the last time he had seen her.

King choked back a sob. He was the spitting image of his father. The discipline and exercise while incarcerated had served him well. He had put on 50 pounds, and looking as though he had taken steroids, his Sean John tightly snugged his massive arms and barrel chest.

"No Mama, it's Cowboy," he replied as a tear slipped down his cheek. He believed it was his fault. He had abandoned his mother, his queen, in a time when she needed him most. For years, she had fought to save everything his father had built for him. She had fought to hold on to his love that had nurtured her heart.

Unfortunately, time and the lack of his gentle touch had left her with a void in her chest that had grown to the size of a crater. Since his father had been killed, he knew his mother had lived with a numbing pain that his presence could at least have soothed her spirit. He knew his incarceration had literally broken her heart and driven her to this point.

"King! Oh... Javon baby," Sticky's eyes piqued at attention at the mention of his name. Though she recognized it, in her mind, it was Redd she was staring at. "I... I tried... I tried. But they took everything!" she cried.

"I know Ma. I know," King replied as he took her by the hand in an effort to comfort her.

Suddenly, she began to ramble, "Redd please, please Redd... 36, 20, 15, 47... Be safe... 36, 20, 15, 47...."

King stood, confused. He hadn't the slightest clue what she was trying to say or what she was thinking about. His thoughts were clouded, overwhelmed with guilt and anger with himself and his family. He was so emotionally caught up, he failed to catch on to the significance of the numbers she chanted. A part of him was filling with rage. It had been months, and nobody had said anything. Not a single word about her health, her diagnosis, or her recent turn for the worse.

After kneeling at his mother's side for what seemed like an eternity, he finally stood to look at his family. One by one, they all dropped their heads in guilt.

"We didn't want—" Blue started to explain.

"Not now!" King snapped, dismissing his grandfather with a brush of the hand.

Under different circumstances, Blue would have taken the gesture as a sign of disrespect. King's interruption was clearly disrespectful and went against everything he had taught him about manners. But then Blue knew from the look in his grandson's eyes, the boy was conflicted with pain and anger with the family's decision to not say anything about Sticky's condition until he came home. He had said enough. Only time would work things out between them.

Chapter 20

"I think you're being too hard on your family," Kay-Kay finally said after listening to King rant about his anger and frustration. His calm and otherwise disciplined demeanor had cracked. Seeing his mother in such a condition had sent him spinning out of control. He had stormed out of his grandparents' house in a fit of rage and copped an ounce of lean to numb his pain. After sitting alone in the park for over an hour and fighting the gorilla, he had mustered up enough strength to pour the concoction onto the ground. He had fought the urge to use and had won round one with his addiction.

Still, he desperately needed something, or someone, to numb his pain. His heart felt as if it had been pierced by a sword of guilt and betrayal. "Goddammit!" he cursed God for taking his father and striking his mother in her prime with such a hideous disease. *Lord, hast Thou forsaken me?* he questioned as he looked to the sky for an answer. It was in that moment that the notion to call Kay-Kay came to him. She was the only person who hadn't betrayed him with secrets. Her letters, which he had kept, had comforted him in his time of need and loneliness while in the Zo.

From the moment her phone rang and she heard his voice, Kay-Kay was anxious to see him. After a few minutes on the phone and sensing he was in pain, she wasted no time making the short drive from her father's shop to the park. As soon as she pulled up, King got out of the *SS* and walked over to her car and got in. It was late, and with the exception of the stars that flickered above them, they were alone.

"Think about it, Javon," she continued as she reached over to turn on the radio. A Trey Songz song began to play. It didn't take long for her to notice something different about him as they sat in the car talking about his mother's condition. He had changed. The King she once had known wouldn't dare lay his feelings out to be judged. Of course, she also noted he was beefy and fine as ever. However, it wasn't his looks that struck her. She had always considered him handsome. There was something more. He now carried himself with a certain depth and maturity that allowed him to speak openly about his feelings. His words and confidence reminded her of spoken word. *He's so in tune with himself as a man standing in his own truth.* This 'new him' appealed to her unlike anything before. His aura called out to her and caused her inner thighs to grow moist.

"Think about it? I have thought about it! That's all I've been doing is thinking, thinking to the point my fucking head hurts. What more could I possibly think of that I haven't already?" King shouted in frustration. He was so emotional he didn't notice that as Kay-Kay turned towards him, she placed a hand on his shoulder.

"Did it ever occur to you that maybe, just maybe..." she paused to lean in closer and whisper in his ear. Her hand slid across his chest and closed the distance between them, "... maybe they were worried that if they said something, it could have caused you to do something stupid?"

If King's confessions and confidence came off as spoken word to her, then she was definitely poetry to his troubled soul. He quickly noted her rhythm and every move she made filled him with ecstasy. He too had noticed her changes. Her letters had grown more and more intimate over time as he gained a great amount of appreciation and respect for their friendship. Still, there was that "onion."

Damn, that onion! The mere thought of it immediately made his dick rise.

Suddenly, Kay-Kay shifted gears and lifted one of her thick, well-shaped thighs to straddle him. It felt as though a wild jungle cat had jumped into his lap. She pulled up her *Baby Phat* mini-skirt and revealed to him she wasn't wearing any panties.

In that moment, King felt like God had answered his every prayer, and though it hadn't been but a year, her country-thick, cornbread and bean eating ass had blossomed into something magnificent.

"Damn, this pussy tight!" He wasted no time gripping her luscious ass and inserting a finger into her moist, velvet folds.

"Mmmmmmmm..." she purred like a kitten, and leaned forward to whisper in his ear, "I saved it for you."

"Pop! Pop! Bang!" The back of his seat suddenly fell backwards has she reached down and pulled the release lever to push him backwards. She was taking charge. Her hips slowly began to gyrate as she ground his fingers deeper and deeper into her honey pot. She could feel his manhood swell between her legs with each grind. Gradually, her rhythm increased and the car windows began to fog up. As her voluptuous ass writhed back and forth, side to side, and made circles on his bulging manhood, her hands gently slithered across his chest and down his abdomen before eventually making their way up to remove her top.

King breathed with childhood wonder. Before him were two of the most perfectly sculptured and firm breasts he had ever seen. He reached up with his free hand and pulled her down on him and began suckling at her perky nipples. They were soft. He gently suckled at each one of them with his full lips and savored her strawberry flavored body oil. He had waited his entire life for this moment and couldn't help but gloat with accomplishment. He smiled, thinking of all the times they had played hide-and-go-get-it and *house* as kids. She had played hard to get and forced him to pursue her for years. *I'm about to lock this pussy in,* he thought to himself as he removed his fingers from her cookie jar to see if it tasted as good.

"Aghhhhhhh! Javon, why did you stop?" she cried, pounding her fist on his chest in frustration as she rose up and opened her eyes to stare at him.

"Ain't no going back at this point," he replied, smelling his finger before putting it into his mouth.

There isn't no going back. I've already crossed the point of no return, she thought to herself as she pulled his hand from his mouth and pressed it to her clit, drawing circle motions with it like it was a sex toy. Her love button was throbbing from the way he had so skillfully fondled her. Her body trembled uncontrollably. She was on the verge of exploding just as he up and left her hanging.

"Stop playing with me!" King complained as he jerked his hand away from her. He seized her by the wrist firmly and stared at her intently. He had been on all three bases with her before. And every time she backed out just as he headed for home base.

"I'm not!" she winced. "You're hurting me. Let me go," she cried as she struggled to free herself of his grip. His hands were strong. Too strong for her to fight. She quickly gave up and he finally released her.

"I'm sorry, I wasn't trying to hurt you," King said softly before taking her by the small of the back with one hand while the other slid down to unbutton his pants.

It all happened so fast. Kay-Kay looked down and gasped in disbelief. Nine inches of hard dick stood firmly between her legs. He then gently stroked her velvet folds with the tip of his manhood before slowly inserting its head. She tensed, biting down on her bottom lip. This was not quite how she had pictured losing her virginity.

"You okay?" he asked as he gently handled her with velvet gloves.

When she didn't respond, he pulled her down onto his barrel chest, wrapping his massive arms around her and give her a slight thrust to get her attention.

Instantly, her insides exploded with ecstasy and he began to thrust again and again, rhythmically and with sure determination. All her tenseness would soon vanish as she began throwing her hips in sync.

"Who's pussy is it?" he said softly and she let out a soft moan. "Who's pussy is it?" he repeated, pounding her harder, faster.

"Y-Yours, yours..." she finally cried out. She couldn't take it anymore. Her legs felt like jelly. Each time he slammed into her, her body grew weaker and ecstasy shot through her thighs.

"Who da one?"

"You... you are. Shit! It h-hurt... Oh shit, it hurts. It hurts so fucking good!" she cried out as her clit began to throb and her pain faded into the pleasure. He was tapping that spot with each thrust.

"Oh yes, yes, yessssss!" she screamed with joy and began throwing her hips back at him. "Grind... Grind that pussy daddy!"

He gloated even more knowing she was enjoying it as much as he was. "You want me to grind?? You want me..." he asked, biting down softly and suckling at the lobe of an ear as he pounded her harder and faster. He was about to explode. "Who's p-p-pussy—"

"Ooooooh FUCK!" Kay-Kay screamed. "I'm coming! I'm coming," she moaned with a final thrust of her hips as King plunged forward for the last time to fill her with his seed as they both exploded with pure ecstasy and collapsed in the seat of the car.

"What! Man you gots to be bullshitting me?" King couldn't believe what he was hearing. It had not been but a few days since Kay-Kay and he had the rendezvous at the park.

"Real spit! Overheard mama on the phone with our people in the Bay Area talking about it. Apparently, the nigga ratted out his team and connect, some Asian mob working out of L.A. Then PC'd up before landing here... compliments of the federal witness protection program," Slim explained. "And that's not all!"

King sat quietly behind the desk in the club's office. He continued to listen as Slim filled him in on Jay-5 and the fact that he and his family had been running since the day they landed in Wewoka. A somber look swept across King's face. He couldn't believe what he was hearing. But then again, he had seen enough in the street to know niggas like Jay-5 had skeletons in the closet. News of his past only made matters that much more complicated between Kay-Kay and him. He had been ignoring her phone calls and text messages all day. He needed time to think about everything that was going on. He had gotten over his anger with his family after realizing that nobody, not even Slim, had wanted to deliver the bad news about his mother's condition. No doubt, it would have caused him to go on one and fuck off his release date. Given her condition, and the fact that his 18th birthday was right around the corner, he now had to hold things down in a real way. He now sat at the driver seat holding the keys to his father's estate, his estate, which meant with everything that was happening, big shit was about to pop off, and he and his team needed to get in a position where they could be on top when the smoke cleared.

"Okay, so these Asians you talking about… How much they put on this nigga's head?" King finally asked, scratching at the palm of his hand. He knew that if they were really about that life, then there was big money on Jay-5's head. With those kinds of enemies it wouldn't be your everyday $10,000 hit. *No, these boys playing with big tickets,* he thought to himself.

"I don't know… But you best believe tthre's going to be some fireworks flying around this bitch when they find out where this nigga been lying his head. Yahmean! Trust I know how they roll. I got a partner, lil' Scooby, in the Bay that run with these crazy rice eating muthafuckas. Before we bounced, I copped some dog food and that 'Barney' from him. Shit raw! Niggaz here ate that shit up as soon as it touched the streets. Plus he got that 'plastic.' That's where I get my 'tract 1's' and 'tract 2's' from."

King sat confused. He knew "dog food" was slang for heroin. This much he had learned from his Uncle Pumpsie.

And, of course, 'Barney' was Bay slang for that Purple Kush those niggas loved to smoke. However, after taking a few seconds to reflect, he looked up, confused, and asked, "Tract 1's, tract 2's... What the fuck is that?"

Slim smiled. When it came to *game*, there were some things his cousin hadn't got up on. "Here..." He tossed King a bundle of sliders after pulling them from his pocket, then said, "DUMPS!" Those are counterfeit..." He pointed to the credit cards just as King removed the rubber band and quickly began to file through them.

"Visa, MasterCard, Discover Platinum! Shit! Bruh... These muthafuckas look real—"

"And they go! The dumps I get from Scooby contain two lines of text, one for each tract on the credit card magstrip. Track 1 is the cardholder's name, address, etc. Track 2 is the credit card number and banking identification and routing number. I use a MSR206 and Reader-Writer software program to program Green Dot cards and... Wala! Each one of these motherfuckers got anywhere from $500 to $1,000 that we can spend," Slim explained.

"What! You bullshittin'?" King looked on with surprise and excitement on his face. "Run it! I want to know the ins-and-outs of the whole operation. And your boy...what's his name?"

"Scooby."

"Yeah... Scooby. You still got a line on him?"

"Yep!"

"Good! We need to holla at these Asians about these cards and this nigga Jay-5. If we play this right... it could put us in the *game* on a whole other level, top shelf, feel me?"

Slim smiled, exposing all 32 platinum and diamond slugs in his mouth. He knew what time it was. His trigger finger began to itch the moment he reached for his cell phone and dialed Scooby's number and said, "Already!"

King fell back in his chair patiently waiting for the call to go through. He had already contemplated his next move, which weighed heavily on his conscience. On one hand, Jay-5 had committed the ultimate sin by violating the code in more ways than one. He was a snitch with no sense of loyalty for his team, which in King's book, made him the worst kind of nigga there was. *A nigga like that… that rats out his team and bites the hand that feeds him deserve to be a dead nigga,* he thought. How Jay-5 had managed to escape a death sentence all these years was beyond belief. He definitely was not to be underestimated. Niggas like that usually washed up at the lake or were found slumped somewhere with a hole in their head. *But here it is… this nigga still standing! Who the fuck this nigga, Sammy the Bull or some goddamn body?*

On the other hand, King thought to himself, *Kay-Kay and I grew up together and are now a lil' something more than friends. This no doubt complicates matters.*

King knew he was about to make a decision that would ultimately lead to her father, and potentially her along with her entire family, getting killed. It was complicated. He was gambling with their lives hoping they would be spared, which depended on how he played his cards. And knowing where Jay-5 laid his head was the only thing keeping them alive.

Still, even if they were spared, if she ever finds out I was the one that put the call in that led to her father's funeral, it would be the end of our relationship.

King couldn't deny the fact that he cared deeply for Kay-Kay and was struggling over the decision he was about to make, knowing it would change her life forever, and forever eat at him, no matter how it worked out.

He slowly drew a breath and exhaled as Slim sat his cell phone on the desk and pushed the speaker button.

"Hello?"

Chapter 21

Agent Sisco sat in a black Ford Crown Victoria parked in the parking lot of the Will Rogers International Airport watching King and Slim as they walked into the airport to board a flight headed for Northern California. Desperate to build a case on Pumpsie before he paroled, he had cast his net wide, and set up surveillance on King after reading the correspondence between the two. While the letters were not incriminating, nonetheless, they were revealing.

He had learned enough from reading them to know that the relationship between them was toxic. Even more, King was the late Reed's son, who, like him, wanted answers as to his father's murder. Jackson was paroling in a matter of weeks, which meant the likelihood of getting an indictment was slim. However, Sisco had remained optimistic about closing the case and was banking on the fact that, after reading the letters, Jackson and his nephew were about to have a little heart-to-heart chit-chat about the events on that fateful day some 15 years ago when six bodies, including Reed's, had been found dead out at the old Nobletown gymnasium. Had Weaver, a.k.a. Jay-5, not lived, there would have been eight bodies, and no conviction in Jackson's case. Still, it wasn't enough for Sisco. Weaver's testimony had only put Pumpsie on the shelf for a few calendars when he deserved to be there, if not on death row, until his last suit.

He sat in the car thinking of that bullshit testimony and how Weaver had taken the stand at the preliminary hearing and lied his ass off.

"Mr. Weaver..." the prosecutor said, then continued, "... could you please explain to the court what you and your friends were doing out at the Nobletow school gymnasium on the day in question?"

"Ah, yes... We were playing basketball with some friends," Jay-5 answered.

"Now while you all were playing basketball, did anyone show up...did something happen?"

"Yes. Pumpsie... I mean Mr. Jackson, showed up and was looking for, I mean, looking to score some dope from one of the other players."

"So what happened next?"

"The next thing I know his brother... the deceased, Mr. Reed, busted through the door, guns blazing. It was a setup...."

Jay-5 lied. That much Sisco was certain of. Redd was no two-bit stick up kid. The story was something the D.A.'s office had spun to get a conviction in the event that case against Jackson went to trial. Plus they were trying to put the squeeze on him and figure out where his brother had hid all the money he made off his bootlegging operation.

Lying on the stand to achieve these ends was something the prosecution did every day when it came to pressuring a witness or a law enforcement officer to get the job done. It was a dirty system.

Nevertheless, Sisco figured he was on the winning side. Both the D.A. and he knew the case against Pumpsie was weak. Still, had it gone to trial, the jury would have bought it so long as it sounded half-ass plausible.

Jay-5 went on to testify that after the first shot rang out, he somehow mustered up the courage to tackle Reed, 'the madman,' and knock the gun from his hand.

"They struggled... Jackson ran out the door, and moments later I heard several gunshots rang out outside the gym. That's when I looked up and saw Jackson aiming the gun... He shot me and his brother in the process of the struggle," Jay-5 had said.

Bullshit, Sisco shook his head thinking about the testimony. He not only knew that the ballistics from the slugs pulled from Reed and Weaver's wounds did not match, but he had also been tipped off by an informant that Jackson had staged the kidnapping, and Weaver had led Redd to the gym to make the exchange for $200,000 for Pumpsie's safe return, which they were to split.

It wouldn't be until years later that he figured out why the D.A.'s office never followed up on the lead. Jay-5 was a federal witness in an ongoing case for some big time dope dealer on the West Coast.

Jackson, on the other hand, would dodge the murder beef for his brother's accidental shooting when he plead out on the attempt. The D.A. was then forced to drop the charge after learning the ballistics did not match up with Weaver's story. Which meant there were six murders Sisco aimed to pin on Pumpsie for the kidnapping plot and subsequent homicides.

Curious, he pulled King's file. Nothing. With the exception of a GTA and possession charge for marijuana, which was dismissed, the kid had a fairly clean record. There was nothing to suggest he was anything other than an adventurous kid looking for a few kicks. Still, someone had murdered his father along with several other poor saps. And from the tone of his letters, Sisco had a gut feeling the kid was about to take it up a notch and try and knock off whoever pulled the trigger. *Not if I get to him first*, he vowed.

"I don't know where in the hell those damn boys are at. I've been trying to call them all morning and all I'm getting is their voicemail," Regina sighed with frustration as she turned to look at her father.

Lenny was sitting at his desk, and both Dekoven and Ole Man Blue were standing at the bar pouring themselves a drink. They had all met up at the Lodge to further discuss the matter pertaining to Jay-5.

"Don't worry yourself about them boys. Hell... They probably out fishing or hunting somewhere," Blue responded, trying to put her mind at the ease.

"Yeah... You're probably right," she said.

"Now, about Jay-5. What's this you say about him and these Asians?" Blue asked.

"Like I was saying... I know him from his hey days, back when he and his crew were Big Tymers in the Bay Area. Those Asians he was hooked up with, that I was telling you about, plugged him in a major way. Not too many niggaz get on like that, you know?" she stated matter-of-factly. "It was big! Bigger than Felix Mitchell or lil' D. They were dropping off packs in 50 states like FedEx. That's until the feds kicked in the door and he turned state. He really gutted their entire operation with that bass mouth. From the top down. How he got on like that is beyond me. Because those Asians don't really fuck with niggaz like that on that level."

"Well that's easy to figure out," Lenny said, scratching at his head. "I bet it has something to do with that half-breed he with. What's her name? Sonya? That's it isn't it?" He looked on for approval, uncertain if that was her name.

"Yeah, that's her. And probably why her name ringing in the streets too," Regina replied. "Word is they got a million dollars on their heads, Jay-5 and her's!"

"What! A mill'?" Blue exclaimed with disbelief. "Now we already knew that boy was dirtier than a muthafucka and ticking on borrowed time. But... Shit! With that kind of money on his head, hers too, it's a wonder they still breathing. I mean—"

"Hold up!" Regina interrupted. "You mean to tell me that you already knew Jay-5 was in Witness Protection?"

"No! We knew he had turned state on some people he was involved with out in California and assumed he ran out here and before they tried to get on his head. We didn't know the details until now, until you showed up," Lenny said.

"I'm sure all this will be news to Pumpsie as well," Blue said.

"He'll be transferring to John Lilly in a few weeks and I'll fill him in then," Lenny added.

"Hold up! I don't get it... I mean, I thought Pumpsie was behind all of this?" Regina questioned as her face twisted in confusion.

Everyone in the room turned to look at each other with solemn faces as they realized no one had filled her in on what actually occurred the day Redd was killed. She knew nothing about Jay-5 and Redd, their beef, or the bullshit testimony Jay-5 had concocted in an attempt to lay blame for Redd's murder on Pumpsie.

"Jay-5 killed Redd," Dekoven finally said.

"What!?!" Regina's mouth hung open with shock. She couldn't believe her ears. "Jay-5 killed Redd!" she repeated.

"Yeah," Dekoven replied as he handed her a drink to take the edge off. He then began to explain everything he had recently learned. When he finished, he lifted his glass and swallowed his drink in one gulp, then turned to Blue and Lenny and said with a troubling look on his face, "And that's not all."

Lenny, Blue, and Regina looked on with shock. What more could he possibly say? That's when he told them what Sticky made him swear not to tell.

"Ugh mum," he cleared his throat, then went on to explain, "After Sis's attorney filed the court documents to buy out Redd's silent partner, she got hit with another bombshell. The partner, she learned, was Jay-5 himself. Apparently, his lawyers were ordered by the court to file a disclosure motion, revealing his name and ownership in the club during the proceedings connected to the tax case. When she bought him out and filed to remove him from ownership, the clerk mistakenly mailed the documents to the club."

"I don't get it. How was she able to put all this together if Jay-5 was in Witness Protection?" Lenny asked.

"The minute Sis opened the envelope and saw his alias on the paperwork, she immediately connected it with the credit card charges he had made over the years at the club, gambling and renting VIP booths. The government had provided him a platinum snitch card. Even more, aside of the protection money he had managed to swindle you out of," Dekoven pointed at Lenny, then continued, ".... he also made a killing off the business that Redd and she literally poured their blood and sweat into."

"I imagine she was speechless when she found out about all this?" Blue asked as he stared into the glass he was holding.

"Yes," Dekoven responded. "At first she wanted to approach both of you about this. However, she quickly realized it would only in add insult to injury. You pretty much already had your hands full trying to maintain appearances and keep Jay-5 sleep to exact Pumpsie's plan to avenge Redd's murder. After giving it some thought, she finally decided that it was best that you all remain clueless as to the matter. She was certain that, if she didn't know Jay-5 had been Redd's silent partner, after years of being at the helm of the ship, then the two of you certainly didn't. With exception of telling me, it was her little secret."

Everybody sat, stunned, taking in what Dekoven had just said. It stung at the heart and soul of them all. What needed to be done was clear. Jay-5 had to pay for the pain he had caused them, *And,* they each quietly vowed, *he's going to pay with his life.*

Chapter 22

Both Slim and King stepped off the plane at the Oakland International Airport looking Dope-Boy fresh. True to form, Slim looked every bit the street thug he was, rocking a pair of fitted True Religion jeans, a cocaine-white T-shirt, and a throwback Avirex leather jacket and shoes.

King, on the other hand, was the epitome of head-to-toe couture and looked as if he had been lifted directly from the catwalk. He had begun to pick up on his uncle's sense of men's fashion and was becoming ever more the businessman his mother had hoped he would grow to be. His action figure physique and chiseled jawline snugged at a Ralph Lauren turtleneck and denim jeans and a Ferragamo sports jacket.

At his feet were his father's gator skin Tony Lama boots, bearing the familiar Masonic insignia. That he was wearing them symbolized more than a mere fashion statement. They had traveled to Oakland to have a sit-down with the Chan Syndicate's underboss. And, as a matter of rite of passage, he now represented not only his father's legacy, but also the secret society of the Freemasons.

"Man, Cuddy... Niggaz out here go swear you country-n-a-muthafucka rocking them boots," Slim smirked, shaking his head at King as they walked over to the baggage claim and waited for their luggage.

"Shit nigga you know what time it is. 'Gator boots and an iced out grill...'" King replied, singing a verse from Cash Money Records classic Hood Rich album.

Between the two, they had enough karats and crushed ice hanging on their ears and platinum grillz to feed a thousand diamond miners in Sierra Leone for a year.

"Anyway... Did you hit your boy up and let him know we touched down?" King asked.

"Yeah, I texted him as soon as we stepped off the plane. Hold up... That's him now I bet," Slim said, reaching for his phone.

While Slim spoke on the phone, King thought of the events of the past few weeks. He hadn't been out of prison a good month and things were happening fast. Kay-Kay and he had taken their relationship to another level, which constantly tugged at his conscience after learning that her entire family was in witness protection.

Then there was the ceremony.

After being home for a week, his grandfather and Uncle Lenny had called a meeting at the Lodge to initiate both Slim and he as Third Degree Master Masons.

Shortly before it began, King stumbled down to the Lodge's basement to retrieve an apron and that's when it hit him. The numbers his mother had been mindlessly chanting were the combination to the old bank vault his father had set in the concrete foundation of the building.

Over and over she had repeated the numbers, "36… 20… 15… 47," until they were all he could remember. He sat in the airport recalling how he removed the boxes stacked in front of the vault and dusted it off before he began twisting and turning its dials with the hopes of opening it.

His stomach turned with excitement as the dials spun back and forth. With each number, he became overwhelmed with uncertainty as he wondered if, in reality, what his mother had been trying to tell him all along was in fact, the combination to the safe. Needless to say, he was eager as a kid on Christmas morning to find out.

Suddenly, there was a long synchronized clicking sound as each of the vaults' tumblers released. Anticipation swept over him as he struggled with the handle to pull it open. Almost immediately, the pungent smell of mold and stale air stung his nostrils. A dim light began to flicker as an electrical current made its way through the old wiring system that lit the inside of the vault.

Finally, the lights came on and he got his first glimpse at what the safe had been holding all these years. Nothing!

He was stunned and disappointed. There were no stacks of gold bullion or any sign of the millions he had been told over the years his father had stashed away. Dust and several duffle bags and a small tin box killed his hopes.

Nothing, King thought as he stood there. Then, as he turned to leave, it hit him. He stopped dead in his tracks, turned and grabbed box off the shelf to inspect it.

As he looked it over, his gut told him it hadn't been left there unintentionally. It was one of those old tin joints with a flimsy clasp on it that could easily be manipulated. He quickly found a screwdriver and pried it open with little effort. Inside was an old leather ledger, tattered and unraveled at the seams.

Carefully, he removed it from the box and began flipping through its brittle pages. With each page, it became clearer and clearer what his mother and father had set in motion some 20 years ago.

That's when the water works turned on. His eyes filled with tears thinking of how his mother had fought for years to maintain everything his father had built; everything he now held the keys to. She had sacrificed so much. She had gambled, devised a plan that not only settled his father's debt with the IRS, but also improved on and restructured his business model.

J.M. Spirits had gone from an illegal bootlegging operation to being distributed throughout liquor chains around the nation. Crown Entertainment, a recent business development, had been set up as part of her restructuring of his father's rodeo events, broadcasting rights, and ownership of the club and Lodge. They were legit, and with the money these ventures alone we're pulling in, comfortable. King couldn't help but contemplate taking the straight and narrow and maintaining his family's legitimacy.

However, that notion was short-lived. The ledger contained a long list of names and contact information to each of his father's former business associates, friends and family. He quickly recognized the name of Chief Brown, several senators whose sons he had grown up with, the bank president, and a number of CEOs that had frequented the lodge or the club over the years. There were also the names of Reed family members. Some he knew, some he didn't. All of which appeared to have gotten their start in politics or business by some means or another with his father's connections or bootleg money.

It was at that moment, while flipping through the ledger, he began to understand what his grandmother had meant when she spoke of the "crown" his father had placed on his head and the hope he wished for in wanting his son to grow into a very powerful man. He thought about the books she had sent him while he was in prison and how they now assisted him to act with prudence and to understand and capitalize on the information he now held in his hand.

Still, as much as he acknowledged the wisdom of his grandmother's words, he struggled, as any kid his age would, with what she had said about the dope-game and how he could never become the man his father had hoped for if he chose that life.

He had seen firsthand what it did to his father and his Uncle Pumpsie. Despite this, like so many young black men, he ignored the warning signs, and instead, began mapping out his traps and contemplating how he could use the ledger to advance his game plan and beat the odds.

Dre got blocks in H-Town and Dallas... Big-D, Tulsa. My other cousin, Ree, OKC... Danny and Heath got every one stoplight town in between on lock. And Slim, the Bay Area. And that's not including this ledger. We got family and just about every major city in the United States, he recounted.

His game plan was simple. *Negotiating Kay-Kay and her mother's life just got that much easier*, he reasoned.

If it was one thing he had learned from the family business, it was the fact that the more turf you covered, the more leverage and appeal you had to *eat* and build connections. The dope-game was no different. He had been in it long enough to know that when it came to getting a major connect, all he had to do was secure blocks, and sooner or later, the cartels would lay their cards on the table.

The Chan Syndicate was no exception. He had done his homework. They were a small band of Cambodian guerillas who had fled southeast Asia to America during the tumultuous 1970s. By the early '80s, Kim Chan, the syndicate's boss, had established himself in the Los Angeles heroin trade, which quickly grew to dominate the West Coast. And despite his incarceration, thanks to Jay-5, Chan had managed to keep the organization afloat and it now supplied the United States with 5% of the nation's heroin.

From the moment Slim had put him on the phone with lil' Scooby, King knew it was about to get major. A week later, Slim's phone rang. Jay-5's name had landed, and a meeting was immediately arranged thereafter.

"Blood! Blood! Snap out of that shit!" Slim tugged at King's jacket sleeve.

Startled, King jumped to his feet and shouted, "What?"

"Come on… That's our ride," Slim pointed as he put his phone in his pocket and grabbed his bag from the baggage claim.

A two-door, jewel green 1971 Ford LTD pulled to the curb and parked in the airport passenger pickup lane.

King looked up and saw the car's 28" rims and asked, "Scooby?"

"Nawl," Slim replied. That's his cousin, Carlos. Scooby in traffic and will meet up with us at the spot."

"7-1?" King asked, eagerly.

He finally was about to see where it all started. King had been feeding 71st and Hamilton for a couple of years now. It was one of several spots in the Bay Area where Slim had managed to get on and undercut the paisas prices on the bammer weed.

For years, he had listened to Slim's stories about how "a hundred niggaz posted on the block with a garbage bag full of HEAD CHANGE, getting it! Swinging '78 Mustangs and Coug' nutz at the side-show."

"Come on," Slim said as he quickly grabbed his bags and began making his way through the crowded airport.

By the time they reached the lobby's sliding doors, they could feel the boom-clap-blonk-clap of the 808 hitting hard in the trunk of the car as the loud music set off car alarms in the parking lot.

"That's Jack's folks," Slim yelled as they walked out the door.

"What?" King asked, unable to hear what he had said on account of the music being so loud.

Suddenly, the music stopped and the car's Lamborghini doors swung open releasing a cloud of dank smoke.

"Now, what was that?" King again asked.

"Carlos... That's Jacka's folks. You know... The rapper I was telling you about that got killed a while back," Slim said, referring to the Pittsburg rapper who was tragically murdered in a case of mistaken identity.

"Pittsburgh?" King questioned as he recalled Slim and his mother had once lived there. "Oh yeah! I remember now. That's where you met 'los and yeah the Jack. I remember. He the one that plugged you with Scooby?"

Before Slim could respond, Carlos had jumped out of the car with a burst of energy and a golden smile to greet them.

"My niggga! What's good, folks?" 'los asked as Slim and he embraced one another. He then turned to King, did a once-over, and again looking at his cowboy boots, said, "Who the fuck is this? Wild Bill or some goddamn body?"

Slim burst into a fit of laughter. He couldn't contain himself. "See I told you niggaz would be clowning about them damn boots."

King shifted about confidently and shot back, "Oh... We got jokes. Oh, okay! Who the fuck you? A hyphy version of Dr. Ken or some goddamn body?"

It was on and cracking. Slim felt like he had a front-row seat at the Laugh Factory. They all fell out laughing as King and 'los took shots at each other, capping and impersonating one another. They were naturals when it came to clowning.

"I guess there's no need for introductions," Slim finally said as he wiped tears from the corner of his eyes. He had to catch his breath. He had laughed so hard, he could barely stand straight as he held his cramping stomach.

"Nah, this must be the 'Cowboy' you always talkin about?' Carlos asked, extending his fist for dap before King and he embraced one another. "Niggaz on the Block know your name like they know Granny's," he added. "Ain't no need for introductions."

"Already!" King said, returning the dap and embrace.

The laughter was good and much-needed. The events of the past few weeks had been stressful to say the least. After taking care of business, King and Slim planned to unwind a bit while in the Bay Area. And the laughter was a sign of a good start.

After a few more laughs, the boys loaded their bags into the car and left the airport to meet up with little Scooby.

The minute Carlos pulled in and parked at the convenience store on the corner of 71st and Hamilton,

King noted it wasn't the 7-1 Slim had once described to him.

A lot had changed while he was in the Zo. California had recently legalized marijuana for recreational use, which had cut the price for a pound of HEAD CHANGE in half. The dispensaries had the market on lock and a lot of street dealers were put out of business. Most of which had now bounced from 71st to 89th Street to push cocaine or heroin, if not both.

"Don't let it fool you cousin! There's still money on the block," Slim said, noting his cousin's disappointment. He then pointed and said, "See—"

King looked in the direction Slim had pointed. Across the street he could see several young hyenas posted, getting it, flagging down cars in broad daylight and dropping off packages like the mailman, as though they didn't have a worry in the world.

"The money still coming in," Slim said as they sat in the car and waited for Scooby to arrive.

"Anybody want anything out of the store?" Carlos asked as he hopped out of the car.

"I'm good. But thanks," King replied as he checked his messages on the phone. There were several missed calls from Kay-Kay. She was the last person he wanted to talk to considering where he was and why he was there. "Out of town. Will call you when I get back," he texted back, hoping that she would kick back and chill.

"Okay, miss you. :(" she texted back a few minutes later.

"Grab me a Coke," Slim replied as Carlos walked towards the store. "So like I was saying… The money still—" Slim turned back to King and started to say.

"Yeah, but the take ain't the same," King interrupted, pulling at the tuffs on his chin before continuing, "At $150,

$200 a pound, we're not seeing but half the money we seen before. And the only good thing about it is the fact that the demand for HEAD CHANGE is still strong despite the dispensaries having took a chunk out of our clientele. It's still moving and it's moving fast. Too fast! Heath and Danny can't grow the shit fast enough to keep the machine up and running."

Faced with the problem of supply and demand, both King and Slim realized that the only way they could keep up with things was to either expand their growth operation or outsource production. This, however, posed two problems. One, cultivating marijuana in Oklahoma was illegal with the exception of the medical marijuana business. Therefore, the larger their operation grew, the more they stood the chance of attracting the attention of the DEA. Second, outsourcing production to legal states meant instead of trafficking HEAD CHANGE into Texas and California from Oklahoma, they would have to move product back into the state, which posed a whole different set of problems in and of itself.

Moving product out of the state had been their advantage. For decades law enforcement had focused primarily on cartel activities that imported drugs into the Heartland. That made Oklahoma and several other states a drug trafficker's Mecca. By the time their product hit the streets of Oklahoma City, Tulsa, Kansas City, or a few other backwood spots like Wewoka, which was a drug trafficking hub for Seminole County, their profit had almost tripled compared to other states.

On the other hand, exporting drugs out of state was almost unheard of. This had made it relatively easy for Slim and King to ship product to California and elsewhere. The feds were not focused on what was shipped out of state. Rather, they were focused on what was being shipped in. So shipping out of state didn't raise any red flags.

"There's Scooby now," Carlos said as he returned to the car.

King looked up, and to his surprise, a tatted-up Asian kid, no older than himself, whipped into the parking lot riding a fully chromed-out, polished Softail Harley-Davidson motorcycle.

The pipes on the bike roared to a stop next to the LTD, giving King a close up of its candy paint and dragon graphics. He had expected some street kid in a souped-up Honda. But after meeting Carlos, he didn't know exactly what to think.

"What it do, fam?" Scooby asked Carlos, setting the bike on its kickstand.

"Shit! Trying to get fresh like you big cousin," Carlos replied as the two dapped and embraced.

"Slim," Scooby acknowledged as he and King got out of the car. "Man that was some real messy shit we had to clean up for you," he added, referring to Detective Li's murder.

"Bruh, I'm just glad to hear your folks were able to take care of it," Slim replied, thankful that Scooby had tapped into the Syndicate's resources and had the evidence linking Peaches and him to the murder destroyed.

"Well…that's all behind us now," Scooby said in a rather nonchalant manner.

Despite the ease to which Scooby had dismissed the matter, Slim knew it came with a hefty price. "Look Fam, I'm forever in debt to you and your people. Whatever you need…you need me to body a nigga, consider it done. You need me to drop off that shit…whatever, just holla!" he said with the utmost sincerity.

"Relax folks! The family already know you blocked tested and certified. You deliver on this Jay-5 business, we good and some. So consider the favor repaid," Scooby said.

"That's why we're here," Slim responded, then turned to introduce King, "This my cousin who you spoke to last week."

Scooby turned to King, who had been quietly observing their brief exchange and was eager to get down to business. A lot was at stake and he felt the sooner they handled things, the quicker he could put his conscience to rest.

"Well," Scooby smiled and said, "... it's good to finally put a face with the name. Your cousin has always spoke highly of you. What's good?" he asked, extending his fist for dap.

"Shit! About to get this money," King replied as he returned the dap and asked, "So when do we meet your boss?"

"Tomorrow!"

"Sounds good. So what now?" King asked. He had seen enough of 7-1 and was anxious for a change of scenery.

"I have something I believe you will find interesting and worth checking out," Scooby replied.

"Yeah?"

"Yeah! My people believe we can work to each other's benefit in more ways than this Jay-5 business. After our discussion last week, I spoke with them and they recognize that it's going to be a vacancy to fill in Oklahoma's drug market after he's removed, if you get what I mean?"

King's palms suddenly began to burn with an itching sensation as superstition foretold of fortune. Without a doubt, the Syndicate and he were thinking along the same lines. Things were definitely looking good. However, he had bigger plans than simply catering to Oklahoma's illicit drug trade.

Chapter 23

Jay-5 sat at his desk staring at the check Sticky's attorney had sent to his lawyers. He had had it photocopied and mounted in a small platinum picture frame, which hung on the office wall at *257 Customs*. It had been a little over a year since he had sold his share in Pooches. After years of playing a silent partner in Redd's business, he had cashed out, tripling his investment and adding to it a small fortune in protection money.

A sinister grin quickly swept across his face as he reached up and massaged the scar. It was numb and cold as his heart. Every time he touched it, it reminded him that no one walked away from the *game* unscathed.

"How many niggaz we done lost to the streets?" he turned to one of his goons and asked.

"Shit man... I don't keep track of that shit. Its taboo," replied the goon as he frowned in deep reflection.

"Well, we about to lose some more if you niggaz keep slipping with these country boys!" Jay-5 snapped.

"What you mean by that?"

"Pumpsie!"

"What about—"

"The nigga about to touchdown—"

"Yeah and—"

"And he a fuckin' loose end!"

"That dope-fiend ass nigga!?!" the goon questioned as his face twisted in confusion. "Everybody know the first thing he go to do when he hit the bricks is cop a balloon."

"You ain't been listening to the streets have you?" Jay-5 asked, then pointed a finger at the goon and said, "That's what I'm talking about right there! Underestimating this nigga was our first mistake. Since that video surfaced, everybody talkin' about him being back on his square," he added, nervously running his hand across his chin.

Pumpsie's homecoming was eating at Jay-5 in the worst way. He knew on occasion the penitentiary would take the man at his worst and provide him that "get back" he needed to hit the bricks on top of his *game*. With his resolve strengthened and drug-free, he knew Pumpsie would be at him out the gates to avenge his brother's murder.

"We got to dead this nigga and dead him quick! Smash him!" Jay-5 growled, slamming his fist down on the desk. He had realized his mistake. Dropping a dime on Pumpsie and sending him up state hadn't accomplished a thing. He had left a loose end untied and could feel the wind changing. He knew he'd have to get out in front of it before it blew. There was about to be a war at his doorstep if he didn't tie things up fast.

"And what about his nephew?" asked the goon.

"What about him?"Jay-5 replied, wanting to avoid the topic. Dealing with King was troubling for him for quite some time. He had overheard Kay-Kay and Sonya talking about him getting out and everything that had happened with his mother. For a split second he had almost felt sorry for him. He knew how close his daughter and the boy had grown over the years, which complicated things. Yet his callous heart was incapable of feeling. This was especially so, given the fact that they were feelings he never had with his own father. In his own twisted mind, killing Redd had been a symbolic killing of his own father. Despite this, it was not personal. It was simply part of the *game*, which now called for him to eliminate his son or stand the chance that he would come gunning for him as well.

"Dead the little nigga too!" Jay-5 finally said. "We got to tie up every loose end and finally put this beef to rest."

Pumpsie lay restless reading the graffiti etched into the bottom of the bunk above him. *Tick 3/21/95, 20 years. Raybone "Vice Lord" 25 to Life. My balls smell like rotten fruit and my armpits smell like cat piss! Give them crack and make them lose their minds. Put liquor and gun stores on every corner, just keep on killing yourself. The whole white power structure, feel it in your bones!, South Side Gangsta Crip*, and so on and so forth the names and profanity read. Superstition about his fate forbid him to add his name to the graffiti, for he was always told that a man who wrote his name on prison walls would always be captive to them. He had spent the last 15 years reading name after name, verse after verse, of the jailhouse poets who dare to bare their souls on concrete and steel which had hardened and broken so many. Their writings certainly seemed to always touch on the hatred that, ironically, kept them alive and optimistic. It had been his hatred for Jay-5 and exacting vengeance for his brother's murder that had been his lifeline all these years.

However, the thought of paroling in less than a month scared him shitless. He hadn't the foggiest idea of what freedom would be like after having spent close to two decades, caged like a dog in a kennel for 23 hours a day. His interaction with human beings had been minimal at most, guarded, non-existent. The majority of the prison guards were animals, psychopaths, who were more cutthroat than the murderers and rapist he was caged with. Unpredictable violence had made him extremely paranoid, skittish, and volatile—PTSD. Without question, the walls were relentless in their ability to drive men insane, to commit suicide, to self-mutilate. The tragedy that came of this constantly consumed him with more violence and suspense than a horror flick. Agony and loud cries for help went unanswered in the night, drawing him closer and closer to the notion to hang himself. His old cellie, Horse, had showed him the easy way out.

"Yo 'P'! I got a fat stick of that 'loud' and a half a gallon of gas. It's my b-day cousin! Let's celebrate," Horse said smiling, looking like a jackass eating cactus, gums, broken teeth and all. He had walked into the cell and tossed a ChapStick cap full of Bobby Brown and a few zigzags at Pumpsie's feet.

A simple farm boy, Horse, a.k.a. Joe Harjo, was a Native American kid who hunted squirrel and rabbit for supper and would occasionally trade the meat for food stamps. His parents were alcoholics, and he too had developed a taste of his own by the time he was 13. His favorite cocktail was a mixture of Everclear and Wild Turkey, which he called Wilder Turkey.

He first went to prison in his late teens after pulling a knife on a man who owed him two dollars, and again in his late twenties following an arrest for a string of burglaries. He eventually landed back in prison for a third time with a life sentence after narrowly escaping the needle on a B&E that went bad after he startled an affluent elderly white woman in her sleep and caused her to have a fatal heart attack.

To the outside world, Joe seemed content with his circumstances. He had a gift for manufacturing spirits that would leave a man with a dry scratchy voice, and blind in one eye for a week. Inside, however, he struggled to find purpose. Prison had done to him what he had done to so many others. It robbed him of everything; family, friends, his girlfriend, his emotions, hope, and his right to self-determination. Like a cold magic trick, they all vanished, disappeared over the years into thin air. So it came as no surprise or lost to the world when, later that evening, while Pumpsie lay in a drunken stupor, Horse, stumbling, climbed atop the desk in their cell and wrapped a bed sheet around his neck and jumped to freedom.

It was a sobering experience, one that caused Pumpsie to clean up and leave the drinking and drugging alone. For years he had used them to cover his pain. Still, there was an occasion or two that he thought to follow suit and end it.

Often, he would stare into the cloudy steel mirror that hung in his cell and cringe at the sight of the struggle written across his face. His addiction haunted him so. Large craters filled his face from years of drug abuse, but, it wasn't his physical appearance that he fought with. Pumpsie was an ugly nigga. It was his emotions he worked hard to keep in check. He struggled to keep caring. His feelings—his caring—were like a rope around his neck that grew tighter and tighter the more he held on to them.

King, his nephew, was the closest blood relative he had. Pumpsie had lived through the whole "Rise & Fall" story of his brother's legacy. And now, it appeared as though his nephew was trying to fill his shoes. He had desperately tried to reach him. But the rendezvous with Captain Barreatto and getting him back in the saddle did little to deter him from following in his father's footsteps. He had struggled to maintain the correspondence with his nephew, yet the boy kept throwing shade at him, venting his frustrations and blaming him for Redd's death.

That King blamed him for his father's murder only added to Pumpsie's grief. To an extent, he did feel responsible, and it was during these times he contemplated suicide. Then the minute he committed to the notion, Redd's blood would appear on his hands and the memory of his baby brother dying in his arms would remind him of his promise.

"Jackson! Bunk and junk and kiss your punk goodbye!" a guard announced over the P.A. system.

Hearing his name called over the intercom, Pumpsie quickly snapped back to the matter at hand, as his cell door slowly opened and the tomb he had been trapped in unsealed after what seemed to be a thousand years. He was being transferred to the John Lilley Correctional Center, where he would be released the following morning.

After 15 years, nine months and 28 days, the only thing he was taking home from prison was years of regret and his nephew's letters.

Chapter 24

King looked on with wonder as he stood on an elevated platform overlooking the entire ground level of the warehouse lil' Scooby had taken them to. Before him were thousands of neatly arranged marijuana plants in various stages of development. Above them a number of mercury vapor lamps radiated artificial sunlight. Timers, fans, and an array of water distribution hoses had been synchronized along with the lamps, to create an artificial climate producing some 500 pounds of top grade dank smoke a week. Despite a state-of-the-art ventilation system, the pungent smell of the high-grade cannabis stung his nostrils as he took in the sight of the elaborate operation.

At the center of the warehouse, he could see there was a processing laboratory set up with a handful of white-coats moving about like mad scientists taking cultures on the plants and examining them under several microscopes.

"What's up with the white-coats?" he asked Scooby.

"Oh that? Well... Come on, let me show you!" Scooby said, turning and waving for them to follow him down a narrow stairway leading to the ground floor of the warehouse.

King, Slim, and Carlos quickly fell in tow, and soon they were all standing in a sawdust-strewn enclosure surrounded by a pantheon of cannabis, microscopes, culture trays, and other lab equipment.

"This is our lead biotech, Lauren," Scooby said, introducing them to a petite Asian woman who had been standing at the table with her head bent over a microscope when they walked in.

"Hey Scooby," she said before giving him a slight hug and turning towards King and Slim and saying, "Hi."

"She's a grad student at UC Berkeley studying the bio-genetics of cannabis to better understand its medicinal effects," Scooby continued.

King did a once-over of the petite lady standing in front of him and noted her round face and handsome features. He had never tripped off the Asian girls as there weren't many in the neighborhood where he was from. As he stood there taking in the scenery, he felt a twitch of "yellow fever" coming on.

Shorty got a nice apple bottom, he thought to himself before finally saying, "What's good." He then introduced himself and Slim after noting how jovial everyone seemed, despite the fact they were standing in the middle of a major indoor grow operation. That's when it hit him! *Marijuana is legal in California. And it was legal for medical purposes in Oklahoma too!* There were over 20 other states where it was also legal. He had made the mistake of thinking only in terms of the illegal markets, when the potential for the legal dope-game and hustle was major.

"Lauren? That's your name right?" King asked.

"Yes."

"I was wondering…. Well this whole legalization thing, it's just getting off the ground, right? So I'm thinking, well…let me ask. Medically, the effects of marijuana I somewhat understand. I mean, I've seen *60 Minutes* talking about how it fights nausea for cancer patients, stimulates the appetite and all that. But what is all the lab equipment for?"

Lauren gave a slight grin. "It's one thing to know the medicinal effects, but it is an entirely different thing to know what molecules make up the chemical genotype of a strand, and what those chemicals actually do, scientifically speaking. This," she pointed to a piece of equipment that looked similar to a microwave, "…this is a PacBio RS II. It reads fragments of DNA as long as 53,000 base pairs and enables us to determine the genetic markers of a particular strand of marijuana."

Sensing King was somewhat at a loss with her explanation, she continued. "For example, their aromas certainly affect the experience of consumption. Did you know that some strains contain myrcene?"

"Myrcene? What's that?" Slim interjected.

Lauren turned to Slim.

"It's one of many chemicals in a particular strain that gives off a distinctive smell. It makes the weed smell like hops and mango and some smokers claim it increases the potency of THC. There's beta-caryophyllen too. It smells like pepper. There's also ocimene, nerolidol, pinene. All these chemicals create whatever distinction that exists between, say… '78 O.G. Affie or Gorilla Glue."

"It effects the potency too! Thirty years ago, the average THC content in a plant was about 3%. Over the years, thanks to the War on Drugs forcing breeders indoors, they started experimenting, crossing breeds and strands, which drove up the THC levels to as much as 37% and created new breeds: White Widow, Purple Kush, Sour Diesel, and many, many, others. And each is as different as Chardonnay and pinot noir. And just as a vintner will rattle off a bottle's tasting notes and terror at a winery, a Denver budtender can sell a smoker on a plant's piney nose and its concentration of crystallized trichomes. Those are the hair like protrusions on the buds that contain high levels of psychoactive cannabinoids. It's all in the science of botany," she added, pointing to a bud on a plant.

"So basically what you are saying is, if we know our plants DNA makeup, then we can grow the plants with the traits we want much faster with extreme precision and potency?" King asked.

"Well... I see somebody paid attention in school," Scooby said with a hint of sarcasm in his voice.

"Kiki ha-ha," King smirked before turning back to Lauren and asking, "I take it I am correct?"

"Yes." she responded. "It's called marker-assisted selection. It's the key to modern-day agriculture."

King stood in silence, staring at the two Cheech and Chong dolls that sat on top of the RS II. He reflected on how the Syndicate's production facility made his operation look like a Toys "R" Us science kit. Granted, Danny had taught him a lot, but as he stood there reviewing the sophisticated, multimillion-dollar pot lab, he realized there was a lot more to learn about the *game* he was in, and the legal side of the hustle.

As the night crept across the sky, Judge Olsen poured his wife a flute of champagne while the two sat in their beach chairs watching the blue ocean waters and the gulls skim freely across the gulf. They had flown down to

Corpus Christi, Texas for a week-long vacation, and had been enjoying the view for the past several days.

"Missy," Olsen said, looking over at his wife.

"Yes dear?"

"I was thinking…with my retirement around the corner, maybe we should start looking at purchasing this share rental or something back on Lake Tenkiller. Our realtor says he can probably get us a waterfront lot for somewhere around $20,000," he said, thinking of his childhood and how the blue ocean waters of the gulf reminded him of the lake.

As a kid, he had grown up in Tahlequah, Oklahoma. There, the lake often became his refuge. All kinds of game surrounded its waters, and it was filled with freshwater fish like bass and perch. Its crystal blue waters covered 27 miles of shoreline and was like an oasis in the Dust Bowl State. As a teenager, and later a student at Northeastern State University, it also held precious memories of his rebellious youth.

"That sounds wonderful darling," Missy said.

"Good, because I've already bought the property and we have an appointment with the contractor to look over the floor plans when we get back. They'll start building as soon as possible. I am sure you will approve. Happy anniversary," Olson said as he reached into his pocket and handed her the key to the front door of their new house.

Missy's face lit up with surprise and she leaned over to give him a passionate hug and kiss.

As the two celebrated and continued to discuss their retirement plans, Dre stood in the foyer of the condo waiting patiently for their return.

"I'm going to run up and get us a couple blankets. It's going to get chilly out here. Is there anything you need while I'm in the house?" Olsen asked, standing up.

"No, I'm good. I'll gather some firewood while you're up there and should have a warm fire going by the time you return."

"Okay. Sounds like a plan. I'll grab some things to make s'mores too."

Dre eagerly watched Olson's every move. The minute he saw him walking towards the condo, he reached in his jacket pocket and pulled out a Gemtech suppressor and began screwing it on the Sig Sauer King had given him shortly before Slim and he left for California.

While at Camp R.E.D., King discovered the extent of Olsen's vendetta against his family and himself. He had learned from Captain Barreatto that his extended stay at the camp wasn't about enforcing the law or on account of lil' Jay and his antics. It was personal. Olsen wanted to shut down everything and everyone connected to his father. He aimed to break King mentally, and the director was in on it.

"Olsen is afraid of what you have been exposed to. It's in your blood," Barreatto explained to King. "See, your father—"

"Hold up! What's the deal with you and my pops?" King asked.

Barreatto shifted about in her chair somewhat uncomfortable, then said, "I grew up with your father and knew him better than most. See everybody knew 'Redd.' I know Javon Sr. before your mother, he and I played *house* as kids. We experimented with sex and drugs as teenagers. And, more importantly, I was one of the few people he trusted."

King blinked in disbelief. Over the years, he had known many people who knew and spoke highly of his father. However, aside from his immediate family, he had not known anyone who could honestly say they were someone his father could trust. What Barreatto was telling him was yet another chapter in his father's life he did not know about.

Up until that point, most of what people had to say about his father was about who Redd was to them: a good dude. Or what he meant to someone; you could count on him. And that he was a top-notch chip getta, OG and solid. Yet what they said was so much more to King. They were reflections of his father that served as a guidepost, a personification of the man he so desperately desired to be.

"My father took your daddy up underneath his wing when he was a shorty like this," she continued as she held out hand about four feet off the floor, indicating how tall Redd was then.

Kings face twisted with curiosity. "Who is your father?"

"Dirty Dick!"

"Dirty Dick Kemp?"

"Yes."

"I know the name, the legend, and the story." King couldn't believe it! He grew up hearing about how Dirty Dick had put his daddy and uncles in the *game*. "Now, what I didn't know was that he was your father. Wow! Talk about a small world."

"Yeah that's my old man. He was my stepfather. Married my mother when I was three years old, rest in peace," Barreatto said proudly. "Now, what you need to understand is, you are part of something that your daddy built and left for you to assume a position in. Olsen aims to break you and destroy that."

It was an ill-kept secret. For years, Olsen had been dismantling Redd's organization. In his eyes, the Freemasons were a gang of thugs, a once noble organization now rotten to the core that had exercised its influence in Oklahoma for far too long. One-by-one, he had personally seen to it that the organization was decapitated, and that those who remained, that he could prosecute or sentence to prison, were sentenced to the fullest extent of the law.

It was then and there that King decided Olsen would pay dearly for crossing his family. It was time to get his "grown man" on and cut his teeth.

Dre held his breath as the handle on the front door of the condo slowly turned and Olsen stepped into the foyer unaware of what awaited him.

A bead of sweat ran down the side of Dre's face as he reflected on his next move. Growing up in the country and surviving 5th Ward, he had grown used to having blood on his hands. He had killed and ate some of everything that walked the face of the earth. *This honky ain't no different,* he thought to himself as he slowly pulled back the hammer on the Sig.

"Click!"

"Push, push," two slugs caught Olsen in the face before Dre's presence registered. His body immediately collapsed to the floor and began convulsing. Blood pooled.

"Shit just got real, baby boy!" Dre said, thinking of King as he walked over and put two more slugs in Olsen's head.

"The higher the monkey get up on a tree, the more it shows his ass! Do you understand the concept of this phrase?" Hai Mei Chan, Kim Chan's nephew, asked King in his heavily Cambodian accented English.

Kim Chan was now 81 years old and had spent the past 16 years in a maximum-security federal lockup thanks to Jay-5. His nephew, Hai Mei, had since taken over the Syndicate's day-to-day operations and was considered by the family as the organization's underboss. Both King and he, along with Slim and Scooby were sitting in a small restaurant located in Chinatown off 8th and Broadway in downtown Oakland.

King looked up as several dried-out ducks hung in the window next to the table where they were sitting. He frowned at Hai Mei's question. After a night on the town, he was not in the mood for rhyming and riddling. Slim and he had spent the evening hitting all the clubs and trap-spots in Oakland and San Francisco after they left the warehouse.

Most of the clubs they hit reminded him of those down south speakeasies he had grown up in. Frisco, however, was XXX. Raves, strip clubs, ho strolls—everything was big in the city lights. And to his surprise, it wasn't simply a city of fags. There was a lot of big city mob shit jumping off in the "Sucker Free." Home to the U.S. Mint, some of the hardest gangsters and hustlers on the West Coast repped the S.F. Before the night was over, Slim had introduced King to every major trap-spot and hustler from Fillmore to 96th & E. Street in East Oakland.

"I have a question for you, Mr. Chan," King said, ignoring Hai Mei.

"A question—"

"Yes, a question. When you look at people do you see puzzles or games?"

The underboss paused for a second to reflect. *Now this is going where, I wonder,* he thought before finally answering. "Good question. Puzzles"

"Well, I see games. And I win every time. Why? For one, I'm not a fucking monkey. And two, last night we hit every trap-spot on both sides of the Golden Gate Bridge. You know what makes me different from those niggaz out there in the street?" King asked, pointing to the street outside.

Hai Mei looked puzzled.

"I see the monkey's ass!"

Everyone at the table broke out in a fit of laughter.

King continued. "I don't need to stunt to let niggaz know my pockets are B.I.G. That's how niggaz get "tipped" in the *game*, stuntin'! See I was blessed into this very much like you. I got mad dough! And a solid team. And, oh! That phrase... That's Zora Neale Hurston, *Their Eyes Were Watching God*," he added, reaching in his jacket pocket and pulling out his father's ledger to sit on the table. "Now, can we get down to business?"

"Sure," Hai Mei said, parting his hands. "So where would you like to start? Jay-5 or our business after he's dealt with?"

King leaned forward and slid the ledger across the table, then said, "Here. I'd like to start with this. I need you to understand the extent of my reach so there is no misunderstanding who benefits who. You will notice I have marked a particular name in the book that I believe you will find interesting."

Hai Mei picked up the ledger and began to flip through its pages. Almost immediately, he recognized the name and asked, "What's your connection to this judge?"

"That's not important. What is, however, is that your organization is willing to pay handsomely to take care of this Jay-5 business and I'm the one holding all the cards right now. That said, I have one condition. Well, two actually," King said looking over at Slim for reassurance knowing he was about to roll the dice with his proposal.

Slim quietly nodded as both Scooby and he stood on edge. Despite breaking the ice, things quickly grew tense once the discussion between King and the underboss got underway.

"What exactly are you proposing Mr. Reed?" Hai Mei asked, somewhat uncertain. "Is it more money?"

"No. The million dollars is more than generous."

"Then what is it?"

"For starters, I don't want your money," King said, noting the confusion that soon spread across the underboss's face.

"I'm confused. Can someone please explain to me exactly what's going on and why we are even sitting here if you are not taking the contract," Hai Mei replied, looking up at his bodyguard for an answer.

"I didn't say we were not going to take care of it. I have my own reasons for wanting to see Jay-5 in the grave."

"Okay, so what about Sonya and her daughter? Uncle wants them dead also. All of them dead!"

"The girls live! That's my first condition," King said with a stern look on his face.

"I don't—"

"I think you may want to hear the second condition before you say anything else," Slim interrupted.

Hai Mei grew quiet, wondering where exactly King was going with all this. "Look, I don't know what your reason is behind wanting to spare the girls. Really, I don't care. Thing is, the contract has been put out by my uncle himself. So whether you take the money or not, there's no getting around it. Besides, what's to stop us from taking a trip down south and taking care of this ourselves, now that we know where this son of a bitch is laying his head?"

'Nothing!" King replied. "However, you would lose an opportunity to expand your operation, and more importantly, free your uncle," he added, then pointed to the ledger and said, "You might want to take a second look at that. We got blocks in OKC, Texas, and just about every major city in the United States. I don't have to spell it out. That's going to take your organization from supplying 5%

to over 90% of the nation's drug trade. That's overnight! Your operation will plug into this overnight. And as far as that judge is concerned, you realize that's the Chief Justice for the Ninth Circuit Court of Appeals?"

Hai Mei again began flipping through the ledger and noting the area codes listed beside the names written in the book, along with a number of politicians whose names he quickly recognized. There were also a number of Fortune 500 CEOs whose names he also noted as well as people he knew to be heavily involved in the drug trafficking business. He couldn't help but be impressed with how this kid was able to get a line on so many politicians and businessmen, including him.

After taking a few minutes to give King's proposal careful consideration, he finally said, "Give me a few days to run this by my Uncle. He'll have to be the one who makes the decision on this."

"Fine," King said. "Now, as for that other business. I think its best that we wait and see what Uncle has to say about my proposal. That way we can better assess everything."

"I agree. How about I give you a call in a few days? I should have everything worked out by then and we can take it from there."

"Bet. You have my number," King stood to shake hands before Slim and he left the restaurant, headed back to Oklahoma.

Chapter 25

"We should just run up and smack the lil' nigga when he show his face. You know, jump out on him in broad daylight. Like New Jack City or O-Dawg or some goddamn body."

"Nah, we don't want to make a legend out the lil' nigga or his team by giving him a *chance*. This ain't about who got the hardest gangsta. We got to get at him correct. See, a lil' nigga like that, he's a live-wire. Look at his pedigree. You just don't run up on a nigga like that."

Two of Jay-5's goons sat in a black sedan with tinted windows parked across the street from the Westside Park. They had been on the lookout for King for almost two weeks.

"Is that that lil' nigga?" questioned one of the goons. "There go the lil nigga right there," he said, pointing.

"About time this nigga show up. That's him for sure money," the other goon said as he looked up and saw

King's *SS* leading a parade of donks, boxes, and muscle cars up Park Street.

Trunks rattled and bass thundered like a marching band. The scene was like a Tonka toy car show. Chrome 28" Dub rims and Giovanni's and Forgiatos rolled out candy coated whips as they pulled up and parked: Los's LTD, Slim's box Chevy, Ziff's drop-top candy brandywine '71 Cutlass, G-Wayne's cotton candy pink *SS* Camaro, and Big-D's tangerine orange and cream '73 Caprice with the ever-popular tear-away flags, which matched the two colors.

"Yeah, that lil' nigga and his team eating!" the goon continued, hating to see a young nigga with it.

"Too bad we got a knock him off his crown. I kind of like the lil' nigga," the other goon said as he looked out across the park. The entire neighborhood had gathered and seemed to be enjoying themselves. Several barbecue pits filled the air with the smell of seasoned ribs and other foodstuffs. A basketball game went full throttle on the court as the Jordan enthusiasts attempted to tear down the goal. "Yeah, you right. We got a get at this nigga correct. It's too many witnesses out here," the goon added.

"Well, at least we know he's back in town. I'm a hit Jay-5 up and let him know we got our red beams locked in."

"Bet. Check with the fam over at Big Mac and see if Pumpsie hit the gates so we can role on that nigga like gang signs, nuh mean?"

The other goon held his hand up in the shape of a shotgun, then said, "Boom boom! We go dead that nigga, fam!"

Across the park, several GRG members posted around the *SS* as King introduced Carlos.

"This our folks, 'los from the Bay," he said. "He family…so treat him like you treat me."

Carlos nodded and, one-by-one, said to everybody, "What's good,"

"So check it out! We finna make a move on Jay-5 and push that nigga out the game," King continued.

"We gon' dead that nigga," Slim stated for clarity.

"Whoa! Hold up now! What you talkin ABOUT?" Ziff snapped. "Man… that's your girl's daddy! An—"

"The niggaz a bitch! Straight up!" Carlos said. "And Sonya and Kay-Kay family. There's a lot you ain't up on, so peep game," he added before explaining how Jay-5 had betrayed the family and fled to Oklahoma.

"You bullshittin!?!" Ziff asked with disbelief once he finished.

"Real Talk! The nigga is a snitch. And that's to say nothing about how he left many of us hanging when we took charges fucking with them cars and dope. Bottom line is, it's matter of principle that this nigga get dealt with," King growled.

Several GRG members nodded their head in agreement and mumbled approvingly. They had all took a hit for Jay-5 only to wind up on the short end of the stick. King was right. It was time they make their own moves. It was time for GRG to grow up and get that "grown man" money.

"So what we go do about the connect?" G-Wayne asked just as Slim passed him a blunt.

"We got a new connect!" King responded.

"Trip this!" Slim tossed 'los and King a knowing smile, then said, "This the business…" he nodded at Carlos who walked over to the LTD, popped the trunk and hit his car alarm to open a stash spot. "We got a thousand pounds of this to move," he continued, pointing to a compressed turkey bag filled with "Gorilla Glue" that Carlos pulled from the trunk.

G-Wayne choked and began to cough violently, after taking a hard pull on the blunt."What!?! You sound like an urban novel right now. Talkin' 'bout a thousand pounds," he continued coughing between words, holding his chest in an attempt to keep the smoke down.

"That's that 'grown man, shit, son!'" King mocked with his best East Coast accent, referring to the tree smoke airing out G's lungs. "We done with that backyard boogie. That shit right there... That's that sticky icky," he said, pointing to the turkey bag Carlos held. Straight out the lab. High grade!"

"Shit fire no doubt!" G snapped before clearing his throat. "Goddamn! But seriously folks, how the fuck we going to move a thousand pounds of this shit without attracting some major heat?"

"Nigga you always lookin' to rain on the nigga's parade," Slim said, disapprovingly.

"This how!" King responded, pulling out a cannabis distribution license and recently filed paperwork to open several cannabis shops.

"What the fuck !?!" Big-D exclaimed as he reached out and grabbed the paperwork.

"Yeah nigga... those L's right there. We finna trap legally in eight states," Slim replied.

It took a few minutes for Big-D and the rest of the crew to look over the paperwork and put two and two together. It was all legit. Like King, the potential for the legal trap game hadn't dawned on them until that moment.

"So what we going legit now?" Ziff asked, still somewhat confused with the whole concept of selling marijuana legally.

"Not exactly," King responded as he reached into his pocket and pulled out a bundle of credit card and tossed them to Ziff.

"Where'd you get these?" Ziff asked, barely able to contain his excitement.

"I made them," Slim responded.

"Made them?"

"Yeah! You country niggaz ain't up on this plastic game?" King quipped with sarcasm as if he himself, hadn't just learned the ins-and-outs of credit card fraud. He was stunting, knowing his connect and the *game* Slim and he had just brought from Oakland was about to change the South.

After taking a few minutes to look over the cards, Ziff finally looked up at both King and Slim and said, "Man, these motherfuckers look real! Big-D, what you know about this here plastic game?"

For all his computer savvy, David knew little about credit card fraud. He had only run across a couple articles about Ukrainian and Russian hackers and online marketplaces like CarderPlanet, which was a thieves market for buying and selling hacked credit card number passwords, stolen bank accounts, and identities.

"To be honest… not much," he finally replied.

"Don't trip! Check it out!" Slim said. He walked over to his car, reached into the back seat and grabbed his backpack. "Here—" he added, opening the bag and pulling out a copy of Kevin Poulson's book *Kingpin: How One Hacker Took Over the Billion-Dollar Cybercrime Underground.* "Now it's time to put your laptop to work with this Reader-Writer software program," he smirked as he handed a copy of the software and book to Big-D.

"Hacker… billion dollar… Cybercrime," one by one, the words slowly rolled off Big-D's tongue.

"So peep this! We doing a test run with these joints this weekend at the mall. Ziff, what's up with those bops your sister be fucking with?" King asked, pointing to the cards, then looking over at Ziff.

"Which ones you talkin about?" he responded.

"The twins."

The twins, a.k.a. Fat Baby and Nanny, a.k.a. "Cookies and Cream," were two country-thick white girls who performed a XXX showcase at Pooches. Come the third Saturday of each month, it would be jam-packed, often with many of the same patrons who, no matter how many times they saw the show, would leave mesmerized at how the two strippers could conceal an object almost the size of a bowling pin between their velvet folds, spin a pole, then turn right around and grip a rope with their tight coochie lips.

Their performance however, wasn't what caught King's attention. Over the years he had come to know that most girls who worked the club had a side hustle. Some had day jobs. Others pedaled dope or pussy, if not both. But with Fat Baby and Nanny, their performance was an extracurricular activity that paled in comparison to the boosting operation they ran. It was this little endeavor that caught his attention and brought them into the fold because he needed a team of skilled runners to get their operation off the ground. Their boosting operation, in and of itself, was just what he needed to accomplish this.

It consisted of recruiting middle-class teenage white girls who unfortunately, had fallen victim to the opiate epidemic. Once hooked, it was easy to persuade them to steal to support their habits. At first they stole from their parents, then their grandparents and other family. When that ran its course, they stole for Fat Baby and Nanny who, seven days a week, sun-up to sun-down, drove them like a team of mules through every strip mall and shopping center between Tulsa and Oklahoma City.

By the end of the day, the Twins had accumulated enough stolen goods to start their own clothing and tech stores. They would dump everything quick, selling it for 50% off the retail price. It was smooth and went without a hitch because mall security often stereotyped shoplifters as poor and black and not rich and strung out.

"You know them 'Hill Hoes' game when it comes to getting paper," Ziff said. "It shouldn't be a problem getting them on board. But, we going to need some IDs because you know they might ID them," he added.

"Don't trip! We going to press them—" Slim said.

"Damn! So what, we DMV? American Express now!?!" Big-D blurted out, then said, "Might as well start a fucking credit card company!"

"—I see you finally catching on. That's exactly what we're going to do, why you bullshittin! And that's not all," Slim continued. "We got that Jiffy too!" he added, holding up a small balloon.

"What's that?" G asked.

"That's that Heron No. 4!" King smiled, and then said, "It's been processed, cut with phynenoyl and condensed to a powder form. And we got it by the fucking boat load."

"So what about this whole Jay-5 thing? And... what, we processing and cutting our own shit now? That's major! But who go process this shit?" G asked.

As if on cue, a '87 Mustang sitting on 22" Ponys drove up on the basketball court and began spinning its wheels before fishtailing into a series of doughnuts.

"Side show!" somebody across the park yelled as a cloud of tire smoke enveloped the court and a small crowd of bystanders went wild with cheer.

The car's primer fenders and hood rattled and roared like a drag car darting for the finish line before it finally stopped and a small crowd surrounded it and cheered on with accolades before lil' Jay at umped out to everyone's surprise.

"That's who!" King responded to G's question and pointed towards the basketball court.

Lil' Jay eventually made his way through the crowd and over to King and the crew. After being introduced, King explained their history and the fact that James had a mean "whip game".

"Now like I said before, we moving on this nigga Jay-5," Slim said. "We have a solid plan. But everyone is going to have to play their part and move when it's time to move!"

"Everybody good with that?" King asked as he looked on to receive approval from each person in the crew.
"Good! Now we only have a few days to wrap this up, then it's time we set up shop and get it in a major way!"

Chapter 26

The ride over from Big Mac to Boley would be filled with a number of revelations and unforgettable memories. After almost twenty years of being behind the *Walls*, the cell block's artificial lighting and constant isolation had caused severe sensory deprivation to set in.

Pumpsie squinted as he struggled with the sunlight to peer through the steel mesh cage he had been placed inside of in the back of the transport van. After a few minutes on the road his eyes eventually adjusted, and for the first time in years, he saw the world.

At first, it was the cars he noticed. He was simply amazed by how much they had changed. He couldn't distinguish a Ford from a Honda, a Chevy from a Toyota. They were all small compact size gas savers. *Tin boxes on wheels*, he laughed, thinking of a time when he considered himself a car buff. Those days, of course, were long gone. He twisted and turned, struggling with his shackles to get a better view of the world before him. Eventually he managed to get a passing view of the people walking along the side streets, driving in their tin boxes, talking on their phones, and moving in and out of the gas stations and surrounding thrift shops that made up the thoroughfare leading to Highway 270. He noted how they were all consumed with their roles. Sure, the world had changed. Yet the puppetry remained the same.

Brother Yusuf, I see it now good brother. I see it, he thought to himself. He had spent years building with the Muslim brothers on the cell block. And seeing the world after all that time definitely assisted him in putting into perspective what Brother Yusuf had always said, "Societies are organized by the roles people often unconsciously assume as consumers and laborers for those at the top of the pecking order. Their titles prescribed, they are puppets on a string."

An hour later the transport van turned off Highway 270, headed to Boley. With each passing field and forest, childhood memories vividly raced through his mind, causing a warm sensation to spread across his chest as he thought of how his brother and he grew strong from years of bailing hay in those very fields.

Suddenly, a loud crash and jolt interrupted his thoughts, sending him flying across the back of the van. The van quickly swerved as the driver struggled for control, but it was useless. It quickly spun out of control and jumped lanes before tumbling off the side of the highway to rest on its side in a field.

Smoke and the smell of gasoline quickly filled the van as Pumpsie shook his head and attempted to gather his senses. His vision spun in and out of focus like a kaleidoscope. After several minutes of being disoriented, he was finally able to retain his vision and survey the damage. He was banged up pretty bad, but miraculously, he had only suffered a few minor scrapes and bruises.

The transport team, however, didn't fare so well. As he turned to look toward the front of the van, shock rapidly spread across his face. To his horror, both guards lay lifeless as flames shot into the driver's compartment and engulfed the entire front half of the van.

Trapped, it took everything in Pumpsie's will not to panic in face of the fact that it was only a matter of time before the flames reached him, and the van exploded. He took a deep breath, exhaled and quickly assessed the situation. *How can I get out of this?* He desperately had to figure something out and do it fast. Time was of the essence.

The stench of the officers' burning flesh stung at his nostrils as the van filled with smoke, causing him to choke violently. His mind raced frantically against time as panic set in. Hopeless, he quickly realized this was it. He glanced out into the blinding sun and began to realize he was going to die, helpless, shackled in the back of a burning van, and never able to avenge his brother's murder.

The irony of Pumpsie's situation was unsettling. He'd spent close to two decades locked in a cage being treated like an animal only to die on the eve of freedom.

Enraged, he desperately struggled to break free of the chains. It was useless. He was no Superman. Nor was there anything he could do but prepare for the worst. Death was at his doorstep. The blistering heat of the flames licked at his skin causing it to glaze with sweat.

He was about to concede his fate when he heard the voices.

"Great! Now I'm losing my fucking mind," he cried out.

At first the voices were faint, muffled and seemingly trapped in his head. They quickly grew louder and louder and were accompanied by what he quickly recognized as footsteps running through the surrounding brush towards the wreck.

There they are again. Only louder and clearer.

"Let's make sure this nigga is dead!"

"What the fuck!" Pumpsie panicked. All hope of being saved evaporated upon hearing those dreaded words.

"This shit about to blow," another voice responded. "If he ain't dead he will be soon!"

"Fuck, fuck, fuck!" Pumpsie cursed again and again, realizing it wasn't his mind playing tricks on him. Nor was it an accident. *It's a hit! Jay-5!*

Despite the fact both men spoke with a Southern drawl, Pumpsie knew Jay-5 was behind it. Twice, he had put money on his head. Twice, the would-be assassins had fumbled and the C.I.U. at Big Mac had found two stiffs in a blind spot.

"Fuck!" Pumpsie cursed again. He had slipped, underestimating the ambitions of his foe. "I ain't even out the gates... And already these niggas shoot—"

"BOOOOOOOOM!" A loud explosion suddenly interrupted Pumpsie's train of thought and sent the hood of the van flying across the field.

The two men outside the wreck immediately held up their arms to shield themselves from the growing flame.

Inside, Pumpsie choked violently as the smoke and fire grew intensely. He finally cracked. "Goddamn it! If you bitch niggas go kill me, let's get it over with!" he screamed like a madman, having resolved to take two to the head instead of suffering the slow, excruciating and torturous death before him.

A minute later, the back of the van flew open.

This is it! Pumpsie shook his head in defeat as he looked up into the blinding sun and started to recite his final prayer, "Ash-hadu Alla Ilasha Il Lal Wa Ash-hada An-na Muhammadan Abduhu Wa Rassuluh." (I bear witness that none is worthy of worship but Allah, and that I testify that Muhammad is the servant and the messenger of Allah.).

His final thought was the realization that Jay-5 had won the war, proving that only the most grittiest of the gritty remained standing in the streets.

"What do you mean Jackson's transfer can't be delayed? We have a fucking judge that's been murdered and he's the prime suspect!" Sisco screamed into his phone. Lieutenant Riley was on the other end. Frustrated, Sisco had repeatedly called Riley's phone that morning only to get his voicemail. He was now a few miles west of Wewoka, about to turn off Highway 10 onto Highway 270, when he finally got through.

"Look! I understand," Lieutenant Riley responded. "Problem is, well…he's already in route. The transport team left about 10, 15 minutes ago. So you're going to have to contact C.I.U. over at—"

"Click!" Sisco abruptly hung up his cell phone and spun the car around, on its wheels and hightailed it back to Highway 10.

The second he learned of Olsen's murder, the alarm had gone off. Almost immediately, he put two and two together and recognized it was no coincidence it occurred within days of Pumpsie's release. Despite the time he had been incarcerated, Pumpsie was well-connected. And the judge had crossed him when he went after his brother and his family. This much Sisco knew.

Over the years, he had discovered the identities of a number of Masons, including Lenny, who formed the J.M. Reed Masonic Order. Many of them he suspected of running a number of criminal enterprises across the country who had maintained contact with Pumpsie to some extent.

As Sisco drove through Wewoka and eventually made his way through the small town of Cromwell, and across the I-40 overpass leading to Highway 48, he couldn't help but wonder why Pumpsie had waited so long to strike. True, revenge was a dish best served cold. But something just didn't feel right. *If he was going to hit Olsen, then why now? Why wait until all the obvious signs point to his release? Something ain't right!* he concluded.

Shortly after he turned off on Highway 48, a black sedan flew pass him. At first, he paid no attention to the car. He was too consumed with his thoughts. A few minutes later, as he drove around a bend about a mile from the prison, what he saw caused him to instantly slam on the brakes.

About a half a mile up the road, the sedan rammed into the back of what appeared to be an O.S.P. transport van. Uncertain as to what was playing out before him, Sisco's mind raced to process what his eyes were telling him. *Was it an accident? Was it a prison break?*

What happened next left no question as to what was happening. The van spun out of control and tumbled off the side of the road. The sedan pulled over and two men quickly emerged with semi-automatic MP5 assault weapons as they ran towards the wreck. That's when it hit him. It wasn't an escape attempt. *It's a hit!*

"Pumpsie! They trying to kill Pumpsie! Oh shit!" Sisco cursed as he grabbed his radio to call for backup. Realizing there was no time to waste, his cruiser came to a screeching halt about 75 yards from the wreck. He quickly jumped out of the car after grabbing an iodized forest green Remington 700 sniper rifle and began to adjust the Leupold 10x tactical scope.

Jay-5's goons never saw it coming.

The Remington barked!

The impact from a high velocity slug pierced the first goon's skull slightly above the right ear just as he stepped back from the burning van. Blood and brain matter exploded some three feet into the air, spraying the surrounding brush and foliage as the slug exited the right side of his face. His body collapsed in a heap of dead weight.

The fate of the second goon would end just as the other. Within a split second of the first shot, the Remington barked again. The slug caught the goon high in the chest and spun him around like a cowboy flick, sending his gun flying through the air. His hands shot up to his chest as he grasped at the wound in agony, gasping for air. Within seconds, his lungs filled with fluid and he choked to death on his own blood.

Pumpsie's eyes quickly adjusted to the blinding sun as the contours of the man's face standing at the back of the van drew into focus. Though it had aged considerably since he last saw it, it was a face he could never forget and was happy to see, given his predicament.

"Sisco!" Pumpsie cried with a sigh of relief as his eyes lit up. After almost 20 years in prison, never in his wildest dreams would it have occurred to him that he would be so happy to see someone in law enforcement. *Fuck the police!* His attitude had little to nothing to do with some street creed and more to do with the fact that America's first police forces were slave catchers. Then again, given the circumstances, if it wasn't for the shackles, he would have happily fallen into Sisco's arms like a damsel in distress.

"This thing is going to blow any second now!" Agent Sisco yelled as he reached into the back of the van and grabbed Pumpsie by the back of the collar.

"Hsssssssssssss!" a long hissing sound immediately caught both men's attention as Sisco struggled to drag Pumpsie to safety.

A split second later, the van erupted into a massive fireball. Flames shot from all directions, causing a mushroom to form an enormous cloud of smoke and fire some 20 feet above the wreck. Debris rapidly came crashing down around them.

Both men went flying through the air from the force of the blast. Hitting the ground hard, they were knocked unconscious.

Chapter 27

King sat up on an elbow as his eyes trailed down the spine of Kay-Kay's back. Her caramel honey complexion and voluptuous feather glistened like a morning dove perched on a hilltop.

"Vizzit, vizzit...." his phone suddenly begins to vibrate.

Damn it, he cursed to himself. He knew who it was before even sliding off the lock to view the message.

"Bruh, you colder than a muthafucka. How you up in that knowing we bout to lay some shit down? You really need to check yourself and quit thinking with your dick head my nigga. We got business to handle!" King quickly read Slim's message and put the phone down just as Kay-Kay rolled over to look up at him with her doey eyes and luscious lips.

"Morning sleepy-head," he said kissing her on the forehead.

"Mmmmm...." Kay-Kay gave a slight moan.

"Vizzit, vizzit...."

"Damn!" she said in a groggy voice. "Who that blowing your shit up this time in the a.m.? It's too early for them hoes, so—"

"Gone with all that," King dismissed her playfully as he reached for his phone.

"Nuh nuh...." she began to protest as she rose up and attempted to grab the phone.

"Back up now! Stop playing shorty," King drew back with the phone in his hand and said, "I've been done told you 'I can get pussy when I can't get nothing to eat.' And you've been throwing that *sweet* on me all night and haven't even tried to feed a nigga some Legos, eggs—"

"I got some pussy for you to eat," Kay-Kay shot back with a seductive grin.

"See that's what's wrong with you now. You need to get your ass up in that kitchenette and burn something."

"I didn't tell you... 'Legacy' ain't into cooking for no nigga," she replied, speaking of herself in third person using her stage name.

"Well... 'Legacy' better get her ass out of that bed and cook something or else I'm going to let my stomach guide me to some pussy that's going to feed me something other than Massengill. You know what they say, the stomach is the way to a man's soul."

"Shish!" Kay-Kay hissed, then said, "Better tell that hoe blowing up your shit up to bring some Mickey D's!"

"Ain't nobody but you and Slim got this number, so gone with all that!"

"What his ass want!?! I swear... you two fucking all the time y'all spend together. Y'all just spent two weeks out of state doing Lord knows—"

"Ahhh... quit crying. Real talk, I need to get this. And afterwards, I need to holla at you about something. It's serious," King said getting up out of the couch-bed and walking out onto the club's balcony.

Kay-Kay set up and twisted her lips in frustration as she began to dress. She was beginning to grow suspicious of King, believing he was back up to his old tricks. Her gut was telling her that he was not keeping it one hundred with her.

"What's good fam?" King asked, answering his phone.

"Bruh! Turn on the fucking TV. Somebody just tried to knock Uncle P's dick in the dirt. It's all over the news!" Slim blurted out.

Anger, shock and confusion gripped at King's chest. He was enraged at the very notion that Slim actually believed he gave a flying fuck about his uncle's predicament. Still, he couldn't deny the shock as he walked back into the office and turned on the TV. *"Two Men Killed by O.S.B.I. Agent in Apparent Murder Plot to Kill Inmate,"* read the subscript on a news report covering the story. *Now, why... Who in the fuck clapping at this nigga!* he thought, shaking his head as he looked on at the story.

"Say bruh... I think this shit got something to do with Jay-5," Slim continued.

"What!?! What the fuck that nig—"

"Mama and Peaches been talking about it all day. Some heavy shit cuz. We need to wrap ASAP!" Slim interrupted.

"It's on! Where you at?" King asked, grabbing his clothes.

"'los and I are on the Northside of Tulsa."

" Bet. Y'all meet me at the lodge in an hour," King replied, before hanging up the phone and turning to Kay-

Kay to say, "Hey, look something just came up. I got to bounce. You—"

"Bounce!?! How you jus—"

"Look!" King snapped.

Kay-Kay quickly picked up on his vibe. She could tell by the look on his face it was something serious. Something was wrong. She had watched the whole event play out in front of her—the message, phone call and news report—but didn't quite understand the extent to which it was connected to her or King.

"What's wrong?"

"It's nothing…. I'll explain to you when I get back," King replied walking out of the office.

The morning after the incident, Pumpsie walked out of the prison infirmary with only a few minor scrapes and bruises. Both Agent Sisco and he had been rushed to the prison hospital immediately after the explosion. It was the closest medical facility within a hundred miles. As with Pumpsie, Sisco's injuries were minor and they both were back up on their feet within hours of the incident.

"Look Jackson," Sisco said to Pumpsie. Both men were sitting across from one another at a table in the prison visiting room. "In a couple of hours you're going to walk out of those gates naked without protection. Now… those wolves I put down yesterday, they run with a pack. And if you know anything about wolves, then you know it's only a matter of time before the rest of the pack returns to finish the kill. Now, I suggest you get to talking and explaining just who the fuck and why the fuck someone trying to cancel your next birthday!"

Pumpsie sat stone-faced seething with vengeance. He was literally within hours of fulfilling the long-awaited promise he had made to his brother some 15 years ago.

"Sisco," he said with an air of calm and great deliberation, "I never would have imagined that there would come a day where I would appreciate seeing your cracker face. You saved my life and I can never thank you enough for that. But if you think for one fucking minute, that after all these years in prison—a hellhole you helped send me too—that that little incident is going to rattle me to the point I would cooperate with your funky pink ass or any fucking pig, black or white, then you're the dumbest sonofabitch I know west of the Mississippi. That wasn't my first... nor will it be my last dance with death. So fuck off!"

"Fuck off!?! Humph! Okay... I don't think you understand what's about to happen once you step outside those gates," Sisco said. His blood boiled at the notion that Pumpsie was about to spring from the cage he had put him in years ago and had worked tirelessly to keep him in. "Here's what I figure," he eventually continued, "We ran the license plate of the sedan those two goons were in that tried to kill you. It came back to a car shop over in Wewoka that just so happens to be owned by your old buddy Ja'Monte Weaver. Now, that's no coincidence."

"Guard, we're finished in here!" Pumpsie snapped at the mention of Jay-5's name.

"Okay, so you don't want to talk? Fine! We've already sent some people to pick up Weaver to have a little chit chat with him about this. Now you and me both know how good he is at putting a spin on things," Sisco said, then continued, "Hell... I wouldn't be surprised that after we're done with him you will be facing two murder charges for those correctional officers that were killed when that transport van crashed."

"Just how the fuck you figure that!?!" Pumpsie said before getting up out of his seat in a fury of aggression. "You just said the license plates—"

"Never mind that," Sisco interrupted, satisfied with the fact he had gotten under Pumpsie's collar. He was flustered and talking. "Now… you got a bounty on your head that someone is aiming to cash in on. And we both know it's connected to what happened with your brother."

"Well… maybe you should take that as an indication that someone doesn't want me alive because of what I know about his murder," Pumpsie said, pacing the floor before calling for the guard again.

"Maybe I will. But I need to hear it from you. So let's talk about it."

"Like I said before, it'll be a cold day in hell before I cozy up with your cracker ass and cooperate," Pumpsie said just as the guard opened the door to release him from the visiting room.

"Well… You're about to learn just how cold hell can get once the bullets get flying and your ass is laying on a cold steel medical examiner's table."

"Yeah… we'll see about that," Pumpsie said as he slipped out of the door with an officer in tow, with only one thing on his mind. *I got to dead this nigga Jay-5 and dead him quick!*

"What the fuck you say?" Jay-5 screamed into the phone. On the other end of the line, one of his goons frantically explained how the hit on Pumpsie had gone south.

"Both CJ and Tic-Booty dead! Talkin' about lucky… They had a tail on the transport van. They never saw it coming," the goon explained.

"Dead! Yeah I seen that shit on the fucking news yesterday," Jay-5 said. *Shit!* he thought to himself. *Good thing I reported that fucking car stolen.*

"And the police everywhere down there," the goon continued.

"CLICK!" Jay-5 slammed the phone down hard.

The following day, two O.S.B.I. agents knocked on his door.

Chapter 28

King stood outside the door of Lenny's office troubled with mixed feelings about his Uncle Pumpsie's situation. After taking a few minutes to gather his thoughts, he took a deep breath and walked into the office. Inside, Lenny, Slim, Carlos, and Pumpsie sat waiting for him.

"Fuck this nigga doing here!?!" King snapped, enraged at the sight of his uncle sitting in the office. If looks could have burned and torn to pieces, Pumpsie would have disappeared that very minute into a few specks of inanimate dust.

"Cuz... You need to turn your ears on and hear this shit out before you go and get to acting up," Slim said as he stood and walked over to King.

"Cowboy!" Pumpsie exclaimed, taken back by his nephew's resemblance to his brother. With exception of the Gucci loafers, Tom Ford jeans and white T-shirt King wore, he would have mistaken him for his dad, Redd, 25 years earlier.

"It's King!" King pronounced in a sonorous tone.

"Boy look at you!" Pumpsie said with a smile as he stood to embrace King.

It was like a stranger had reached out to King. His body stiffened as his uncle's massive arms wrapped around him.

Pumpsie, noting how tense his nephew stood, pulled back. He had come to know the cold embrace of far too many men in prison. There was an elephant in the room. He forced a smile and threw his arms back around his nephew in an attempt to ease the tension. It was useless. The fuse had been lit.

"Look at you... Looking like your pops, man!" Pumpsie said, reflectively.

"Yeah! I get that a lot," King replied, twisting his lips sourly.

Both voices were throaty, drawling, tinged with uneasiness.

The fuse burned.

"Well..., take a seat," Pumpsie motioned to a chair, somewhat clueless as what to say.

"Nah... I'm good. Don't plan on staying long," King responded.

The fuse burned.

"Suit yourself!" Pumpsie said, tossing a hopeless hand to the air. *This is going to be a lot harder than I thought,* he thought to himself looking to Lenny for support. He was struggling to find words to explain to King what he had so desperately sought answers to over the years. He was at a loss for ways to compensate for what he had taken from his family, himself, and ultimately, his nephew.

The fuse grew shorter.

"Aiight!" Pumpsie continued. "I guess it ain't no need in beating around the bush about—"

"Yeah! It ain't. So let's cut to the chase," King said, his voice sharp. His face tightened. A vein at the side of his neck swelled. His fists clenched.

Lenny sensed the dangerous energy stirring about the room and stood from his desk to walk over to the bar and pour himself a drink. It was about to jump off. Pumpsie, despite his imperfections, was no punk. He knew he would tolerate only so much of King's antics. He was trying to make amends, but if the boy wasn't willing to forgive, Lenny knew Pumpsie wasn't going to kiss his ass. And he certainly wasn't going to allow him to keep throwing shade.

The fuse grew shorter and shorter. Suspense hung in the air like poisonous gas. It was toxic. King's contempt for his uncle had grown into something lethal with each passing year.

How do you explain to a curious child why his father was murdered in cold-blood? Lenny thought of how he had tried and failed. It was now Pumpsie's turn.

"Son..." Pumpsie began, "I need you to understand that up until this point, I've insisted the family leave it to me to explain what happened that day your father was killed. And more importantly, who did it."

King's chest began to tighten with frustration and rage. Tears welled in his eyes as his hands repeatedly clenched into fists.

"You see..." Pumpsie continued, "When you become a factor in those streets, the world closes in around you. It gets cold! Your friends start plotting on you. And your family can have unrealistic expect—"

"Look nigga! Spare me the fucking lecture," King interrupted. You of all people should know that my innocence was shattered the day my daddy was killed. So miss me with all that and let's get to it. Did you kill my pops? Did you set him up?"

"No! Fuck no!" Pumpsie said nervously. He could see things were now out of his control. The last thing he wanted was to fight with his nephew.

"Then why is it that for all these years my mama—"

"Look! I'm trying to explain," Pumpsie interrupted. "A lot of people, even your mother, bless her soul, had these misgivings about your father and who he was. Sob stories and scams... He was a target from jump!"

"Target?" King questioned.

"Yes... Target. He had a bull's-eye on his back for sob stories and scams because he was so damn generous. When I fell off and got tore up off that dog food, I found myself owing the wrong people. Your father always bailed me out. Before long... It became, how can I say this... Well, those hyenas fed off his love for me. Your ma, she hated me because my addiction made me a liability. That's why she blames me. My addiction allowed people to extort your father. So eventually they upped the ante from a drug debt to a kidnap—"

"Blammmm!" chaos suddenly erupted in the room as flesh clashed with flesh, stopping Pumpsie mid-sentence as an explosion went off in his head.

King had exploded into a series of vicious combinations. The first punch, a stiff right, landed just below Pumpsie's temple. The next, caught him on the chin.

"Oooooo wee, shiiit!" Pumpsie winced in pain before saying, "'Godamnit!, that lil' nigga hit hard!"

"Awl fuck!" Lenny cried out load. "I knew this shit was about to go south. Well godamnit, get it off your muthafuckin' chest!" he yelled, clearing the way as

Pumpsie recuperated and went after King with a straight right to the forehead.

"Cuz... You gots to bob and weave... Bob and weave!" Slim shouted.

"Yeah... Bob and weave," 'los repeated. Never had he seen two human beings more calculated to strike terror into each other's heart than Pumpsie and King, who stomped like raging bulls, pawing the ground before charging at one another.

Instantly, they met with a clash, and in the breakaway, King closed Pumpsie's left eye with another powerful blow.

Dazed and blind in one eye, Pumpsie realized his only hope of coming out on top against the youngster was landing a chance blow to either his stomach or head with hopes that it would knock the fight out of the boy. With his guard high, he tempted King to lead for his ribs. King bit. And as he did Pumpsie lashed out with all his weight for his jaw with a left hook, which was the equal of any man's punch, bar none. It landed squarely against the temple, sending King falling into his arms, then dropping to the floor, face down.

A few seconds later, King rolled over on his back dazed.

Pumpsie stood over him and placed a foot on his chest and said, "Now we can continue to do this the hard way or you can listen to what I have to say. Either way you're going to hear me out. So which one is it?" he asked as he looked down at his nephew.

"You got me on that one... I'll give you that," King replied, "But if you think for one minute I'm going to sit here and accept some sob story about your addiction and it being some sort of excuse to account for my father's murder, then you got life and bullshit twisted and got me fucked up!"

"Look son," Pumpsie said removing his foot from the boy's chest and extending his hand to help him up. "This shit ain't easy for none of us. Now I've explained to the best of my ability why, why your father... my brother, was killed. Now... I need you to listen..." he paused for effect, and then spoke the name of the one person King despised more than his uncle. "Jay-5 killed your father!"

"Can I help you?" Sonya asked as she opened the door to greet the two O.S.B.I. agents standing on her porch.

"Yes..." said one of the agents holding up his badge. We would like to speak with your husband, Mr. Ja'Monte Weaver. Can we please come in?"

"Could you please wait here," Sonya said, motioning for the agents to step into the foyer. She then turned to disappear to summon Jay-5.

A few minutes later he appeared calm and collective. "Good morning officers. Can I help you gentlemen with something?" he asked. "Please... Let's take this into my study," he added as Sonya and he turned in the direction of his office.

"That won't be necessary Mr. Weaver," said one of the agents. "We actually request that you accompany us down to headquarters so that—"

"Headquarters!?!" Jay-5 asked as his demeanor suddenly changed from calm and collective to guarded. "Is this about the car I reported stolen?"

"Yes and no!" responded the other agent. "We need to speak with you in regard to an incident that occurred a couple days ago involving the murder of two correctional officers and the attempted murder of a prisoner."

"Oh... I heard about that on the evening news. Terrible," Jay-5 said, shaking his head before adding, "Let me grab my keys and—"

"Oh that won't be necessary," interrupted the agent. "We'll be providing the transportation," he added, holding up a pair of handcuffs.

"We have a warrant for your arrest," said the other agent.

Before Jay-5 could even get a word of protest out of his mouth he was shoved up against the wall and slapped in handcuffs.

"Warrant!? Arrest!? What?" Jay-5 protested as he struggled with the officers trying to figure out what the hell was going on.

"Yes... Please turn around—"

"What are the charges? What is he being arrested for?" Sonya asked with little surprise. She knew all about the mess he had gotten himself into with Redd and Pumpsie.

"Bitch, never mind that! Get my fucking lawyer on the phone," Jay-5 demanded.

Sonya calmly walked over to his desk and reluctantly began to dial their attorney's phone number as the two agents turned to escort Jay-5 out of the house. She seriously doubted he was going to be able to talk his way out of this one. He had used all his bargaining chips. *Enough is enough,* she began to reflect. Slowly she sat the phone down. She was done. She had spent over 20 years living in constant fear for her daughter's and her lives only to be treated with contempt by a man who had proved pussy when the feds came knocking. *Enough is enough. It's time his bitch ass pay the piper!* She quietly sat wishing, as she listened to Jay-5 struggle with the agents, it would be the last time she saw his face. Unknowingly, it was a wish she did not realize was about to be granted.

"Look! I told you we already set it in motion," King said after explaining to Pumpsie the arrangement with the Chan Syndicate. Both Pumpsie and he sat licking their wounds. After the fight and the bomb dropping revelation of Jay-5's involvement in Redd's murder, they had come to terms quick.

"But you just don't get at a nigga like Jay-5 any ole kind of way. The nigga is dangerous and slimy as fuck! You just don't get at—" Pumpsie insisted.

"I'm telling you we got this," Slim interrupted.

"Got this? This is personal. You don't want to cross that line," Pumpsie said, disapprovingly. "You... You two are way in over your head. There's consequences to this shit! You get caught up...then what? What happens if you get burned like—"

"Like who? My father?" King snapped jumping to his feet.

"Y-Y-Yes," Pumpsie stammered, sensing King's rage.

Things were happening fast. Too fast! While he and King had come to terms with one another, the wound wasn't going to heal overnight. Pumpsie felt the heat as the fuse reignited.

"Okay, okay. Look..." he continued. "I get it. We both want to dead this nigga. But nephew... I need you to understand—"

"I don't understand shit!" King shouted.

Pumpsie ground his teeth as he struggled to maintain his composure. "Okay... Listen here 'lil nigga! Your pops died in my hands... My fucking hands! I just did 20 calendars behind this grimy ass nigga Jay-5. Now... I'm telling you... You just don't think you can jump out on a nigga like that and start airing shit out. He's a fucking federal stool pigeon for Christ's sake! So if you move on him and you not on point we're talking about the fucking death penalty. You understand what I'm saying?"

"Nigga you sounding like a real bitch right now!" Slim smirked.

"Bitch?" Pumpsie sighed, shaking his head. Both King and Slim had stretched his patience to its limits. He was fighting hard to hold it together knowing that he had to in order to get them to focus on the bigger issue at hand. "Look… You can't be half steppin' with this nigga—"

"Oh… we on point… We on point!" Carlos said, looking at his watch. "We should be getting a phone call any fucking minute now just to show you how on point we are!"

"Who the fuck this!?!" Pumpsie finally snapped as he looked to King and Lenny to explain just who Carlos was and why he was there in the mix of family business.

Before anyone could answer, the phone rang and a wide grin swept across King's face. "Like my boy said… we on point," he said before picking up his phone and answering it. A minute later he turned and said to everyone in the room, "We got Jay-5!"

Chapter 29

"They'll be here in an hour," Danny said, hanging up his phone as he looked up at Askari, then Jay-5, who sat struggling against the duct tape they had bound him with.

"Man... It's amazing what miracles a shave and bath did in transforming you from a Hells Angel into a badge waving cop," Askari said, still processing the dramatic transformation Danny had undergone. "Just amazing..." he added, shaking his head in disbelief as he thought of how convincing they both had been when they knocked on Jay-5's door and arrested him.

Jay-5 never saw it coming. Askari and Danny stood at his door dressed as O.S.B.I agents. The minute the door slammed on the police cruiser Dre and Big-D had stolen, Askari plunged a hypodermic needle filled with propofol into Jay-5's neck. He would struggle only briefly before the tranquilizer rendered him paralyzed with fear as his captors sped off to an abandoned warehouse in west Tulsa.

"I'm telling you... this shit almost got me feeling like Blue Lives Matter," Danny replied, admiring the attire they were dressed in.

"Yeah... King called it right on this one," Askari said.

"What the fuuuck..." Jay-5 began to mumble while shaking his head in an attempt to regain his senses. "Fuck that lil' nig—"

"Smaaaack!" Askari's fist smashed into Jay-5's face before he could get King's name out of his mouth.

"See... That's the problem with muthafuckas like you..." Askari said, playing the bad cop. "You don't know when to keep your fucking mouth shut... Always running off at the mouth with the fucking police."

"Okay... Okay, man what... What this shit about!?!" Jay-5 cried, spitting a mouth full of blood onto the floor. "What... the lil' nigga tripping because—"

"Smack, smack, smack!" three jaw breaking blows caught Jay-5 square on the bridge of his nose. Blood instantaneously sprayed across Askari's button-up dress shirt.

"I think you might want to remain silent partner," Danny said to Jay-5, playing the good cop.

"King new we couldn't just get at you any old kind of way. That's why we got these badges and shit," Askari said, holding up a fake badge before continuing, "Considering how comfortable you are with the police, he knew you would bite... drop your guard and walk right into this trap."

"Walked right into it like a kid walking into a candy store," Danny laughed before saying, "But you damn sure are not walking out with no candy this time!"

"Okay man look…" Jay-5 paused anticipating another blow to the face.

Askari stood poised ready to strike but held back wanting to hear Jay-5 plead for his life.

"Okay…" Jay-5 finally said, sensing Askari's reluctance to let loose. "What the lil' nigga trippin' because I never looked out?" he asked. His tough-guy act had all but vanished. "Look… We can work some—"

"Check this out you grimy ass motherfucker…" Danny snapped. The good cop act had run its course. "This isn't about that crumb shit. You out bitch! We know all about your snitching ass—"

"This about Kim Chan muthafucka!" Askari said, sending another crushing blow into Jay-5's face.

"Chan!" Jay-5 exclaimed after coming around. His stomach turned in no time. Fear swept across his face, and his eyes cue balled. He was speechless. All presumption of being a ruffian vanished with the mention of the Chan name. Despite the façade he had put on over the years, it was the one name next to Pumpsie's that haunted him. He looked on, terrified, realizing the hour of reckoning with his past was finally upon him.

"So what now?" Pumpsie asked King as he hung up the phone. "You realize that once you cross that line… There's no turning back."

"Cross that line?" King replied sarcastically. "That line was crossed the day my daddy and mama decided to bring me into this chaotic world. It's a little too late for all that."

"Look… I get it. You're right. You're dealing with some shit your father and I should have dealt with long before you came along. But I got this." Pumpsie was intent on seeing his promise through to avenge his brother's murder. At the same time, he desperately needed to deter his nephew from making a decision he knew would ultimately send him deeper into the *game*.

"Like I said…" King paused, thinking of the hit he had just ordered on Judge Olson. "I'm in too deep! Ain't no turning back at—"

"It's never too late to turn around son," Pumpsie interrupted. "Look… Whatever you have—"

"I SAID, ain't no turning back at this point!" King snapped. "Now either you riding or sitting on the bench. Which one is it?" he added, extending an olive branch to Pumpsie before turning to exit the office.

Despite the drama, everything he and his uncle had gone through now seemed inconsequential. King realized that his uncle was not the man he had grown up to despise. It was Jay-5. His uncle was the truth and the only person that could truly lace him. He had come to a point in his life where he had begun to recognize wisdom was shaped by his ability to take the lessons, the experiences—good and bad—taught by those around him, and apply them to the image of the man he so desperately needed to be.

He had heard the stories. His uncle Pumpsie had taught his father everything he knew about those streets. Pumpsie had survived the fire, literally. And he was the only person King could look to for a better understanding of the boy, the man, the legend his father had become from jump.

All this, of course, forced King to reckon with what his uncle had just put to him about choices. He had a decision to make and it was weighing on him heavily. On one hand, he was driven by vengeance, emotion. On the other, logic was telling him everything his uncle had told him was right; he had a decision to make that would change the course of his life forever.

Behind him, King heard a door open.

"I can't let you go at this alone nephew," Pumpsie said. He followed King to his ride, opened the passenger side door and jumped into the *SS*.

"Understand this," King said, reaching down to turn up the music, "This chapter—only I can finish it. It's time to finally close the book on this nigga Jay-5."

As King and Pumpsie exited the Turner Turnpike into Tulsa, Agent Sisco eagerly trailed behind them in hot pursuit.

At the same time, Regina and Peaches pulled up in a rental van at the Tulsa International Airport. Within minutes of parking, Hai Mei and lil' Scooby appeared from the lobby's sliding doors with a small entourage of Asian goons in tow.

"There they go..." Peaches said, recognizing them as she hung up her phone after lil' Scooby had called her to let them know they had arrived.

Within minutes, they had loaded up the van, briefly introduced themselves, and were headed to the warehouse where Jay-5 awaited his fate.

Chapter 30

Agent Sisco pulled up and parked down the street from the warehouse just as King and his entourage got out of their cars and walked into the building. He noted there was a van and an unmarked police cruiser parked outside as well. As he reached over and grabbed his Remington rifle, he had a gut feeling that whatever it was that had led them there, it was the key to finally indicting Pumpsie.

Unknowingly, the two O.S.B.I. agents he had sent to pick up Jay-5, were across town taking a report from Sonya, who was explaining how she was under the impression they had just visited her home a few hours ago and arrested him.

Inside the warehouse, Jay-5 frantically prayed for his life. "Please, please… just hear me out," he pled as Hai Mei stood before him with contempt written across his face. "I was a kid... I didn't know any better when I got caught up with your uncle... I'm sorry... Man, I'm sorry, please—"

"And what about me? What about when you testified on me... you bitch-made muthafucka!" Pumpsie growled as he and King stepped from the shadows to join the small circle of onlookers who had gathered around Jay-5.

"Well?" King insisted, wasting no time as he reached into the small of his back and removed his father's Llama. "Click!" He pulled back the hammer and pressed the cold steel to the back of Jay-5's head and then said, "What about my father? What about all the grimy ass shit you did after you killed him?"

Pumpsie stared at the Llama. He knew that if King pulled the trigger, it would be the beginning of the end. "Son..." he said calmly before continuing, "Knowledge has taught you how to load a gun. But only wisdom can tell you when to pull the trigger. Be wise with your next move."

Sisco could hear the men talking as he eased into the building with his pistol drawn. The minute he recognized Jay-5's voice, he heard the gun click and he realized he was within seconds of witnessing an execution if he did not act, and act fast. He quickly reached for his rifle.

"Cliiiick!"

"I suggest you put down that a hammer and get up 'reeeeeal' slow with your hands up!" Askari said, standing behind Sisco with a MP5 pointed at his head.

"Okay... Okay, take it easy there partner, " Sisco replied, lowering his pistol and rifle to the ground before saying, "I'm with the State Bureau of—"

"Smaaaaack!" the butt of Askari's pistol struck violently sending Sisco crashing to the floor. Stars exploded behind Sisco's eyes before he hit the floor with a loud bang.

"Hey! Check it out!" Askari shouted as he stepped from behind several barrels to wave King over. "We have a problem."

King slowly lowered the Llama and took a few steps back, turning to walk over to where the Askari stood. "Who the fuck this?" he asked upon seeing Sisco sprawled out across the floor unconscious.

"This son of a bitch is the reason why I spent the past 15 years in prison and why your pops got indicted," Pumpsie replied as he walked over to where King and Askari stood. He then reached down to grab Sisco's handcuffs to handcuff him. "He's O.S.B.I."

"Sisco?" King asked somewhat uncertain.

"Yes!" Pumpsie replied.

"Well... today's his lucky day," King replied. "This the muthafucka who worked with Olsen to destroy everything my Ma and Pop's built. String him up with his stool pigeon. They both about to get it!" he added, motioning for Pumpsie and Slim to drag Sisco over to where Jay-5 sat awaiting his fate.

"Shit just got real fo' sho," Slim said as he and Pumpsie reached down to grab Sisco under the arms and drag him over to where Jay-5 was before throwing him on the floor.

"Okay... so back to where we left off," King said after walking back over to Jay-5, and again placing the barrel of the Llama to the back of his head. "Is there anything, anything yo' bitch ass got to say before I blow yo' shit back nigga!?!"

It was in that moment Jay-5's life began to flash before him. It was déjà vu, same gun, same scenario. Except this time he was certain he was going to die, short of a miracle.

"L-L-Look kid..." he stammered. "This whole thing with your pops, it was never personal. You see... your

Uncle Pumpsie... he hasn't told you the entire story. Neither has those rice eating muthafuckas standing over there," he added, looking over at Hai Mei.

"Fuck this nigga talking about," King snapped as he looked over at his uncle, then Hai Mei. His hands trembled for the first time as the Llama shook and he began to question whether there was more to the story. *Did Pumpsie have something to do with my father's murder? What did Hai Mei have to do with all this?* These questions and more began running through his mind.

"He's playing on you son... Trying to buy some time," Pumpsie replied.

"Kill the motherfucker!" Hai Mei shouted in broken English before turning to one of his goons and giving him the signal to execute Jay-5.

The goon wasted no time reaching into his coat, pulling out a gun, and stepping to Jay-5.

"Hold up godamnit!" King said, pointing the Llama at the goon, stopping him dead in his tracks.

Guns instantaneously went up around the room as King found himself at the center of a Mexican standoff.

"Now... Just hold up, hold up!" Pumpsie shouted. "Everybody be cool," he added, motioning with his hands for everyone to put their guns down.

Nobody budged.

Jay-5 saw his opportunity and went for it. "Now... I know I haven't been on the square with you youngsta," he said to King whose hands now trembled violently as the Llama went back and forth between Jay-5 and the goon. "But the truth is... your uncle here was the mastermind behind the whole plot that led to your father getting killed. I didn't pull the trigger. He did!"

"That's bull fucking shit. Cowboy... I mean King don't—" Pumpsie began to protest.

King held a hand up signaling to Pumpsie there was no reason or need to explain. "Stop! I have only one question," he said, turning to Jay-5. "There's only going to be one truth that comes away from this situation today. You want to know what that truth is?"

A long, eerie silence fell across the warehouse as everyone looked on in anticipation. The moment of reckoning had arrived. King stood firm, certain of his position in his father's legacy. He was certain that the man who sat before him, bound with tape, had been at the center of all his pain and all the misfortune he and his family had suffered over the years.

His hands no longer trembled as he uncocked the hammer on the Llama and handed it to his uncle.

"As much as I want to be the one to bury his muthafucka... Finish what you started!"

King turned and walked out of the warehouse as gunshots erupted, ending the first chapter of his legacy

Coming Soon!

KING

Too Hollywood For a Small Town

Book #2: graphic novel and animation film short
by Ivan Kilgore
Graphics by Santos

Blessed into the Game, King struggles to walk away from becoming a legacy to the most ruthless drug lord and cybercriminals in Seminole County. His crew, the Get Rich Gang, fall into the lure of money and power, and one by one, they turn on each other. As a matter of principle, this forces King to murder one of his lieutenants. This lands him in the box. Facing a capital murder charge, he discovers the streets of Wewoka, where necessity knows no law, are not big enough to feed his dreams and finally comes to grip with the lessons that his mother and family have imparted to him....

by Ivan Kilgore

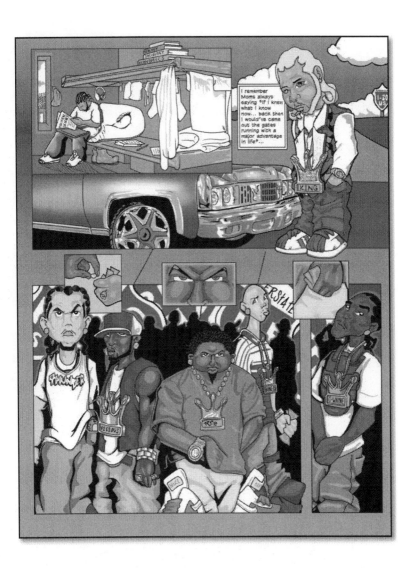

ivankilgore.com

Available on Kindle and Paperback at Amazon.com

A twist on the hustle in the Dirty South, the black rodeo circuit and Prince Hall Masons elevate King's father to the top of the Game. One-by-one, Daddy Redd buries his enemies as they attempt to tip at his $tack. Betrayed by his brother's heroin addiction, the Game God eventually claims his life and leaves King without a father. A mere child, he grows up in the shadow of his father's legacy. The streets call and he answers, playing the Game for keeps with only one thing in mind--Exacting Vengeance!

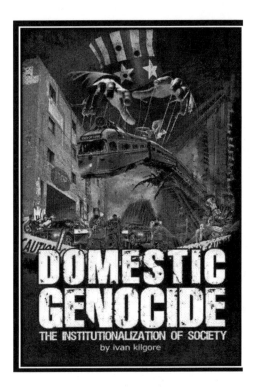

Available on Kindle and Paperback
At Amazon.com

In what has become a highly controversial topic, American institutions have come under fire as a growing number of committed scholars and advocates for social justice have caught the vapors and awoke to the fact that these institutions have been designed with the sole intent of organizing American social and economic life to the advantage of its predominantly white ruling class. In the case of many Black Americans and other people of color, this often means that their communities and lives will be exploited to the fullest.

In his highly critical analysis of these institutions, Ivan Kilgore explains in Domestic Genocide: The Institutionalization of Society the various cultural and institutional forces that have operated to preserve this agenda. Here, the backdrop of this thesis centers around his 39 years of a short life and experiences in the streets of American ghettos, college hallways, and prison dwellings where the day-to-day struggle to rise above the mire of poverty, injustice, racism, miseducation, and violence in American society have taken him on a journey that, prior to his 26th birthday, had placed him before two separate juries for capital murder; sent him across the continental United States and into the bowels of Mexico to traffic illicit drugs and other forms of destruction prior to a life commitment to the California Department of Corrections.

You can find
KING: THE EARLY YEARS
and
DOMESTIC GENOCIDE: THE INSTITUTIONALZATION OF SOCIETY
by Ivan Kilgore
at:
Amazon.com
or
The United Black Family Scholarship Foundation
https://www.ubfsf.org

Or you can purchase by mail
Send check or credit card information to:
United Black Family Scholarship Foundation
P.O. Box 862
Bristow, OK 74010 USA

DESCRIPTION	UNIT PRICE	QTY.	TOTAL ITEM(S) COST
King: the Early Years	US 14.95		
	CANADA 19.95		
Domestic Genocide: the	US 19.95		
Institutionalization of Society	CANADA 24.95		
CREDIT CARD INFORMATION		SUBTOTAL	
Cardholder Name: _____ Billing Address: _____ Card Type: ▢ MasterCard ▢ VISA ▢ Discover ▢ AMEX Card Number: _____ Expiration Date: _____ CVV (on back of card): _____ Customer Signature: _____ Date: _____		(one time fee) Shipping	4.95
		TOTAL CHARGES	

Made in the USA
Lexington, KY
12 November 2019

56884198R00185